THE SILVER MUSIC BOX

The Silver Music Box

MINA BAITES

TRANSLATED BY ALISON LAYLAND

amazon crossing

This is a work of fiction. Names, characters, organizations, places, events, and incidents are either products of the author's imagination or are used fictitiously. Any resemblance to actual persons, living or dead, or actual events is purely coincidental.

Previously published as *Die Silberne Spieldose* by Amazon Publishing in Germany in 2017. Translated from German by Alison Layland. First published in English by AmazonCrossing in 2017.

Published by AmazonCrossing, Seattle

www.apub.com

ISBN-13: 9781542048484
ISBN-10: 1542048486

Cover design by Shasti O'Leary Soudant

Printed in the United States of America

For Ele, with love

List of Characters

Johann Blumenthal: silversmith at Blumenthal & Sons in Altona
Lotte Blumenthal: Johann's wife
Max Blumenthal: Johann's brother and manager of the family firm in Lübeck
Alma Schott: Max's housekeeper
Martha Severin, née Blumenthal: Johann and Max's sister
Hermann Severin: Martha's husband
Robert and Michael Severin: Martha and Hermann's sons
Jakob Baer: employee at Blumenthal & Sons in Lübeck
Gregor Oetting: Johann's friend and comrade
August Konrad: Johann's friend and comrade
Toni, Piet, Herbert, and Hans: Johann's comrades in the war
Paul Blumenthal: silversmith, son of Johann and Lotte
Clara Blumenthal, née Fisch: Paul's wife
Margarethe Blumenthal: daughter of Paul and Clara
Karl Schumann: employee at Blumenthal & Sons in Altona
Alfons Färber: sales assistant in the Altona shop
Dr. Nathan Fisch: Clara's father
Friedrich Lükemeier: farmer
Lilian Morrison: translator from London
Sam Flynt: Lilian Morrison's best friend

Chapter 1

Johann

Altona, near Hamburg, August 1914

The light from the workbench lamp shone down on an ingot of pure silver. Strong hands had extracted the sharp-edged ore from a mine in Saxony, and others had toiled to stow it in a rail truck. It had crossed the German Empire to be melted and shaped into an ingot and had finally found its way here. This fine silver was no different from any that Johann Blumenthal had held in his skilled hands before, but as the young silversmith bent low over the bench and narrowed his eyes to inspect it beneath his magnifying glass, an idea of what it would become was already forming in his mind. A melancholy smile came to his lips as his sensitive fingers gently brushed the surface. How could Johann imagine the ways this piece would affect his family, that its value would far exceed all the jewelry and ornaments he had ever crafted?

Johann was a striking man, not so much because of his fine features or his above-average height, but because his light-blue eyes were like windows to his thoughts. Maybe it was also the way he tilted his head when listening, giving everyone he spoke to the impression of his undivided attention.

His back prematurely bent by work, thirty-year-old Johann was sitting in the workshop of Blumenthal & Sons. He loved the evenings, when the day's work was done and he was free to experiment, innovate, and create fine works of art. As he studied the silver on his bench, the final piece took shape in his mind's eye. His hands flew to a sketchbook, and a deep crease formed between his brows as he drew the two parts of a little box. This would be something special, unique—not destined for the display window of Blumenthal & Sons. It was to be a gift for his four-year-old son, Paul. His farewell gift.

Johann dashed tears from the corners of his eyes. From the upper floor, where his family lived, he heard his son's pattering footsteps. Over them came the voice of his wife, Lotte, probably warning her little rascal not to disturb his father's work. If only Johann knew how to tell them about his decision.

He waited until Paul was asleep, then went up to the living room and sat down next to his wife on the Biedermeier sofa—a wedding present from his older brother, Max.

Lotte smiled absently before lowering her head back to her embroidery. A few curly locks had come loose from her braid, falling over her pretty, gentle face. Once again, Johann thought how fortunate he was that he could call the most warmhearted, intelligent woman in the whole town his own. He had loved her for as long as he could remember, since they'd first met in the synagogue at the tender age of ten. Even then, he had declared to his father with utter conviction that, one day, she would be his wife. He had achieved his heart's desire five years ago.

"French Planes Over Nuremberg!" screamed the front page of the *Neue Hamburger Zeitung*. "Traitors Face the Firing Squad!" it proclaimed farther down.

The newspaper was four days old. Since then, the Blumenthals had observed the long lines waiting outside the post office. People were withdrawing their life savings, rushing as though pursued through the shops, and squabbling over goods at the market stalls. There were ever more frequent brawls, and the post office had closed for lack of money.

People were preparing themselves for war.

Silently, Johann reached into his dark jacket and threw a new edition of the newspaper onto the table.

"To the German People!" it proclaimed. "The sword must now decide. In the midst of peace, the enemy has now descended upon us. So let us arise! Let us take up arms! Any hesitation, any hint of weakness, is a betrayal of the fatherland! Let us go forth with God, who will be with us, as He was with our fathers! Berlin, 6 August 1914. Wilhelm."

As Lotte skimmed the words, she sighed in dismay.

Johann placed his arm around her. "All the protests and demonstrations for peace have come to nothing," he said, as though to himself. "Our kaiser has allowed us to slip into war."

"Has the world gone mad?" Lotte exclaimed. "Yesterday, outside the union headquarters on the Besenbinderhof, I saw a crowd of men furiously debating the latest developments. Herr Volkmann was there, too. You remember him?"

"Our old neighbor, the police officer."

"Right," Lotte said. "He told me about a recent scuffle on Jungfernstieg between a gang of flag wavers who were beating up a Serb, and a group of protesters cursing them as warmongers." Her delicate features were clouded with worry. "The atmosphere on the streets is more frightening every day." She shuddered. "I was so relieved to get back home safely with Paul."

Johann stroked her narrow back. Only a few months ago, their life had been full of promise, aglow with new possibilities. Since the coming of the railway, the world seemed a little smaller. Johann thought of the trips to visit friends and relations in Salzburg and Munich, little Paul finally old enough to travel. But since the assassination of the heir to the Austro-Hungarian throne and his wife in Sarajevo in June, an ice-cold wind had been blowing through the German Empire. Austria-Hungary had declared war on Serbia, and the kaiser had promised his unconditional support. By now Russia, Great Britain, Serbia, and France had come together to oppose Austria-Hungary and the German Empire.

Johann kissed Lotte's hair. He felt an unpleasant creeping sensation in the pit of his stomach, knowing the storm that his next words would unleash. He raised her chin, forcing her to meet his eyes. "I have something important to tell you."

She searched his face. "What is it, Johann?"

"I intend to volunteer for military service."

At first she appeared dazed, only the rapid fluttering of her eyelashes betraying her agitation. But then her fingers dug into the sleeve of his jacket and she shook her head violently. "You can't be so stupid!"

With a sigh, he pulled away from her. "Am I to leave our friends and neighbors to face the enemy alone?"

She stared at him incredulously with her big gray eyes. "But darling, we're Jews. This isn't our affair."

"Being Jewish has nothing to do with it. Besides, don't forget that Max and I trained for a year as reservists." He traced the lines of her face with his thumb. "This is our homeland, where we're fortunate enough to lead a good life with two shops and a team of employees. We live in a beautiful home, and young Paul will take over the business one day." His throat tightened as he saw the fear growing in Lotte's eyes. "It's time to express my gratitude. I can't just stand by as our Christian friends fight. It's my duty as a citizen to protect and defend our country."

Lotte's lips quivered, but she remained silent and laid her head on his breast.

"Don't worry." Johann tried to sound confident, realizing that he was seeking to reassure not only Lotte, but also himself. "I'll make sure the two of you want for nothing while I'm away. I'm going to talk to Max tomorrow morning and arrange for Alfons to take over the management as long as needed."

Johann kissed his wife passionately. "Be brave and look to the future with optimism. Please. For the sake of us and our son."

"You're asking a lot of me," Lotte whispered through tears. "War brings nothing but sorrow and misery. Tell me, how am I going to explain to Paul why his father's going away for so long?"

"Tell him I'm doing it for his sake."

❧

The next morning, Johann went down to the shop earlier than usual. He looked at the telephone on the counter, near the till. Max, four years older than he, managed the main shop on Holstenstrasse in Lübeck. They had been fiercely proud when, two years ago, they had become one of the first businesses to install a telephone.

Johann asked the operator for a connection, and a short time later, he heard a crackling on the line, through which he could make out his brother's scratchy voice.

"Johann. You're at work early! Imagine this, I was roused from my bed at five in the morning by a group of rowdy fools. What were they doing, you may ask? Singing at the tops of their voices—some patriotic nonsense, I don't know what. All of them boys, really, still wet behind the ears, but they certainly knew how to use their lungs."

"Five, eh? So you'd just gone to bed?" Johann teased. He imagined his brother, always dressed according to the latest fashion, with a Cuban cigar in the corner of his mouth. But behind the dapper façade was a shrewd businessman with a strong sense of family.

Max laughed. "How did you guess? I won a tidy little sum at baccarat." When Johann didn't reply, he continued, "It seems you got out of bed on the wrong side this morning, little brother. Tell me, what's wrong?"

Johann hated being called "little," but he wasn't going to take Max's bait. Not today.

Max listened attentively as Johann told him of his plans. "I admire your courage," he said finally. "But I'm not going. Someone has to keep the business afloat—leave everything to me, Johann. You can be the one to bring honor to our clan. But listen, have you really thought this through?"

"I have. My mind is made up."

"Then that's that." Max cleared his throat loudly. "Come and see me on Shabbat. Martha, Hermann, and the children are coming, too. We can talk over everything then."

Martha, their younger sister, looked after the accounts at the Lübeck shop. Her husband, Hermann Severin, worked for them as a jewelry buyer, and together, they had two young sons.

"OK, Max. I'm sure Paul will be delighted about visiting his uncle again. We'll see you on Friday."

Johann cut the connection and allowed his gaze to wander out of the window, where people were hurrying past on their way to work. A horse and cart, loaded with sacks of flour and salt, came into view. "Make way! Food for the front!" cried the driver, forcing his way through the crowd. His horse whinnied and shied, earning a crack of the whip. As the cart clattered away, Johann's eye was caught by a boy of about ten, who was playing harmonica on the other side of the street, a threadbare cap lying at his feet. His shoes were far too big, probably borrowed. Johann had often seen him begging. He had chosen his time of day well, as all of Altona seemed to be afoot, and a few people paused to throw the child a coin.

The little beggar always triggered an uneasy feeling in Johann. Did his parents know what he was doing out on the streets? The boy seemed to sense he was being watched, and looked up. When Johann nodded to him, he quickly tucked the harmonica away in his pocket.

A gang of adolescents appeared, crowding around him and laughing raucously. They shoved the child down onto the wet pavement. Horrified, Johann moved closer to the window. One of the attackers took the opportunity to give the boy a kick in the stomach. As he doubled up with pain, another grabbed him by the hair. Johann seized his walking stick and hurried out. As soon as the gang saw him, his stick raised menacingly, they made to leave, but Johann managed to plant himself in their way. A few passersby watched curiously.

"Not so fast! What do you think you're doing?" Johann grabbed the gang's apparent leader by the collar. "If you ever lay a finger on him again, I'll call the police!" Johann pulled the delinquent in even closer. "Now leave him in peace!"

"Sure, whatever," he muttered, dangling from Johann's grasp like a fish on a line.

Johann let him go and the gang immediately dissolved into the crowd. He helped the tearful boy to his feet. "Are you OK?"

The boy nodded.

"What's your name and where do you live?"

"Martin—Martin Holz. We live a few blocks down that way." He pointed with a grubby finger.

Johann asked him to wait a moment while he locked up the shop, then put an arm around the boy's shoulders. "Come along, I'll see you home."

Chapter 2

Johann sat at his workbench and regarded his creation with satisfaction. The shape and size of each of the pieces were finally perfect, and he had polished them with potash until they gleamed. He had no need of his usual scale drawings for the ornamentation—every dimension and detail was imprinted in his mind. Johann positioned the lower part in a vise, angled his small chisel, took a hammer in hand, and began tapping out a heart-shaped motif.

The young father lost all notion of time and space as the sky gradually grew light over Altona. Since making his decision to volunteer, he'd hardly slept. Last night, too, he had crept on tiptoe from the bedroom to the workshop with a pot of strong tea. He couldn't stop thinking of yesterday's encounter with the young beggar. Martin's family of six lived in two drafty rooms. His father worked as a day laborer, and his mother still hadn't fully recovered from giving birth to her latest baby. They had been shaken to the core when Johann told them what had happened. They had no idea their son begged on the street instead of going to school, although they had wondered about the money Martin sometimes claimed to have found.

Johann fell to brooding. A while later, he looked at his watch, quickly covered his work with a soft cloth, climbed the stairs to the storeroom, and filled a basket with flour, salted herring, eggs, and summer vegetables.

He ran into Lotte on the way out. Although she did not show it, he could feel her despair and her anger.

"Where are you taking that food?"

Dark shadows under her eyes revealed that Lotte had been crying—something Johann knew she rarely did. He told her about the incident with Martin.

Lotte immediately added some potatoes and a bottle of milk. "How dreadful. Where does the Holz family live? I'll deliver the basket to them later."

"Thank you," he said, noting the address on a piece of paper and kissing her.

❧

His first customers of the morning were two well-dressed gentlemen.

"Good morning. What can I do for you?" he greeted the brothers, whom he had known since childhood. Walter and Richard Sattler were the third-generation owners of a local roofing business.

"Morning, Johann. I've come to fetch the silverware for my daughter's wedding," Walter replied, rubbing his stout belly with his hands.

"Ah yes, that's right. The dinner service with the family coat of arms. Wait, I'll fetch it myself. My assistant won't be in until later."

When he returned, Walter let out an appreciative whistle. "Magnificent work."

Johann gave a slight bow. "Thank you. That's always good to hear."

"So, Johann, this war, eh? It's time we put those Frenchies in their place!" Richard declared. Ten years younger than his brother, and slimmer, he sported a neatly trimmed handlebar mustache that lent a touch of masculinity to his soft features.

A frown came to Walter's round face. "I'd gladly take up arms, you know, but I'm sorry to say I'm too old for that now." He clapped his brother on the shoulder. "But our Richard will make up for that."

"Got my call-up papers yesterday," Richard agreed with undisguised pride. "I'll be on my way next week. I can hardly wait. The only good Frenchman is a dead Frenchman, eh?"

Johann forced a smile.

"Have you heard?" Walter continued with a smug grin. "The Café Belvedere on the Ballindamm has been renamed Kaffee Vaterland! Isn't that great? And since yesterday, no more French Camembert in the stores!"

"Just you wait," Richard added. "The same thing's going to happen with the Russian hotels. Rightly so, I say!"

Johann glanced up from wrapping the silverware in tissue paper. "What does your wife have to say about your call-up, Richard?"

"Hanne? Couldn't be more delighted! We celebrated with a glass of fine wine."

Johann blinked at Richard. *The world's gone mad,* he thought. Still, it was important for him to support his countrymen and demonstrate loyalty to the kaiser. "I'm volunteering myself, actually."

"You?" Walter slammed his palm down on the counter. "That's tremendous, Johann! I've heard of a number of Jews who are marching to the front. Young David Lüneburg, for example, the son of the moneylender on Billrothstrasse, and Leopold, the leather manufacturer Süssmann's youngest."

"Maybe we'll run into each other out there. I'm pleased to hear of your decision," Richard said, taking his leave with a firm handshake.

"All the best," Walter said. "If you're as skilled with a weapon as you are with your tools, there'll be no cause for worry."

"I hope your daughter's wedding goes well."

Johann smiled weakly and accompanied them to the door. Deep in thought, he watched the brothers make their way along Königstrasse, heads held high, as though they had just accepted an award. He was uneasy about the rejoicing with which his fellow citizens greeted the war.

He was torn from his thoughts by the arrival of Alfons Färber. The slim sales assistant was in his late forties, was always well dressed, and parted his hair sharply on one side. He had worked for many years in the Altona shop and was reliable and well liked. A true Hamburg man, Alfons belonged to the Protestant majority and spoke with the broad accent of his home city.

"Morning, Herr Blumenthal. What a beautiful day. How's your family?"

"They're well, thank you," Johann replied absently. "Has my brother spoken to you?"

"No. About what?"

At that moment, a few people entered the shop. "Come and see me when you have a moment."

"Of course." Alfons moved toward a young woman who had stopped in front of a display case, while Johann hurried into his workshop. Taking a deep breath, he shut the door behind him. This was where he felt most at home, where the buzz of voices and the clanging of the bell over the door faded to a low background noise, leaving him alone with his beautiful works.

Later that morning, Alfons Färber came to the workshop and Johann gave him the news. "I'm sure I'll be back home in a few months. They say we can look forward to a swift victory," he finished.

"Let's hope for the best, Herr Blumenthal. Thank you for your confidence; you can rely on me." Alfons shook his head with concern. "This damned war. When will you report for service?"

"Probably in the next few weeks." Johann gazed into the distance. "But before then, I have something important to finish. You can discuss the details of your position with my brother."

"Of course." Färber nodded and left the workshop.

The next few hours flew by as Johann lost all track of time. He was determined to complete the pieces for this year's showcase collection. The past two years, it had been an overwhelming success in both shops, their well-heeled customers literally snatching the precious creations from one another's hands. It was also important to uphold Blumenthal & Sons' reputation to ensure that Lotte and Paul could live comfortably in his absence. Johann hunched over his bench with grim determination.

When Lotte came to collect her husband that evening, Paul tore himself from her hand and fell into his father's arms. Moved by this outburst of emotion, Johann tousled the boy's hair and sat him on his knee. Paul had his mother's gentle features, but his light-blue eyes were Johann's.

"Can we go to see the swans, Papa?"

Johann and Lotte smiled. Their son loved birds more than anything else and could spend hours watching them and feeding them bread crumbs. "Of course we can," Johann replied, touching him playfully on the nose.

As the three of them left the shop, Johann caught a brief glimpse of Martin. The boy waved shyly and disappeared around a corner. They took a detour to a small park near Elbstrasse. The sky was cloudless and the air filled with the busy sounds of the port and the cries of the seagulls. At this time of year, the fresh breeze off the Elbe was a great relief. Mothers with small children were enjoying the summer sunshine on the banks.

Behind them, bicycle wheels clattered along the sandy path. Looking around, Johann saw three horse-drawn carts. As they drew nearer, he realized they were Red Cross. Two of them were loaded high with plank beds and chests, while on the third sat rows of women in nurses' uniforms.

"God bless you. Where are you heading?" Lotte called out to them.

"The station, and on from there to the front, to save the lives of our brave soldiers," a young, chubby-cheeked girl replied. She began to sing and the others joined in, waving, as the vehicles rolled away.

Johann was filled with a sense of foreboding, which even the peaceful evening atmosphere could not relieve.

"Look, Papa, there they are!" Paul broke free from his hand and ran into the park, at the center of which was a pretty, reed-edged pond.

Johann and his wife followed, and sat down on a nearby bench.

"Don't get too close to the swans," Lotte warned, "or you'll get a nasty bite."

"I won't," Paul replied cheerfully.

"Did you deliver the basket?" Johann asked.

"Of course, darling. At first, Herr Holz didn't want to accept it. He said they didn't want charity. But when I passed on your greeting and assured him that our shelves are well stocked, he came around. He sends you his heartfelt thanks."

Johann smiled with pleasure. He and Lotte sat peacefully, watching their son playing with blades of grass while never letting the pair of swans and their five cygnets out of his sight. Lost in thought, Johann watched the gray cygnets follow their parents to the reedy bank. An idea suddenly shot into his head, sending a tingle of delight to his fingertips. He could hardly wait to set his thoughts down on paper.

When the sun sank low over the rooftops, the family rose to make their way home. But in the Rathausplatz, they came upon a strange scene. Here, where the people of Altona held their daily market, where brides and grooms were greeted by their families, was a tightly packed crowd of men, women, and children—hundreds of them.

"The mobilization has lit up the darkness like a bolt of lightning." A booming voice split the tense silence. "Our souls are touched with emotion. With God giving us the strength to defy our enemies, we will triumph. Germans, I implore you, trust in God's strength and keep up the fight until victory is ours!"

Lotte and Johann glanced at one another in dismay. A pulpit had been set up on a platform in front of the city hall, and behind it they saw a pastor in a black cassock and white collar.

Paul clutched his father's hand. "What's that man doing up there?"

"That's a pastor addressing his congregation," Johann replied carefully. How could he explain to his son why a pastor was giving the rumbling of German guns his blessing? He put his arm around his wife and signaled to her to keep moving before the child could ask more questions.

"Come, let's go and see if the young swallows in our garden are learning to fly yet." Ignoring the boy's protests, Lotte picked up the four-year-old. Their house on Königstrasse was only a few minutes from the city hall.

"I've got to work a while longer," Johann said to Lotte as she hung her hat on the peg in the hallway.

She regarded him for a moment. "If you must."

Johann kissed her, then hurried to his workshop. He took out his sketchbooks and began outlining his new idea. For the first time in days he felt something approaching optimism.

That evening, he and Lotte went to bed early. Lotte lay with her back to him, breathing deeply, but Johann was fully aware that she was no more asleep than he. In all the years of their marriage, they had never gone to sleep without feeling close to each other. But since Johann's confession, a gulf had opened up between them. The oppressive silence in the bedroom was broken occasionally by the sound of the wind rustling the fruit trees in the garden.

Johann edged closer. How pointlessly they were wasting their time together! They should be savoring every hour, every minute left to them, instead of allowing themselves to be overcome by their fears, which would probably turn out to be unfounded.

Johann curled an arm about her waist. Lotte didn't move, but the rise and fall of her chest beneath his fingers had an incredibly soothing effect.

"Please don't be angry with me," he whispered. "Don't think that the defense of our country, or honor and glory, are more important to me than you are. That's not it at all." He heard Lotte sigh, and in the next moment she turned to him.

Their eyes met in the moonlight.

"I know." Her mouth was set in a pained line.

Johann longed with every fiber of his being to kiss away the bitterness from her face. But he simply nodded, letting her express her feelings.

"I don't hold it against you," she continued. "In truth, I wish I could be angry with you." Her voice wavered slightly as she spoke.

"Why, Lotte? Why do you want to be angry with me?"

"Because that would make it easier to let you go," she began, her eyelids lowered. "I could reproach you for being blinded by patriotic ideals, or hate you for being so thoughtless that you'd long for battlefield glory. But you're not."

He slid his hand up to stroke the hollow at her throat, feeling the rapid heartbeat there. "No, truly I'm not."

Suddenly, she threw her arms around his neck and nestled her cheek against his. His heart leapt for joy. "Do you know what you are, Johann Blumenthal?"

"Tell me," he murmured, her delicate scent fogging his mind.

"You're a man who's getting involved in a conflict that isn't yours. You could step back and wait until this dreadful war is over, look after your business. But you feel responsible for the people of this country that means so much to you. More than you feel responsible for us."

Johann sat up and kissed the soft skin of her neck. "Not at all. Now listen to me carefully," he implored. "Our son deserves to grow up knowing that homeland and family mean more than social status or religious affiliation. I'm his father. Who's going to teach him that if I don't?"

Lotte stared at him, motionless.

"With your help, Paul will come to terms with the situation," he continued. "And I'll be home before you know it." Feeling her coming around, he kissed her gently. "Will you grant me another wish?"

Lotte drew him close. “Anything.”

“Our family isn’t complete. I want a little brother or sister for Paul,” he said, tracing the delicate lines of her body.

Her features softened as she ran her hands over his muscular back. “If it pleases the Lord, I would be the happiest woman in the world.”

With a sigh of pleasure she snuggled up to Johann and, for a few moments, all his cares were forgotten.

Chapter 3

The following Friday, Johann closed the shop early, and he, Paul, and Lotte took the train to Lübeck to see their family for Shabbat.

The road from the rail station led directly to the Holsten Gate. Beyond the gate, the ornate lettering of the "Blumenthal & Sons" sign could be seen from afar. The narrow, three-story building stood at the top of lower Holstenstrasse, which was lined with renowned shops. Max lived on the first floor above the shop and rented the upper floors to his goldsmith, Jakob Baer, and his wife, Dorit.

Lotte knocked on the door, which was opened by a shapely young woman with brown hair. Alma Schott was Max's housekeeper and had her own room in the spacious apartment.

The man of the house met them with arms spread wide in greeting. "Johann! Lovely to see you. Lotte, you get prettier by the day! Come in, my dears." He swept his nephew, who was giggling with delight, up onto his broad shoulders.

A little later, Martha and Hermann came in with their five- and six-year-old sons, Robert and Michael. As Johann greeted his sister with a warm embrace, he could tell from her open smile that Max had not told her about his plans. Martha was a resolute but sensitive woman, and Johann was worried about how she would react.

The large dining table was spread with a white damask tablecloth, Shabbat candles, and the best cutlery. Lotte lit the candles and began singing "Shalom Aleichem." As she did so, the housekeeper bustled about making sure the guests were comfortable.

Once Alma had served the soup and withdrawn, Martha leaned forward over the table. Like Max, she had the Slavic features of their Polish mother, who had arrived in Lübeck almost forty years earlier as a migrant worker and found work in Dietrich Blumenthal's jewelry shop, later also winning his heart. Johann, on the other hand, resembled his German father.

"You have a lovely home, Max," Martha said softly, trying to look stern, "but if you were a decent man, you would long since have found yourself a nice Jewish girl to look after you."

Max smiled indulgently. "Marriage isn't for me, dear sister. I'm happy with things the way they are. Now, don't let the food go cold. Enjoy your meal!"

Martha patted Max's arm across the table. "I'll never give up hope."

Johann grinned. Their sister had always been the most observant of the three siblings, and all too ready to play the role of mother. All her attempts to bring Max around to a less secular way of life had so far fallen on deaf ears.

The second course was a slow-cooked stew of meat, beans, barley, and potatoes.

"Anyway, why do I need a wife when Alma makes cholent like a Jew!" Max boasted, making the young Christian woman blush.

After the family had enjoyed dessert, finishing the meal with a blessing, the three boys settled down on the carpet and played with the tin figures that Max had collected. Meanwhile, Hermann and Max were talking politics.

Max waved his housekeeper over to pour him more red wine. "With our Christian colleagues going off to war, it's up to us to keep the businesses going. I'm telling you, there are hard times coming."

"Which begs the question, who will be left to buy silver if the soldiers' wives have to save their money for food and clothing," Hermann remarked, his expression clouding.

Martha kissed her husband's cheek. "Don't worry, darling. I've saved up enough that we can get by for quite some time."

A brief silence descended and Johann thought the time had come. Lotte reached for his hand beneath the table as he broke the news to his sister and Hermann.

Every drop of blood seemed to drain from Martha's lovely face. Her eyes wide, she stared at Johann in speechless disbelief.

Hermann ran a hand pensively over his thinning hair. "I agree with everything you say, Johann. I've also toyed with the idea of joining up."

Martha turned to him. "You can't be serious, Hermann. Don't you dare leave us here alone!" She pushed her plate away, rose, and flashed a look of anger at him and Johann. "Do either of you think that anyone will thank you for risking your lives?" She threw her napkin down onto the plate. "Your drivel about honor and homeland makes me sick! War isn't a playground. Robert, Michael, we're going home."

Robert pouted. "But we want to keep playing."

"Come on. Thank you for the invitation, Max," she said, sweeping the two boys from the dining room.

Hermann made to follow, but Max, who was sitting next to him, pressed him back into his seat. "Give her a bit of time," he said to his brother-in-law. "She'll calm down."

"I know. Especially since I've decided against enlisting. But she didn't give me the chance to tell her that." Hermann raised his glass. "We should drink a toast, my dear ones. To being reunited before too long. Our thoughts and wishes will go with you, Johann."

Lotte's eyes grew moist as their glasses clinked together, but she kept her fears to herself, and Johann loved her all the more for it.

The next few days were hectic. Johann worked feverishly, and by mid-week, he was adding the finishing touches to the new collection, feeling very satisfied with the imaginatively ornamented powder and tobacco tins, Jewish menorahs, brooches with inset sapphires, and tie pins. He stayed in the workshop until late, and now his final piece was almost complete.

When Lotte came to find him one evening, he covered it up quickly, earning himself a look of reproach. "Isn't it enough that I hardly ever see you before dinnertime? Now you're even hiding your work from me."

Johann gave her a weary smile. "I'm sorry. You'll see it soon enough."

Lotte drew up a stool and sat down. "What is it?"

"A little something for Paul. I want to give him a farewell gift."

She turned abruptly and made to go. He reached out and took her arm.

"Don't cry, my love."

A hint of humidity still hung in the air as Johann made his way to the makeshift recruiting office housed in a building near the train station. Despite the early hour, a long line of men had already formed in front of the desk bearing the sign "Volunteers." Among them, Johann saw some men with whom he had a passing acquaintance. He watched two uniformed men ask to see the identification papers of a young man, barely eighteen, with an eager face. After a brief exchange, he was handed a stamped form and stepped aside to make way for the next in line.

An hour later it was Johann's turn. A brave man like he was, who had already completed voluntary training, was enthusiastically received. He was told to report immediately for a medical examination. If there were no health problems, he would be called up.

Johann completed all the formalities and even managed to be back at the shop before opening time. His mind racing, he muttered a greeting to Alfons and withdrew into his refuge at the back of the shop. From his bag he took Paul's gift—now that his decision had become reality, he had to complete the piece. Johann's hands were trembling slightly as he gathered everything he needed.

The pattern on the lid was not yet finished. With a small magnifying glass clamped before his eye, he added a few details and worked the central figure to make it more clearly defined. Noises reached him from the shop; Alfons seemed to have his hands full.

Around midday Johann finished the motif. He smiled wistfully as he imagined Paul's amazement. Next was the trigger mechanism, intricate work that gave him some trouble. But once he had it working, a sense of well-being spread through his body. The only thing left was to attach the feet, which he had given the shape of long, rolled-up leaves. He soldered them carefully in place. An indefinable feeling took hold of him. Johann polished the gift, although it already shone immaculately, and examined every detail again and again. When there really was nothing else left to do, he wiped beads of sweat from his brow and leaned back in his seat. If his son took proper care of the memento, it would stand the test of time. He would have a piece of his father with him always. The thought was so comforting that Johann allowed his head to sink onto the bench, where he stayed until he felt calm inside.

The jangling of the bell over the door stirred Johann back to reality. He rose and went into the shop, where he found his employee deep in conversation with a few summer vacationers. A few seconds later, a slim woman with a wide, swinging skirt and a fashionable hat came in.

"Martha!" Johann cried as he hurried over. "What are you doing here?"

She kissed him on the cheek. "I've come to see you. Do you have a few minutes to spare?"

He turned to Alfons. "I'll be next door if you need me."

"Of course, Herr Blumenthal." The assistant smiled at Martha. "Enjoy yourselves."

In the café next door to the shop, they found a quiet table in the corner and ordered coffee with cream puffs.

Martha looked at him with remorse. "I want to apologize to you. I let my temper get the best of me on Shabbat. It was terribly rude of me. Are you angry?"

"No, but poor Hermann was rather upset."

"I know." Their food arrived, and Martha waited until the waitress had left. "Your news came as quite a shock," she said. "I wasn't really angry with you. In truth I'm simply amazed by your determination. You're the bravest of us all. But the very idea: my dear brother, fighting, somewhere in a foreign country . . . I know I can't do anything to change your mind. But I needed to see you again and wish you well."

Johann tried to smile but failed miserably. "Thank you, Martha. Don't worry. It'll all turn out well."

She stirred her coffee thoughtfully. "Have you told Paul yet?"

"No. I don't intend to until I know when I'll be leaving. He's still so young. I hope I'll be able to find the right words."

"You will," she said gently. He thought he saw a tear in her eye, but maybe it was just the sun. "Will you let us know before you leave?"

"Of course."

Martha handed him a small leather pouch. "So you won't forget us."

The pouch contained a photograph. Johann felt a lump in his throat as he looked at the picture of the family of four in their best clothes. "Thank you, but I don't need a picture to remember you."

She pressed his hand, then took a sharp breath and broke away. "My goodness, it's getting late. Hermann's taken our two little terrors with him to the shop. I have to get back before they drive him mad."

Johann found himself back in her warm embrace.

"Look after yourself."

"I promise I will."

Chapter 4

Paul

A week later, it was time to say goodbye. The night before, Johann and Lotte had made love right through until the dawn. All the arrangements had been made, and the kit bag with Johann's old reservist uniform stood packed in the hallway. They had talked about everything under the sun, yet he felt there was still so much he couldn't put into words. Now Lotte was standing in front of him, pale, in the dark calf-length dress that emphasized her delicate figure. Like a drowning woman she clung to him and kissed him until he freed himself gently but firmly.

"What am I going to do without you, Johann Blumenthal?"

He studied the lines of her face until he believed he could draw her. "Live, my angel," he replied softly. "Live and look forward to the day we meet again. But now it's not only ourselves we have to think of."

She nodded and went to fetch Paul for breakfast. As she did so, Johann weighed the letter in his hands and read the official text, although he already knew the words by heart.

> *You have been assigned to Reserve Infantry Regiment Unit 212, Altona. Report on Monday, August 24, at 10 o'clock to the barracks at Zeiseweg 9 in Altona, where you will be given further instructions.*

He'd been dreading this day and at times even wished it had already come and gone.

After breakfast, Paul came to sit on his lap and looked up at him trustingly. The boy made it easy for him by pointing to the bag near the door. "Are you going away like the other men?"

"What makes you think that?" Johann asked carefully.

"Big Anne next door says that nearly all our fathers are going away to fight. Is that what you're doing, too?"

He kissed the top of his son's head, avoiding Lotte's eyes. "Yes, that's right. Maybe I'll be back home by the new year."

Paul's big eyes were fixed on him inquiringly. "But that's a long time."

God bless children, who don't yet understand the ways of the world, Johann thought, and promised his son that he would write as often as he could. "In return you have to promise me you'll be good. You're a big boy now and you have to help your mother. Can I rely on you?"

Paul nodded enthusiastically.

"Good. Then I have something for you." Johann set him down, went over to a drawer in the bureau, and took out a little package wrapped in tissue paper, which fitted perfectly into his outstretched hand.

"A present?" Paul hopped from foot to foot.

"Yes. So that you know I'll always be thinking of you."

The four-year-old began to unwrap the paper with his little hands. Johann could tell how difficult it was for him to resist tearing it to shreds.

Lotte came closer and peered at the silver object Paul held reverently in his hands. In addition to the heart and ivy motifs, each side was ornamented with silver angels.

Lotte let out a cry of wonder. "Johann! It's beautiful!"

"What is it, Papa?" Paul asked in amazement. He pointed to the engraved figure in the center of the lid, where there was a circular opening.

"It's a little boy like you. Do you see? He's holding a notebook open in his lap. That's a conductor's baton in his hand."

"And there are two birds!" Paul's eyes gleamed.

His parents exchanged a smile.

"Indeed, my son," Johann replied. "The boy's playing the birds a tune. You see, it's a music box. Look, I'll show you something." He put his arm around the boy. "You see the pin here? Pull it."

The round lid sprang open and a small black bird emerged, twittering brightly. It disappeared a few seconds later, and the lid snapped shut.

Paul clapped his hands in delight. "Again, again!"

Johann took his shoulders gently. "You must take great care of it. The lid with the bird could easily break."

"I will," the boy said seriously.

"There's something else." Johann turned the music box over. "If you turn this knob a little, you'll find a hidden compartment. You can keep all your secrets in there—all the things you don't want your mother to see."

Paul grinned mischievously. "What do those words say?"

"They say: 'Johann Blumenthal, Altona 1914. For Paul, with love.'"

The boy planted a wet kiss on his father's cheek.

"And now we'd best go or we'll be late." Johann cleared his throat and smoothed his fine black pants. With his family watching closely, he threw the kit bag over his shoulder.

Hand in hand, the three of them left the house. They were met by the sound of a cheering crowd. Observers lined Königstrasse, which was filled with countless soldiers streaming toward the barracks with their families. Among them Johann saw Oskar Hofmeier, the eldest son of the baker around the corner. Holding himself erect as he walked, and with a confident smile, the sixteen-year-old seemed to be drinking in the cheers like sunbeams. Johann wondered if the schoolboy had lied about his age to enlist.

A young girl with blonde braids emerged from the flag-waving crowd to hand Oskar a bouquet of flowers and blow him a kiss.

Lotte squeezed Johann's hand more tightly.

The three of them made their way in silence toward Zeiseweg, and half an hour later they reached the barracks. A stocky man with light-blond hair was waving to his wife and three tearful children.

In front of the barracks, Johann crouched down to be on eye level with Paul.

"Are you going away now, Papa?"

Johann wanted to reply but was unable to utter a word. He held his son tightly in his arms and kissed him.

Lotte stared at her husband, motionless. He cupped her face in his hands. "See you soon."

"Wait. I have something for you." She handed him a small photograph. "So we'll always be with you."

The photo showed Lotte and Paul, laughing and hugging each other affectionately. Johann tucked the picture into Martha's pouch, which he wore around his neck, and kissed his wife. Then he filed into the stream of men and walked past the guard. Before the gates closed behind him, he looked back one last time and glimpsed Lotte and Paul leaving the square.

He took a deep breath.

The stocky blond man approached and greeted him politely. He must have been around Johann's age. "Gregor Oetting," he announced.

"Johann Blumenthal. Are you a reservist, too?"

"I am." Blue eyes studied him with a hint of suspicion. "No offense, but I get the impression you're not like the men I've met here so far, who can think of nothing but seeing some action—am I right?"

"You are."

Oetting grinned and extended his hand. "Call me Gregor. Pleased to meet you."

Johann shook his hand and felt as though a slight weight had been lifted.

The two men joined the other new arrivals, who gathered in the training building, where the captain gave a rousing speech. "We Germans fear only God—nothing and no one else," he concluded.

A group of sergeants then divided the men into groups, and Johann was relieved to see Gregor in the same brigade.

Every volunteer was to be issued a field-gray uniform, marching boots, a spiked helmet, and other equipment they needed for battle. Gregor and Johann surveyed the ragged gear, then looked at one another in alarm. It didn't take a military genius to see that the barracks were woefully ill-equipped. They were told that the next two weeks would be spent preparing them to face the enemy. They should report immediately for the first drill.

Later that evening, Johann and his new friend were standing on the parade ground. Gregor was smoking a cigarette, blowing small clouds of smoke into the air. He had a thoughtful expression on his angular face with its high brow. "Have you noticed? Some of the men haven't been given helmets."

"Yes, and I see that when it came to some of the youngsters," Johann indicated the portly eighteen-year-old Hans Stillwasser, "they even ran out of boots."

"It's alarming," Oetting replied. "But I'm sure they'll bring in more supplies before we leave. In any case, the victory by our troops at Mulhouse and the reports of the occupation of Brussels and Leuven should give us courage."

"That's true." Johann glanced sidelong at him. "You've got three children, right?"

"It'll be four in spring." Gregor stamped his cigarette out and stared up into the starry sky.

"Lucky man," Johann replied. "We have a son. At this time I'd usually be reading him a bedtime story." He could feel how mirthless his smile must look. "That's why we're fighting—for our children's future."

Gregor nodded. "That's the attitude."

When the two men entered the dormitory, which they shared with eighteen recruits, they found the others standing around talking or playing cards. Neither Gregor nor Johann were feeling sociable, but they introduced themselves, knowing they'd be spending a lot of time in close company with these men. There was the wheelwright, Piet, a man of around Johann's age, but already graying at the temples. Johann took to him immediately. And then there was Toni, a father of six in his forties, who worked at the Holsten Brewery. Two of his sons had already been called up. Toni was a born entertainer and managed effortlessly to lighten the mood. There was also tubby Hans Stillwasser, a forester and the youngest in the brigade. August Konrad was another who caught Johann's eye, not only because he was already a master carpenter at such a young age; Johann was also struck by his reserved manner as he played cards. And he seemed to lack the unbridled thirst for the battlefield Johann had observed among so many others. After Piet won several hands in a row, the game broke up.

As Oetting stretched out on his bunk with a book, Johann sketched the room and the men.

During the days that followed, their commanding officer, Sergeant Brandt, drilled the men on marching in step and battle formation, and out on the muddy field, they learned to obey orders such as "Shoulder arms!" and "Take cover! Down!" Piet and Toni's impatience gradually grew; the eager men were itching for weapons training. But the first shooting practice sessions soon put them in their place. Even Johann struggled with the heavy gun.

"It was as though I'd forgotten all my reserves training. You were far more skillful," he said to Gregor at lunch in the canteen.

His friend clapped him on the back. "It's just practice. Guess I learned a thing or two during my two years' military service." He gestured toward his plate. "Pretty good pea soup, don't you think?"

Johann studied the contents of his bowl. "Um, yes." He knew there was no hope of getting kosher food, a fact that had deterred some more observant Jews from enlisting. His family had always been fairly assimilated, but living so completely outside of halacha, the religious laws that governed daily Jewish life, came as a shock. But Johann felt sure that setting aside his own faith to defend the country that had given him so much was righteous in the eyes of the Lord. Johann took another spoonful of soup and smiled to himself.

The next few days passed in practice maneuvers that pushed many of the inexperienced volunteers to the limits of their endurance. Sergeant Brandt had them training until every movement came instinctively. When Johann sank onto his bunk in the evenings, his muscles burned and his head throbbed with the sound of gunfire. In moments such as those he took solace in the Torah that he always carried, and read the verses he'd learned long ago for his bar mitzvah. They gave him a sense of consolation and peace. His last thoughts before dropping off to sleep were always of Lotte and Paul.

Chapter 5

The moment three weeks before, when Paul was given the music box, would be his first clear memory. Lotte sensed it with a certainty that she couldn't explain. Johann's exact words might fade, resonating indistinctly inside the boy as if through cotton wadding, but the moment would lie dormant in Paul's mind, ready to spring back at the slightest trigger.

In the first few days following Johann's departure, the boy wouldn't let the music box out of his hands—it even had to remain in sight during his nightly bath. When Lotte finally put him to bed, the bird's song came floating from his room over and over again. She even caught him cradling it under the sheets. The silver toy was sacred to Paul, and to ever take it away from him would be an impossibly harsh punishment.

That morning, Lotte was kneading dough. Her eyes drifted to the window. In the garden, the apples were ripening in the midday sun and the swallows were beginning to leave for their journey south. With every day that dawned, her heart grew heavier.

Paul burst into the kitchen. "May I go and play in the yard with Fritz, Mama?"

Fritz was the youngest son of their neighbor, Elise Steinfeld, and Paul's best friend. Her husband, Josef, had been deemed unfit for military service due to an eye defect. When Lotte helped out in the shop from time to time, Paul would go to the Steinfelds'. Elise insisted that since she had four children in her house already, a fifth wouldn't make any difference.

Lotte looked carefully at her son. "You may. But how many times do I have to tell you—please leave your music box here."

Paul pouted and shook his head vehemently. "No. I want to keep it with me."

Lotte wiped her hands on her apron and bent down to him. "If you were to trip and fall . . ."

"I'll be careful," he said firmly, and threw his arms around her neck. "Please, Mama."

But Lotte insisted, as she always did, and finally managed to persuade him to leave the music box in the bureau. She listened as he ran down the steps two at a time.

Lotte was covering the dough with a cloth when the doorbell rang. She opened the front door to find a boy with a battered bicycle, who lifted his cap in greeting. "Forces' mail for you."

Her hands trembling, she took the letter and hurried back up to the apartment.

> *My dear Lotte,*
> *I send you my love from en route. The day before yesterday we finished our training, although I doubt that those two weeks have been enough to prepare us to survive the front. The sergeant told us the evening before we left that we will be fighting in West Flanders by a river called the Yser.*
>
> *As time is pressing, all we can do is trust those in charge. As well as a number of rather euphoric volunteers, there are fortunately also some who haven't been infected by the general enthusiasm. One of those is my friend Gregor, who works in a bank in Altona. When we're back*

home, you must meet him. Just imagine, the freight train to Flanders was covered in graffiti such as "Free passage to Paris" and "A bullet for every Frenchman." Truly grotesque. I hope my letter will reach you soon. Be brave. My thoughts are with you always. With love, Johann

Lotte read it again before lowering the letter. Flanders. He was well. She let out a deep sigh and sat down until her racing pulse calmed. Her thoughts flew back to that evening when they'd shared their fears. *Our family isn't complete. I want a little brother or sister for Paul,* he'd said. She had hoped fervently that her long-held desire for a second child would finally be realized. But those hopes had burst like soap bubbles. The cheerful laughter of the two boys drifted in from outside, but this time it brought her a stabbing pain.

She needed something to distract her. In the shop she only got under Alfons's feet, and sales were already noticeably down. On a sudden impulse, she threw on a cloak against the gusty wind and left the house. She left the dough on the kitchen table and paused only to let Elise know she'd be back shortly.

The synagogue on Breite Strasse was only a ten-minute walk from the Blumenthals' house.

Samuel Spitzer was about to lock up the office when he saw Lotte. "Shalom, Frau Blumenthal. Were you looking for me? Please come in."

She sat down opposite the forty-year-old chief rabbi.

"Rabbi, as you know, my family has not been the most devout. We have perhaps been too distracted by our business, complacent in our personal joy, neglectful of our customs and our duties to the Lord. But now, with so much suffering, my thoughts turn to *tzedakah*, to what charitable work I might do to relieve my people's pain."

Spitzer nodded. "In times of need, the voices of our ancestors remind us who we are, and we must find worthwhile activities to bring us light in the darkness." He leaned across the desk. "Perhaps you would like to come here to cook for the needy in our community three times a week, and help to serve the meals?"

"Oh, thank you, Rabbi. I'd love to."

She left the rabbi's office in a buoyant mood. The idea of making her own small contribution took away some of the helplessness that had been clouding her days.

Over dinner that evening, Paul's eyes shone as she told him about Johann's letter. "Mama, can you write a letter to Papa for me?"

Lotte was amazed. Sometimes Paul almost frightened her. He had changed since Johann's departure, often seeming too serious and introspective for his age. It was only when he was playing with his friends that he changed back into the lively little boy with perpetually skinned knees. "Of course, darling. What would you like to tell your father?"

She fetched a pen and paper and looked at her son expectantly.

"Dear Papa," he dictated, incessantly turning the music box around in his hands. "Is Flanders a foreign country? I'm being good most of the time. I love the music box. Please come home soon. Love, Paul."

Lotte suppressed a sob as she noted down the message on good deckle-edged paper. Paul had always favored Johann. It wasn't that he didn't love her, but he looked up to his father with pure adulation. She'd often had to battle Paul's obstinacy, but as soon as his father entered the room, the little rascal acted as though butter wouldn't melt in his mouth.

After putting Paul to bed, Lotte sat down at the bureau and wrote her own letter to her husband. Of course she kept quiet about her cares and sorrows; after all, they were nothing compared to what Johann would be facing. She chose her words carefully, since he knew her so well and could read between the lines. Her longing for him was overpowering, the silence of the room oppressive. If she could only catch the faintest scent of him in the living room, it would be a comfort. She slid the letter into its envelope, went over to the window, and stared out into the darkness. The sound of hooves drifted up to her as riders trotted along Königstrasse below, despite the late hour. *Horses for the cavalry,* Lotte thought with a hint of bitterness. The animals had previously been used in forestry, but had now been commandeered for the front.

At some point that night, she heard Paul begin to cry. He crept beneath her blanket and was soon fast asleep in her arms.

The following morning, Lotte and Paul paid Alfons Färber a visit. As the boy headed for a case where the most elaborate pieces of jewelry were displayed, showing no interest in the play area Johann had set up at one end of the showroom, Lotte joined Alfons at the counter.

"Thank you very much. But if you can't help me here and now, I'll take my business elsewhere," hissed a middle-aged woman as she hurried out.

Lotte looked to Alfons. "What was that about?"

"She's a regular customer," Alfons explained. "Her parents have bought a lot from us in the past. She came here today to have a platinum chain repaired."

"But we agreed that we'd collect orders like these together and send them off to my brother-in-law in Lübeck," Lotte said.

"That would take too long for her," he replied, worry clouding his face. "Since most of the mailmen have been conscripted, letters and packages are piling up in the warehouses. Unfortunately she's not the first disappointed customer. I'm afraid she'll be going around looking for a shop where they still have a resident gold- or silversmith."

Lotte saw Paul pressing his nose against the glass of the display case, and gently told him to stop. "What can we do, Alfons?"

"Employ a specialist until Herr Blumenthal returns. I can't see any other way."

"That begs the question of where we'll find someone." She looked around. Though the work in the cases still glittered and shone, the atmosphere in the exclusive shop seemed to have changed. It lacked its soul. The man who had breathed life into it with his skill and passion was no longer there. "I'll ask around, Alfons. Please offer our customers a discount on their next purchase as an incentive if they have their jewelry repaired at Blumenthal and Sons."

His face lit up. "That's an excellent plan, if I may say so."

Lotte smiled. "You may. Listen, could Paul spend an hour or so here with you?"

"But of course," he replied with unconcealed pleasure. "You know I always enjoy Paul's visits. In any case, I've got all the time in the world this morning. You can see how quiet it is."

"Wonderful, thank you."

Paul was happy, too, when he heard he could stay with kindly Alfons, who usually kept a few sweets tucked away in his pocket.

Lotte made her way to the mikvah, the ritual bath next to the synagogue. There, she would wash away all the worries burdening her soul, ready to face her new duties with renewed strength.

Chapter 6

For days on end the brigade hurtled across unknown country in a windowless freight car. Packed tightly together, the soldiers had at first engaged in animated speculation on what might await them. Fortunately, the missing gear had been supplied shortly before their departure.

But the longer the men were on the move, the more monosyllabic they became. Johann hardly knew anymore whether it was day or night, as scarcely a beam of light penetrated the freight car. After what felt like an eternity, the train suddenly came to a screeching halt. The door opened and the tall figure of Sergeant Brandt could be made out in the moonlight.

"Everyone out!" he roared, chasing away the last shreds of Johann's fitful sleep.

The twenty men shouldered their packs and guns and got into formation in front of a rickety building.

"Looks like an abandoned barn," Gregor murmured. The words had hardly left his lips when the air was torn apart by the earsplitting explosion of a shell.

Piet, standing next to Johann, nearly threw himself to the ground.

But the sergeant was clearly unmoved. "Stand still and listen! Go to the hut and await your orders!" He shoved a cloth sack at gaunt, big-nosed Herbert. "Off you go!"

Moonlight slipped through a couple of cracks in the field hut, giving enough light for them to orient themselves by. Gregor's guess seemed right, as the floor was strewn with grains and broken stalks. Johann pressed his hand to his nose. Judging from the stink, vermin had colonized the abandoned building. He spread his blanket in a corner and caught a fleeting glimpse of a plump rat as it scurried off, squeaking.

"What's in the bag, Herbert? Open up," Toni said.

"Two loaves of bread and a few canteens of water."

"Just bread and water?" Gritting his teeth, Hans Stillwasser tore open the bag. "That's not enough for a meal."

"Don't be a brat, man," Piet teased. "You're not at home being spoiled by Mama anymore."

The others hooted; only August turned away.

"Be patient with him," Johann whispered to Piet. "He'll have to accept soon enough that the times of plenty are over."

"By his age I was a father of two," Toni said, shaking his head.

"Quiet, guys. We're all hungry and tired," Gregor said as he began to slice the bread.

A sudden infernal noise rocked the building.

Herbert screamed. The men threw themselves down on their bellies and pressed their hands over their ears. Johann was overcome by trembling. When all was quiet and they dared to venture back onto their feet, they found the slices of bread scattered in the dirt.

"Sorry." Gregor looked remorseful. "That damn shell made me drop them."

Toni waved away his apology, brushed sand and grains of corn from a slice, and took a hearty bite.

Johann looked up and gasped. "Look!" He pointed to a hole in the roof, through which black earth was trickling softly down.

The others followed his gaze.

Gregor whistled through his teeth. "It must have been caused by shrapnel."

A tense silence spread through the company. "At least we won't be short of fresh air now," Toni remarked with a grin that was more like a grimace.

No one laughed. Herbert passed around a canteen of water. Johann took a quick gulp, then sat down by Hans, who was staring at his bread, lost in thought and trembling like a leaf. Johann nudged him gently. "Do you want some?"

Hans drank and passed the bottle on. Johann turned to look at him. "Why did you enlist, son?" he asked, voicing the question that had been preoccupying him since they first met.

"For the kaiser, God, and the fatherland," the young forester intoned, as though he had learned the response by rote.

Johann decided not to press him further. It was now the middle of the night, and the men stretched out on their blankets. Silence had descended outside. The soldiers on the front line were probably sleeping, too, Johann thought, as he felt in the darkness for his leather pouch. The sounds of snoring soon filled the hut. He laid his helmet over his face to shut out the world and eventually slipped into exhausted sleep.

Then the door banged open.

"Move! Marching orders!" Sergeant Brandt barked.

The men sat up, blinking.

August and Hans were still buttoning up their uniforms as they set off, and Piet scrambled to don his helmet. A truck was waiting for them outside the hut. The first hints of dawn showed in the sky as they drove through a bare landscape. In the middle of no-man's-land a solitary tree stood among charred bushes, its branches still bearing purple plums as if the war had passed it by.

Even Toni, whose mouth was rarely still, remained silent as he looked around.

"Where are we going?" Herbert asked.

"You're going to attack tonight. The damned English have positioned themselves just a few miles away," Brandt replied. "The trench is around five hundred feet to the east. You're to await your instructions there."

They got out at the side of the road, and immediately, a howling noise rocked the earth around Johann. He ducked involuntarily. Hans was whimpering beside him. August's lips were pressed tightly together. Bent low, the men set off at a run. Johann's pulse was racing as he fought his way doggedly across the muddy ground. The way seemed endless. He glanced up and froze. Not a hundred yards away a shell was heading straight for the men. The French had seen them.

"Faster!" Brandt yelled.

Johann saw Piet stumble. "Keep going!" he cried out in horror.

"My foot." Piet groaned. "I twisted my ankle."

Johann dragged him upright and supported the man as he ran.

He heard an unbearable screeching over their heads. The safety of the trench was only a few yards away now. *But we'll never make it,* he thought. Then a barrage of artillery fire broke out right before his eyes. Clods of earth flew up and robbed him of his sight. All he could make out was the muddy ground beneath his feet and Piet's body pressed against his own.

The next moment he saw helmets below him. Men were pulling him and the others down. His feet found purchase. Brandt, whose blackened face meant he could only be recognized by his stripes, clapped him on the shoulder. They had reached the trench. Breathing heavily, the two men pressed themselves against the rocky wall.

"That was close," Johann whispered, but he received no reply.

Piet stared at him in silence, one hand pressed to his right ear. Blood seeped between his fingers.

"Here, drink this." Johann handed him his water canteen. "Let me see. The bullet only grazed you."

The wheelwright's eyes became noticeably less clouded. "I thought the . . . the bastards had got us," he whispered incredulously. "Thank you, friend."

Johann nodded, though he would have put it differently. *It seems war brings our deepest, most primitive characteristics to the fore,* he thought.

In the meantime August, Hans, Herbert, Gregor, Toni, and most of the others had also reached the trench. Johann could see the last three men of their company still struggling toward them.

The sergeant demanded attention with an unequivocal gesture. "As soon as Stoss, Weber, and Schliemacher make it in, head for the reservists' trench." He ordered Herbert and August to go ahead and take up the first watch.

Johann doubted that Herbert was in a fit state for watch duty. His comrade looked completely dazed.

"I mean today!" Brandt snapped, breaking the spell that was paralyzing the man Johann and Gregor secretly called "the Nose."

"Go, now!"

August and Herbert scampered off like startled rabbits. Piet and Johann watched them go.

"Where are the last three?" the wheelwright whispered, climbing onto a stone to look.

Johann, who was a head taller, held him fast. "Are you crazy? Stay down!"

His warning came not a moment too soon, as a second round of artillery fire sprayed the ground.

Scarcely twenty yards separated the last three men from the safety of the trench. One of them pointed to the dugouts, presumably to encourage the others. Then several shells hit the ground right at their feet. The soldiers flew into the air, and seconds later fell in a shower of mud and earth to the ground, like marionettes whose strings had snapped.

A dull silence spread through the trench. Someone vomited.

Gregor stared at Johann with horror. "Did you see that arm in the air? Like it was waving at us."

But Johann did not respond; he was murmuring the Kaddish, the Jewish prayer for the dead.

One of the men approached Brandt. "Shouldn't we at least drag the bodies out of the firing line?"

The sergeant scowled. "There's not a lot left of them. There'll be many more to come. You'd better get used to it, and quick."

The soldier lowered his eyes sheepishly, and then they all hurried along the connecting passage to the reservists' trench.

Brandt indicated a hole in the ground, lined with makeshift boards. "Until you're ordered into action, you'll be digging a mine chamber." The men moved nearer so they could hear his low voice. "We think the damned French rabble are no more than two hundred yards away. If we all pull together, we can blow them to kingdom come. But not a sound down there. Otherwise it'll be us in the air!" He looked at each of them sternly. "Oetting and Blumenthal, you'll relieve the watch in two hours."

The men peered dubiously down the shaft, which led no more than ten yards into the earth. Some were ordered to fetch munitions, while others saw to the food. Later they were to split up into groups of four to relieve Gregor, Johann, Toni, and Piet digging the tunnel.

Wielding pickaxes, Gregor and Toni began to enlarge the tunnel. Johann and Piet's task was to shovel the sand into jute sacks. In silence they began their backbreaking, dangerous work, taking special care to avoid the large stones that regularly loosened themselves from the soil—a difficult task in the sparse light from their lamps.

The first hour passed and Johann's skin was itching with sweat that mixed with the soil to form a solid crust. He felt clayey crumbs of earth falling down the back of his neck. His back was sore from the unaccustomed labor, but that was nothing compared to the eerie silence broken only by the rhythmic sounds of the pickaxes. He fought to suppress grunts as he hoisted the sacks of sand over his shoulder to stack them up against the wall. He and Piet kept exchanging glances. How must it be for Gregor and Toni, slaving away down there? When their shift came to an end and the next four sent them out with a wordless wave, they blinked in the daylight like moles.

An unearthly calm hung over the battlefield. Fleecy clouds floated lazily overhead. Someone handed them cups of instant coffee; another offered cigarettes.

Johann coughed—even his lungs seemed full of grit. He sipped the hot coffee and grimaced, his throat sore.

He looked over at August, Hans, and Herbert who, guns at the ready, were scouring their surroundings with narrowed eyes. Hans gripped his rifle desperately, his hands trembling with the effort. The young forester was swaying like a birch tree that could be felled by a mere gust of wind. He went over to them. "I'll take over here, Herbert. You're needed for the digging."

The Nose turned to him, his expression blank. "Thanks." Then he nodded toward Hans with a wry smile. "Our baby's having a bad time of it. Look, he's pissed himself."

"He's scared to death. And you're not?" Johann said coolly. "You ought to be looking after the kid, not laughing at him. We have to depend on each other here."

Herbert glared at him. "OK, OK. I didn't mean any harm, Jew."

Johann took the gun without a word and watched him go. At that moment it occurred to him that there were more theaters of war than he could ever have imagined. One of them was being waged among the men.

Chapter 7

April 1917

Wearing a scarf around her head, Lotte stood over the steaming pots by the side entrance to the synagogue, ladling the turnip soup into bowls, her every move followed by the eyes of hollow-cheeked men, women, and children. The people's need grew daily now that ration books had been introduced for bread, butter, eggs, milk, and other necessities. The quantities per head were nowhere near enough, and Lotte was worried for Paul. He was too pale and thin for his age, even though she always gave him some of her own rations on top of his. In the past, they had been able to depend on grain and vegetables grown by the farmers, but now the fields lay fallow and untended. As she looked at the murky broth with disgust, her stomach turned. Everyone else surely felt the same, but turnips were the only vegetable available now with the British naval blockade. The winter had been long, and since turnips were much less nutritious than potatoes, many people looked as if they had one foot in the grave.

Chief Rabbi Spitzer had told her about the increasing number of starvation deaths in the region. It was a scandal, Lotte thought. The cold east wind tugged at her coat, making her shiver. At first there had been no more than fifty people in line at the soup kitchen, but there were now at least three times that number. She and the cooks, Binah and Chaya, did their best to prepare decent meals with ever-scarcer ingredients. Meat was only available on public holidays. In the evenings when Paul was asleep, Lotte baked bread. Flour was still available, and it filled the stomach.

Deep in thought, she studied the expectant faces filled with fear and hunger. Once again she felt grateful that the German-Jewish community was responsible for Paul's school, which he had been attending since the previous summer. Lotte's thoughts drifted to her seven-year-old, who was the spitting image of his father. Even his mischievous smile was Johann's.

She saw her husband in her mind's eye, his image stoking the burning pain that had smoldered inside her since he'd enlisted, becoming a part of her, hardened at the edges. If only the war would finally end, if only he could come back to them. She wouldn't feel whole again until he walked through the door, and maybe then Paul would smile and laugh the way he used to.

The previous summer, Johann's division had been moved from Flanders to northern France, by a river called the Somme. She had heard nothing from him since then. At first she'd thought she would go mad with worry. Her thoughts turned again and again to whether he was safe. Or whether her husband, who was used to intricate silversmithing, could have come to terms with having to aim heavy weapons at human targets. But when Lotte heard from the other women that the Forces' mail had been held up by the cold spell and the thick snow that covered the hills of northern France, she forced herself to remain calm. There were so many soldiers' wives, and they were feeling the same things.

In his last letter, Johann had talked of young Hans, who had volunteered because he wanted to impress his girlfriend. Of August, who had not yet seen his firstborn son. Of Herbert, who had developed a burning hatred for the enemy and fired at them with disconcerting joy. And of his friend Gregor, who made no secret of his yearning to be home. He had only written a sentence about Piet and Toni, saying they had fallen at Ypres. Lotte knew her husband. The fewer words he used, the worse he felt. Day after day she read in the newspapers about new horrors from the western front. Whenever she thought about what her husband must be experiencing on the battlefield, her chest tightened in fear.

"Are you ill?" a girl of Paul's age asked her.

Lotte forced a smile. "No, thank you, Esther," she replied, handing her a bowl and a crust of bread.

"Please excuse my daughter. She can sometimes be a bit impertinent," the girl's mother said.

"No need to apologize," Lotte protested. "A little concern goes a long way these days. How's your husband doing, Frau Rosenfeld?"

The Rosenfelds had lived for generations in a grand, multistory house near the synagogue. Lotte could never have imagined serving thin soup to the textile merchant's family. But Wilhelm Rosenfeld had been forced to give up his business a few months earlier after artillery fire in the East had torn away both his legs below the knee.

"As you'd expect; thank you for asking," the merchant's wife replied. "We all have to accept our fate. Have you heard anything from your husband?"

"No. His last letter came in July. Please take a portion for your husband." Lotte filled a second bowl.

"Thank you, Frau Blumenthal. May the Lord watch over you." The mother and daughter disappeared into the crowd.

Lotte had no time to watch them leave, as the line in front of the soup kitchen seemed to have no end. The familiar figure of a boy caught her eye. Martin Holz and his mother were hanging back a short distance away. She had told the young beggar about the Jewish soup kitchen, and now they came regularly in the hope of leftovers. Lotte often kept back a few portions without anyone knowing. She no longer saw Martin begging on the street.

When all the people waiting in line had been served, she waved them over. "Shalom, Frau Holz. You're in luck today." She reached for a small metal pot from under the table. "Please, could you bring the container back for me?"

Frau Holz's expression brightened. "Of course."

The relief on her prematurely aged features moved Lotte, but she nevertheless felt a pang of guilt. The Holzes were not members of the Jewish community. *But doesn't hunger affect all people equally?* Lotte asked herself. *Hundreds of thousands of soldiers are dying like flies on the battlefields, and we all share the responsibility for their families' well-being.*

"When does Paul get home from school today?" Martin asked shyly.

Despite their different temperaments, the two had become friends in recent months. Lotte imagined her son must see Martin as the big brother he had always wished for. "Three o'clock," she replied. "You're welcome to come to call for him. Paul will be delighted."

"I will," Martin said with a radiant smile, before following his mother down the nearest side street.

On the way home, Lotte passed a newspaper stand, where the vendor was calling out the latest news of the war at the top of his lungs. But she hurried past.

Lotte had become accustomed to visiting the family business once a day to make sure everything was in order. When she entered the shop that day, she was welcomed by their employee Karl Schumann, a young man with a goatee, who then bustled away into the workshop.

Alfons greeted her.

Lotte indicated the workshop door. "I'm glad to see Karl getting on so well."

"Indeed, Frau Blumenthal. Two days a week isn't much, but it's enough for repairs and small items of silversmithing. We can't afford to lose any more regular customers."

"That won't happen, Alfons." Lotte made every effort to sound confident. She hadn't the slightest idea how she was going to continue paying Karl, but she would find a way. If necessary, she would sell the coin collection she had inherited from her parents. Lotte would make the sacrifice with pleasure—this shop was Johann and Max's life's work. She wanted her husband to be proud of her when he returned home, and if it were possible for the effects of his dreadful experience to fade with time, he should be able to continue his skilled craftsmanship. There must still be people who could use wonderful gifts like Paul's music box to remember their loved ones.

She suddenly remembered a scene from the previous Friday. Paul was always off school in the afternoon before Shabbat. That day, Hermann, Martha, and their two boys had come to Altona to celebrate with them. Max had stayed home as usual; he was always reluctant to leave Lübeck. It was a trait that always surprised Lotte, since Johann's elder brother gave the impression of being so worldly. Max had told her on the telephone that their main shop was struggling, too. He had been forced to let his sales assistant go, and since then it had been Martha who served the customers. Other than that, they were still able to live much as they had before—for the time being, at least.

As she talked with Martha and Hermann, Lotte had noticed Paul listening closely, his music box in his hand. He was so mature for his years that it was getting harder and harder to keep things from him. He'd sat there deep in thought, tracing the patterns on the silver box with his fingers. She knew he slept with the keepsake under his pillow. *If only Johann would come home,* she thought.

Alfons met her faraway gaze with a look of sympathy. "I hope they'll soon bring an end to this senseless bloodshed. Remember their loud promises of a swift victory? What a joke! How's the next harvest going to be brought in without our young men? What's going to happen when so many people face another winter of starvation? I'm also worried about that wretched matter with the Reichsbank."

For some time the Reichsbank had been tempting people to exchange their gold and silver jewelry for paper money by awarding them a medal for their services.

"They're using the gold and silver to finance this disastrous war, Frau Blumenthal," he said, his cheeks reddening with anger. "It's driving us slowly but surely to ruin."

"Last week I was on the Bornplatz, near the synagogue, and I saw a woman exchanging a gold chain for an old stained winter coat for her daughter," Lotte replied. "People's need is being shamelessly exploited. It's shocking." She looked at the clock on the wall. "Oh, goodness. Paul will be home soon. Will you be needing my help later?"

"No, I can manage just fine."

"Good, then I'll see you at closing time. Bye for now, Alfons."

Fortunately, the children were fed a hot lunch at school, and Paul generally came home bursting with news about his day and what he had learned. Lotte had never known anyone with such a thirst for knowledge. School had changed Paul, distracting him from his worries, especially since the other children's fathers were away fighting, too, making him feel less alone.

Lotte set a small pan on the stove. Paul loved hot milk. The doorbell rang twice. She hesitated and looked down at the street, but could see no one. *Forces' mail,* she thought, throwing her apron carelessly onto the back of a kitchen chair and hurrying to the front door.

She saw a young man in a brown suit too short for him, leaning heavily on a stick. It seemed an effort for him to keep himself upright.

"Hello. Am I speaking to Frau Lotte Blumenthal?"

"You are."

His eyes were rimmed with black shadows and seemed to have difficulty focusing. "Konrad's the name. May I come in for a moment?"

The brittle tone of his voice set the hairs on the back of Lotte's neck on end. "Of course. Can you climb the stairs OK?"

"I'll manage." His face set, he followed her up the stairs.

She invited him to sit at the dining table. The young man could hardly meet her eyes.

"Please tell me what this is about, Herr Konrad. What's brought you here?" Her heart was caught in a vise. "Do you have news of my husband?"

The ticking of the kitchen clock was suddenly the only sound in the room. Then she heard Paul dashing up the stairs. He hurtled in and flung his school satchel on the floor.

"Shalom, Mama. Can I go and play with Martin for a while?" His big eyes moved inquiringly between her and the stranger.

"Yes, off you go," Lotte replied. "But make sure you're home by five."

Chapter 8

Lotte was left alone again with her visitor. She looked at him expectantly, her hands clasped in her lap because she didn't know how else to keep her impatience in check.

"I only got home yesterday; I was in the hospital for months after the English shot my left knee to pieces," he began. "I . . . I fought in the same brigade as your husband, Johann. My name is August Konrad."

"August. Yes, of course," she murmured. The carpenter whose little son had been born during the war. A coldness crept through her, and she felt like demanding then and there that he come to the point. But her visitor seemed to be suffering from shock.

"For the first year we were in Flanders, in Ypres by the river Yser," he continued softly. "We spent a lot of time digging a mine chamber like moles." He paused briefly. "In March they sent us south to St. Eloi. We were almost in the trench when we were blown into the air, and our comrades Piet and Toni were killed. We saw soldiers with horse-drawn carts hauling away the mountains of corpses and tipping them into mass graves like so much trash, and then the rats and crows trying to get to them. If your husband hadn't taken such good care of me, I'm sure I'd be in an asylum by now. It was a dreadful time." His lips trembled.

Lotte made to interrupt him, but August raised a hand. "Please bear with me. I know how difficult it must be for you, but I want you to hear the whole story."

Did he have any idea what he was asking of her? But she nodded and he continued.

"At the end of August we were called to northern France, to the Somme, where we were to relieve five exhausted units. In Courcelette on September 15 we met two Canadian divisions and the British II Corps." He was clearly fighting for words. "They intended to overrun us. Later, the British forces even used tanks."

Lotte pressed a hand to her mouth in horror.

"The enemy infantry closed in on us from both sides." August closed his eyes. "I screamed when we caught sight of them. That could have cost me my life, and it put my comrades at risk, too."

The terror on his face made Lotte's heart leap painfully.

Her visitor continued. "Johann and Gregor warned me to stay calm, and made me walk between them. It was foggy, and we couldn't see more than fifty yards. We were standing by the machine guns and my knees were trembling."

He suddenly began to shake violently, staring into space as he relived the dark memories.

"Johann was the first to see the damn thing. He yelled, 'On the ground!' The noise of the shell above us was horrific. I must have passed out. When I came around"—he swallowed hard—"I couldn't move my left leg. There was a bullet in my knee. I was bleeding like a stuck pig and I thought I'd go mad with the pain. Gregor bound my leg with a scrap of fabric. Then the order came to advance. Johann asked, 'And what's to become of Konrad?' And Sergeant Brandt yelled, 'I said, advance!' But Johann, he drew himself up before the sergeant. 'Permission to take my comrade to the field hospital, sir.'"

Lotte moaned softly.

"Please, do you have a stool I could use?" August asked with a grimace. After putting his leg up, he sighed loudly. "Brandt was furious with Johann. Said, 'His life isn't worth a damn now. Leave him there.'

But the enemy was close and there was no time to argue, so he gave in. Gregor wanted to go, too, but Brandt forced him to obey orders."

Beads of sweat had broken out on his brow. Then he leaned forward across the table. "Frau Blumenthal, your husband spent a whole day dragging me through mud to the hospital, across open country and enemy territory."

"Lord almighty," Lotte muttered. Her stomach clenched at the thought.

"When the pain became unbearable, I begged him to leave me to die. But Johann wouldn't have it. Sometimes I heard him praying. Later, I passed out. I'd lost too much blood. But he slapped me awake again. He was completely spent, but managed to say, 'Now look here, friend. It's only a few more miserable yards. Hold on.' But then . . ." He stopped.

Lotte shook his shoulder gently. "Then what?"

He grabbed her arm. "Suddenly a volley of shots rang out. I assume they were trying to take out the hospital." He took a deep breath. "Anyway, Johann jerked suddenly as he was hit, and collapsed by my side." His voice sounded strangled. "If it weren't for your husband, I wouldn't be alive today. My comrades and I are so grateful to him. I'm very sorry, Frau Blumenthal. Johann is dead. He died saving my life."

Lotte sat rigid in her chair. All she could do was stare at the young man. "No! It's not true!" She shook her head vehemently. "Johann . . . He can't be . . . dead." Her words echoed in her own ears. There must have been some dreadful mistake. He was still alive in her dreams. Only the night before he had held her in his arms as she had listened to Paul practicing his reading. She looked up and the room appeared to have been plunged into darkness. "Please tell me it isn't true."

"I'm afraid I can't, Frau Blumenthal. Johann is with our Lord in Heaven." He dug into an inside pocket of his jacket and produced a brown envelope, which he laid on the table. "I wanted to save you from having to hear the news from someone who didn't know him. You have my heartfelt sympathy, and I can say the same for Gregor and Herbert."

Lotte knew she should thank him, but she couldn't say a word. Her eyes were glued to the envelope. She felt cold all over.

"Johann was the best man of all of us. He never had a bad word for anyone, not even the enemy. Even in the most difficult situations, he gave us the courage to carry on. I don't know where he got his strength from. Whenever there was some quiet, he wrote letters or just looked at his family photos."

A sob rose up in Lotte, which she suppressed forcibly. She had to keep control and concentrate on August's words. As her vision cleared, she noticed that his left leg was a few inches shorter than the other.

"It could so easily have been me." August was silent for a moment as he furtively wiped tears from his eyes. "I don't know how I made it the last few yards to the hospital. But I do remember that they were going to throw Johann's body into a pit. I persuaded a man in a white coat to dig a grave for him. He said I should worry about myself, and he was about to put me on a stretcher. But I told him that if I couldn't bury my friend according to Jewish custom, the least I could do was to make sure I gave him an honorable send-off. He said he had also lost a good friend in action, and so he buried Johann near the hospital."

Lotte got up stiffly and went to the window for a few minutes. When she finally sat down again, her limbs were reluctant to obey.

He was turning the envelope over and over in his hands. "Your husband kept a diary. Did you know that?"

Lotte shook her head.

"He once told Gregor that he should destroy it if anything happened to him. But the man at the hospital found it in his jacket, and I just couldn't." August rubbed his knee. Then he took a small book from his pocket and handed it to her.

Lotte couldn't take her eyes off the dark stains on the cover of the book.

August rose awkwardly. "Perhaps Johann's thoughts will help you come to terms with his death. I've tucked my address inside the book in case there's anything else you want to ask."

As she stood to see him out, Lotte grasped the back of a chair, willing herself not to faint in the soldier's presence. She took a deep breath and looked up. "I'm very grateful to you for doing this difficult thing," she heard herself saying in a voice that didn't sound like her own. "If ever you pass this way again, you'll be most welcome here. My . . . my husband would be very pleased."

He tried to smile. "I certainly will. In any case, I'll never forget Johann. I wish you all the best, Frau Blumenthal."

A little later, after the sound of his heavy boots had receded, Lotte allowed herself to sink onto a chair. The icy cold spread throughout her body until she was nothing but a lump of unfeeling flesh. Unaware of the passage of time, she didn't notice the last rays of the afternoon sun bathing the living room in hazy light.

She had to call Max and Martha, preferably before Paul got home. Paul.

Adonai, help me to find the right words.

As if guided by a puppeteer's string, she staggered to the bathroom, splashed some water on her face, and tidied her hair as she had always done.

Chapter 9

November 1929

Paul was sitting in the Blumenthal & Sons workshop eating lunch. Anyone who remembered Johann would, at first glance, have thought that he'd returned. The silversmith's resemblance to his father was not only in his bright blue eyes and tall, slim figure. His family was also constantly amazed by the similarity of his gestures and expressions, even though Paul had lost his father at such a young age. But the nineteen-year-old could see none of this. When he looked in the mirror, he saw a young man with gentle features, whose soft facial hair wasn't even thick enough for a goatee. It was a face that held neither Johann's calm composure nor his uncle Max's urbane gravity. But one thing that did bind him to the two men was his devotion to Blumenthal & Sons.

Paul pushed back a light-brown lock of hair and gazed pensively at the music box that he kept in a glass case above the workbench. From time to time he would take it out and polish the dust or tarnish from it, amazed at how it had weathered the years. Sure, it bore a few marks testifying to the exuberance of its young owner. As a boy, he had carried it with him everywhere, and it had slipped from his pocket more than once.

The young jeweler suppressed a curse. Since the stock market crash on Wall Street two weeks ago, the economy had been on its knees. Their customer list included a substantial number of businessmen who had invested in up-and-coming companies and now faced ruin. He looked darkly at the drawer containing completed orders. It wasn't only that the number of repaired items waiting in vain for collection grew daily. After the war, when no one in Germany could buy anything and even repair work was scarce, Uncle Max had spent years trying to sell their jewelry abroad. When he'd finally made a deal with an American distributor a few years ago, he'd held a lavish party to celebrate. Everyone had been invited—business contacts, neighbors, and, of course, regular customers like the roofers Richard and Walter Sattler, and Frau Herbartz of the shoe store on the Rathausplatz. Paul had been so proud to think of people so far away admiring his artistry. But since the crash, the Americans had canceled all their orders.

Paul's heart felt heavy. He was sure that the people's need and hunger experienced in the immediate postwar period would return with the far-reaching austerity measures following the crash. He was reminded of the first street fights shortly after the war ended. The brave men who had fought for their fatherland were enraged because their jobs had been taken by women, forced labor, and, increasingly, machines. They stormed through the streets, attacking anyone who got in their way, incensed by the thanks they'd received for putting their lives on the line.

Paul had gripped his mother's hand in fear when the men came too close. Now, years later, unemployment was again rising sharply, and feelings on the streets were more raw than ever.

Paul thought back to last summer, when he and his mother had personally felt the effects of the aggression. Walking in the park, they had stumbled across an altercation between National Socialist and Communist gangs of thugs. Hurling insults, the two sides brandished batons. When Paul asked politely for permission to pass, the Communist faction grew enraged and encircled them, hurling slurs. He had somehow managed to extricate his mother and himself before things got worse, but ever since then, they had been reluctant to leave the house. Paul was certain that the country was heading for disaster.

Uncle Max was particularly disturbed by the situation. While the Altona branch was scraping by on sales to people emigrating to America from the port in Hamburg, the Lübeck shop was operating at a loss. It was only Aunt Martha's thriftiness that enabled Uncle Max to keep it open.

Paul adored his uncle; he had always secretly modeled himself on him. Fiercely independent and with an air of mystery, he was still quite a ladies' man.

But over the years, the war and all its aftershocks had drained Uncle Max of his vitality. His well-stocked wine cellar had emptied dramatically, and when Paul visited Lübeck, he was met with the smell of stale alcohol and cigar smoke. Fortunately, Max's housekeeper, Alma, kept a watchful eye on him and made sure that he didn't go too far astray.

Paul's gaze fell on the magnifying glass that had belonged to his father. Johann's death had left a gaping void in the family. Uncle Max probably felt guilty for failing to talk his brother out of volunteering. Deep in thought, Paul picked up the magnifying glass. His visual memories were limited to a vague image of his father in a suit, a serious expression on his face. But the sound of his voice was ever present in Paul's head. He heard his words as clearly as the day they had been spoken. *So that you know I'll always be thinking of you,* he'd said as he gave his son the music box. When Paul heard about Johann's death, he had thrown it to the ground in distress.

Now, he looked wistfully at the little silver box, the focus of so many of his thoughts. His initial anger had, of course, been the inability of a little boy to come to terms with his loss. Paul thought tenderly of his mother. Since that day when August had brought her the news, something seemed to have died in her, too. When Paul had been unable to sleep at night and tiptoed into the living room, he would watch his mother studying his father's diary. He had often been tempted to ask what his father had written that could make her smile tenderly and then shed tears or start in fright. But she had never spoken a word about it, and over time his curiosity faded. To a growing boy, old, yellowed books were nothing more than nostalgia, and his new experiences at school were much more interesting.

The thin face of Martin Holz appeared unexpectedly before his mind's eye, and with him, memories that still made Paul grin. When he was a boy, his friend, eight years older than he was, had taught him such indispensable skills as spitting long distances, peeing in the open air without getting his feet wet, and tricks to attract the attention of a pretty girl. Ten years ago, his friend's family had moved from Altona to the center of Hamburg. They hadn't seen each other since, and sometimes Paul wondered what had become of Martin and whether he had a family of his own by now.

Another childhood memory rose in his mind. Paul had been seven. He remembered that solemn moment when a company commander had handed his mother the Iron Cross and a certificate for his father. Johann Blumenthal had served his brigade with outstanding merit. Courageously, and putting his own life at risk, he had dragged August Konrad across enemy territory. He had given his own life to save that of his comrade. "Johann Blumenthal died as a hero and an example to us all," the company commander concluded. His mother's face was expressionless, betraying nothing of the emotion underneath.

"The medal won't bring your father back to life," Lotte Blumenthal had told her son later. "But it should comfort us to know that his efforts and his service have been recognized."

It was only years later that Paul was able to grasp what that small case with the silver cross on its ribbon actually meant. Although Lotte bore her fate bravely and was a loving mother to him, even as a child he had been disturbed by the way she spoke of his father on a daily basis. She was probably driven by a fear that Paul might one day forget him.

But, of course, he had the music box as a daily reminder. Whenever he was feeling low or lonely, the treasure had given him consolation, and reading his father's dedication on its base always brought a smile to his lips. And then there were his father's former brothers-in-arms, August and Gregor, who had become adopted members of the family and whose regular visits had kept his father's memory alive. Despite his disability, August had built a house for his wife and two children, Emil and Friedel, as well as a workshop for himself. Paul's admiration of him had grown beyond measure when he had once observed him adapting a bicycle so that he could use it with his injured leg.

When Gregor had appeared at their door one day, after the war, Paul and his mother knew immediately what had made him Johann's best friend.

"Johann asked me to watch out for his family if anything happened to him. May I come in for a moment?"

His open manner and loyalty had ensured him a special place in Paul's heart from the first time they met. On the surface, Gregor gave the impression of a man who had his feet planted firmly on the ground. But Paul soon noticed the constant tremor in his left hand, and how it embarrassed him. In spite of all the years that had passed, Gregor still refused vehemently to talk about his experiences on the battlefield.

Paul's mother had for a long time protected her little boy from the reprisals against their people. Shielded by the walls of the community school, Paul had felt safe, believing that anti-Semitism was a thing of the past. After all, his father and thousands of Jews like him had proved their loyalty and, in many cases, even laid down their lives. Over the years, Paul had been buoyed by the belief that his father had died a hero. As he grew older, though, his mother gently told him the truth. He learned about the census of Jews in the German forces during the war, and of the numerous German populist leaflets that were being distributed throughout Hamburg, which claimed that the Jews had been cowards, shirking their duties at the front, and carrying out shady deals while there. Paul's shock at the brazen lies had never waned. How could people give the slightest credence to these rags? Looking back, he realized that, with the painful realization that people did believe them, he had grown up at a stroke.

As his mother had made him aware of the hostility, he began to see things that had escaped his attention before: people deliberately crossing the street when he came out of the synagogue with his mother, Alfons carefully removing graffiti from the shop's window or door. It wasn't until he was thirteen that he realized these were slogans of hate.

And things kept getting worse. Three years ago, his mother had cried bitterly because the Jews had been called "maggots in a rotting corpse." Regular customers suddenly began to stride past their shop without so much as a glance.

Paul looked again at the music box. As he had grown, he had found a further use for his father's poignant gift. Dorothea was the name of the first girl he had fallen in love with, six years ago. In the secret compartment in the bottom of the box, he had hidden the childish love letters he had written to her but never sent, together with a faded photograph of his father.

Paul turned decisively back to his repair job. Positioning the magnifying glass in front of his eye, he inserted a new gold link into the chain before replacing the clasp.

When he heard the entrance bell ring, he stood quickly, as Alfons had broken an ankle climbing the stairs and Karl only worked on Tuesday and Friday mornings. Storm clouds were gathering in the sky, bathing the shop in an eerie light. Paul closed the workshop door behind him and switched on the light behind the counter.

He was captivated by the dainty young woman who approached. Her long brown hair shone like ripe chestnuts. Her simple clothes highlighted her natural grace.

She smiled politely. "Shalom. Has Dr. Fisch been here?"

Dr. Nathan Fisch was the community doctor. For several years, he and Paul's mother had been involved in caring for orphans and destitute girls.

As the young woman looked at Paul inquiringly with her gray eyes, he found it hard to look away. She was the most beautiful woman he had ever seen.

"Dr. Fisch?" he replied, distracted. "No, I haven't seen him today. Can I do anything for you?"

"Yes, please. If you don't mind, could I wait here for my father? He was going to come and fetch the watch you repaired for him. We arranged to meet here."

Paul blinked in surprise. Dr. Fisch was her father? Then she must be Clara. He hadn't seen her in years. The last time they'd met, she'd still been a scrawny kid with blemished skin. "Clara? I'm so sorry, I didn't recognize you. It's me, Paul."

Her smile broadened. "Oh, you're Paul with the little girl's curls, who never missed an opportunity to pull my braids?"

His ears glowed. "I admit I could be a bit of a devil at times."

She offered her hand. "And I could be a little brat."

His heart pounded. "Can I get you a cup of tea or coffee?"

Clara declined politely and sat down on the soft armchair by the window. Paul learned that she had gone to the girls' high school, and after leaving, had spent two years keeping house for a widowed colleague of her father's and looking after his children. She crossed her long legs. "Now I work as my father's assistant," she concluded, with a grimace as though she had bitten into a lemon.

"Don't you like the work?"

"No, not at all. To be frank, I can't find a good thing to say about it—being surrounded by sick, ailing people all day. My father would love me to marry a doctor one day, someone who could take over his practice in time. But that's not for me."

Paul was about to reply when Dr. Fisch entered the store with his doctor's bag and greeted him. "Have you been waiting long, Clara?"

She kissed him on the cheek. "Don't worry, Papa. I've only been here a few minutes."

"I met old Jochebed on my way here. She sends her regards." He turned to Paul. "Is my watch ready?"

"Of course. I'll go and fetch it for you."

After strapping his watch to his wrist, Dr. Fisch turned to his daughter. "Shall we go, Clara? We have a few home visits waiting for us. I wish you a good day, Paul. Shalom."

As the doctor placed his arm around his daughter's shoulders, she looked at Paul wistfully through lowered lashes.

They turned to leave, but their way was barred by an elderly couple.

The man stopped and looked Clara and her father up and down disparagingly. "We've come to the wrong place," he hissed to his wife. "Let's go find another jeweler."

"But why?"

"Didn't you see the shop sign? I don't do business with Jews."

"But they have the most beautiful jewelry here," the woman pouted. "I've seen some wonderful earrings in the window."

The man followed her, grim-faced, to the counter.

Paul watched Dr. Fisch and Clara go before turning reluctantly to his customers. If it were up to him, he would have asked the couple to leave on the spot. But as the state of the order book didn't allow it, he forced a polite smile, especially since he could sense the woman's discomfort at her husband's behavior. While Paul showed them one item of jewelry after another, he caught her giving him surreptitious glances.

When they left the shop, Paul dropped banknotes into the till with a sigh of relief. At least the vile man had bought the most expensive pair of earrings they had. He should have been able to put the day down as a successful one, but it had cost him a great deal not to reveal his disgust at the man's bigotry. For as long as he had been running the business, he had never encountered such an overt display. *The man's clearly been taken in by the hateful lies used to turn people against us,* Paul thought bitterly as he turned out the lights in the shop.

At home, Gregor greeted him with widespread arms. He was doing really well in his career at the bank, but still found time to visit regularly for afternoon tea and a chat. His light-blond hair was now streaked with white, but his broad smile was the same as it had been on the first day they'd met. Paul sometimes feared that Gregor would attract the displeasure of the anti-Semites by coming to visit them, but his friend didn't seem worried in the slightest. They spent a pleasant hour chatting, not least because Paul stayed silent about that afternoon's events. Paul decided it would be best if he forgot the disagreeable encounter. He was only too pleased to be diverted by the hilarious anecdotes his father's comrade related about his five-year-old grandson, Rudi. Even Paul's mother seemed more settled when Gregor was there.

When Paul went to bed that evening, he still felt echoes of unbridled joy at seeing Clara again. As he slipped into sleep, it was her voice he heard in his dreams.

Chapter 10

Days went by, then weeks. At first, Paul just happened to pass by Dr. Fisch's practice every day. Clara's eyes shone whenever she caught sight of him. And soon, what the two of them had felt from the moment they met was a secret no longer: they belonged together. Clara's concerns about her father's reservations proved unfounded. If he had hoped for a successor in his practice, he kept it to himself.

The very next week, Lotte invited Clara and her father over for Shabbat dinner. As they gathered around the table, Paul's eyes flicked from his mother to Dr. Fisch, finally settling on Clara's expressive face, and his heart beat faster with happiness.

After the meal and the blessings, Dr. Fisch took his leave, as he wanted to visit his elder brother who lived out on the edge of the town.

No sooner had he left than Lotte drew Clara into a conversation about her plans for the future.

"I'd like to work with children. I've always wanted to, ever since I was a little girl," Clara said. "There are too many children who are left to their own devices because their parents have to work round the clock to put bread in their stomachs."

Lotte paused in pouring the tea. Her smile lit up her face, softening her features. "You're so right, Clara. Oh, how wonderful it is to hear you say it! Why don't you think about joining our work at the synagogue helping poor children? For ages now we've been looking for a bright young woman like you."

Paul looked affectionately at the two women. His mother seemed to have found a soul mate in Clara.

Clara lowered her teacup. "I thank you from the bottom of my heart, Frau Blumenthal. Maybe one day. But I have a different dream. I'd like to train as a kindergarten teacher."

Lotte smiled in understanding, and tapped her fingers. "That's a wonderful profession. But there's no use losing yourself in dreams."

A shadow passed across the younger woman's face.

"Jewish women aren't admitted to the profession, darling," Paul said gently.

"You don't need to tell me that," Clara replied. "My father's been trying for years to talk me out of these 'flights of fancy,' as he calls them."

He detected grim determination in her features.

"Paul, you've said you'd like to marry me. Do you really mean it?"

Surprised by her direct question, he sputtered a moment. "Of course! You know I do."

Clara nodded thoughtfully and fiddled with her napkin. When she looked up, tears were shimmering in her eyes. "I love you, Paul. But I don't want to spend my life clinging to impossible dreams. I want them to become reality. Do you understand?"

"Of course. Please don't be sad. We'll find a way for you to work with children," Paul said in a soothing voice.

"Yes," Lotte said. "And I'll ask around the community the next opportunity I get."

"Thank you," Clara replied firmly. "But it won't be necessary. I've got my eyes fixed on my goal and I'll do whatever I must to achieve it—with or without support."

"What do you mean?" Paul asked hoarsely.

Clara folded her hands together. "I intend to convert."

Lotte froze like a pillar of salt.

Paul loosened the tie he always wore on Shabbat. "They'll make you renounce our ways and customs, darling," he said, trying to grasp the situation. "You won't be able to celebrate with us anymore."

"Oh, that's the least of it." His mother turned to Clara. "Could you suddenly forget what the Lord above has taught us, all that we live and strive for? Could you tear Adonai from your heart for this worldly career ambition? You want to become a Christian, even though they treat us like second-class citizens? Have you forgotten how they slander us in their schools? About the National Socialist Schoolchildren's League?" Lotte had turned pale. "You can't be serious!"

"I understand what you're saying, Frau Blumenthal," Clara said. "And I won't hold it against you or Paul if you want nothing more to do with me."

"Nonsense," Paul replied indignantly. "We're just trying to understand."

Clara waved her hand in a broad gesture. "I want to become a Christian *because* I don't want to be treated like a second-class citizen. All my life, they've told terrible lies about us, barred us from professions and schools, sneered at us in the street. Why should I live this way? And, Frau Blumenthal, the truth is that my family was never much for strict observance of the laws and customs anyway. Especially since my mother died, my father and I have, well, fallen away a bit. I love the Lord, but deep down, it doesn't make any difference to me if I pray to Him in a synagogue or a church. Whether I fast or not, observe the Sabbath on Saturday or Sunday, in my heart I believe we're ultimately praying to the same God."

Lotte raised a hand. "Don't ever let the rabbi hear you speak this way," she replied with a ragged edge to her voice. "There are vast differences between the two religions. They're not even—"

Paul interrupted his mother's torrent of words and gestured for her to let Clara speak.

"I don't deny that at all," the young woman said. "But please allow me to point out that there are also similarities. Their messiah was a Jew, was he not?"

Paul looked at Clara tenderly. Her fighting spirit made him love her all the more. Surely her openness must have a disarming effect on his mother.

But then he caught a hard gleam in Clara's eyes that scared him. "I won't wait any longer. You yourself know the abuse our people are forced to endure. And if we defend ourselves against it, we risk ending up in jail."

At this, Paul's mother muttered reluctant assent.

"I'm tired of having to walk through life with my head lowered, living in constant fear of the future. I want to be happy, and I know that teaching is my vocation." Clara held her chin high. "I can't let anything stand in my way."

Her words pierced Paul. The silence in the living room weighed heavily on him.

"Does your father know of these plans?" Lotte asked, her voice hollow.

"Not yet. I wanted to discuss it with Paul first."

Lotte stood stiffly and smoothed her skirt. "I'm tired. Paul, will you walk Clara home?"

"Of course. Good night, Mama."

After Lotte had left the room, he moved to sit by Clara. "How do you intend to convert without half the town knowing?"

She looked at him, gently stroking his cheek. "I'll say I'm going to a boarding school in Rostock for three months to further my education and training. That should be plausible enough. When I return, I'll have my certificate of baptism in my bag." She sighed. "What about us, Paul?"

He kissed her eyelids, her straight nose, and finally, her soft lips. "We belong together. That won't change."

She looked at him, her eyes full of questions.

"I'll convert with you," he said. "And once we have all the obstacles out of the way, we'll marry."

Clara's eyes widened. "Are you sure? Your business, your family. Your father . . ."

He waved her concerns away. "My father made a far greater sacrifice. He'd understand mine. My heritage may be Jewish, but my heart belongs to you. I love you, Clara."

She took him in her arms and, although shaken by her confession, he felt a calm certainty. No one and nothing would ever come between them.

Chapter 11

Paul's decision pained his mother, and he heard her up at night weeping. Still, she didn't broach the subject again, possibly hoping he would change his mind. But when he announced to her a week later that, at the beginning of the new year, he intended to go to Kiel for a three-month course in accounting, she looked heartbroken.

"Don't worry, Mama. I'll pay for the room from my savings," Paul said gently. "Alfons knows what he's doing in the shop, and I'm sure Karl will be delighted to work an extra day a week. The customers like his work."

"If your father were alive . . ." Lotte broke off, fighting back tears.

"I love her, Mama. I'd do anything to keep her safe and help her fulfill her dreams. This is the way to do it. Papa would understand that I have to follow my heart."

Lotte took her son's face in her hands. "I refuse to lose you too. If I can't persuade you to change your mind about this, I will try to accept it. Just promise me that, even if you turn your back on your heritage, you will never turn your back on your family."

"I promise, Mama," Paul said gratefully, wrapping his arms around her.

Clara had a much harder time with her father. She told Paul later that they'd never had a serious argument before. On the contrary, since her mother had died eight years ago, Clara had benefited from her father's liberal ideas, enjoying far more freedom than most girls her age. But this was different. Dr. Fisch wouldn't even discuss it seriously, but accused her of being foolish and ungrateful.

Paul knew how this rift pained Clara, but he also knew her well enough to trust that she would find a way to bring her father around. One morning two weeks later, he was at the counter of Blumenthal & Sons, sorting the change in the till and arranging a handful of handmade gold watches artfully in the display case. He looked up and recognized Clara's distinctive figure in her tailored black coat. Each morning, they would meet at the shop for a few brief moments before going to their own work. A cap covered her beautiful hair to protect her from the frosty cold. She was treading carefully, as a thin layer of ice had turned the street into a skating rink.

Paul spotted two youths sauntering over from the other side of the street. One of them cupped his hands around his mouth and called out to her. Clara hastened her steps. Just before she reached the door of the shop, the men had caught up and surrounded her.

Paul stormed out.

"Leave me alone," she was stammering, recoiling from them. "What do you want?"

"Can I help you, gentlemen?" Paul placed himself in front of Clara, edging her toward the door.

"Is that your Jewish slut?" one of them sneered.

Paul drew himself up straight. "My future wife," he replied coolly. "I suggest you leave right now."

One took a step closer. "And if we don't? This is a public place. We can go where we want." He leaned forward, the tips of their noses almost touching.

The next thing Paul knew, a fist landed in his face. He felt as though his head would explode. Clara screamed, and the thug stepped back. The two walked away, laughing.

Paul took her in his arms. "Are you OK?"

"I'm fine." Clara examined his nose, her lips pressed tight, and dabbed at it with a handkerchief. "You're bleeding."

"It's nothing. Come in," he said, drawing her into the shop. Paul could feel his nose swelling. Something had happened to his left eye, too. But he wouldn't let Clara see how deeply shaken he was by the incident. For the first time, he longed for the day when they would return to Hamburg as Christians, knowing that they could finally walk through the world unafraid.

The two lovers stood for a few moments in the shop, holding hands in stunned silence, before Alfons came in with his usual cheery greeting.

He saw Paul and froze. "Herr Blumenthal, what happened to your face?"

"I have to get to work." Clara tried to conceal her agitation, but the tremor in her voice gave her away.

Paul turned to Alfons and asked him to look after the shop for a while.

Ignoring the disapproving looks from passersby, Paul placed his arm around Clara's waist. They walked the short distance without speaking. As they reached the two-story building that housed the doctor's practice, she turned to say goodbye, but he led her determinedly to the side door.

"What are you doing?"

"Wait here, Clara."

Inside, a couple with a whining infant were already waiting for the doctor. Ignoring their protests, he knocked and, after a brief pause, entered.

Dr. Fisch was in the middle of buttoning up his white coat. A fleeting look of surprise crossed his face, turning almost immediately to alarm. "Shalom, Paul. What happened? Sit down; I'll take a look."

"That won't be necessary, thank you." He gave him a brief account of the incident.

Dr. Fisch's face turned an unhealthy red, but Paul implored him to stay calm.

"Forgive me if I'm causing you offense," Paul said carefully. "I don't know what insults those men threw at her before I stepped in. But one thing's for certain: they were ready for violence."

"I understand," the doctor replied.

Paul studied Clara's father closely. The man's dark eyes were glowing with rage. "May I speak openly, Dr. Fisch?"

The doctor indicated for him to sit at the desk, then looked at him expectantly.

"You probably no longer approve of me and think I'm the one encouraging Clara to convert," he said, the words tumbling out. "That's not the case, but I intend to support her, and even to convert, too. I want her to be happy."

The two men's eyes met.

"We love each other," Paul continued. "I want Clara to live in safety. This morning makes it clear how bad things have become and how important it is to do something soon. Clara and I will each make our own peace with the Lord, and we will mourn the loss of our community, but it would be too much to lose our families as well. Please say you won't turn your back on your daughter?"

Dr. Fisch folded his hands on the desk and sat in a pensive silence for several long moments.

"You're wrong, Paul. I like you very much; it's these plans I don't like. But I must confess that I'm disturbed by the way things are going, too. In recent weeks my patients have been complaining that they can't get served in shops anymore. One of them even told me that a good friend refused to be seen with him in public. These things have always happened, but it's increasingly difficult to convince myself that they're isolated incidents." He tapped the surface of the desk in agitation, then suddenly stood. "Of course I want Clara to be happy. And I cannot

disown my only child. I only ask that you both look realit
The community will not be as softhearted as I."

"We're ready for that," Paul replied calmly. "But I'm co
tolerance will win in the end. And who knows how many
follow our example?"

The doctor shook his head vehemently. "No. You and
grown up on the outskirts of the community here, in famili
perhaps too liberal. Most of our people, especially the old
have grown up within the traditions that bind our comm
never betray their ancestors, their way of life."

Paul wanted to argue, but decided not to pursue it fu
was one point he was certainly willing to concede to his futu
law: the younger generation, who had grown up with acces
German society, who already chafed at the demands of the
of Jewish life, they were far more prepared than their elders
familiar behind.

"The Jewish community will see you as traitors, and the
will consider you outsiders who need to be watched carefully
observed.

"Time will tell." Paul sensed the older man watching h

"This decision pains me deeply, but I understand the e
the times and I won't stand in your way. She is my daughter
already consider my son." The doctor came around the des
returned his firm handshake.

"There's one thing I'd ask of you," Dr. Fisch said. "I
observe Shabbat together as a family before you two no longe
His breath caught in his throat and he was silent for a lon
before looking up and meeting Paul's eye. "I believe your mo
be very pleased."

"I'm sure she will," Paul replied warmly.

Back at his workshop, Paul had difficulty concentrating
the brooch a customer had ordered. It was to have a teardr

ıber stone at its heart. As he clipped the magnifying glass in front of ; eye, his thoughts wandered to his mother, who had a similar silver ooch made by his father. His attention was drawn by the music box its glass case above him. Until that moment he had thought it best keep it there, since that meant it would always be safe, and close by he worked. But as he left the store that evening, he tucked it into the side pocket of his jacket.

ıd so it came about that Lotte, Clara, and Paul gathered for Shabbat nner in Nathan Fisch's house. As darkness fell over the roofs of amburg, Lotte lit the candles and began the blessings. Then they ared a delicious meal and drank the doctor's best wine.

But the gathering was overshadowed by a sad event that had caught otte and Paul unawares. Alfons had given his notice that morning.

"I hope you can forgive me," Alfons had said, frowning as he arched for the right words. "Your family has always been good to me. n truly sorry that I have to leave you now, after almost thirty years."

The announcement had shaken Paul to the core. He had to fight a mp in his throat as he told Dr. Fisch and Clara about it that evening.

"I don't understand," Clara said. "Why is he resigning so soon efore retirement age?"

Lotte leaned forward. The corners of her finely curved mouth were dged with deep lines of sorrow. "Because his Hedwig can't bear the tuation anymore."

"What do you mean, Frau Blumenthal?" Nathan Fisch asked.

"Her friends and family are snubbing her or constantly making asty comments," Lotte replied. "Because Alfons works for the 'filthy wish rabble,' as they put it."

The doctor breathed in sharply. "I'd have expected Alfons to have ıore backbone than that."

"That's easy enough to say," Paul replied. "Please don't hold it against Alfons. After all, Clara and I are also taking an unconventional route toward a peaceful future."

Clara smiled at him affectionately across the table. Her eyes drifted to the window. A streetlamp lit up the deserted sidewalk, making its icy surface glitter. "But it's a particular blow now, when Paul's going to be away for three months," she said, turning to Lotte. "Who's going to look after your customers?"

"Karl will be in the workshop three or four mornings a week," Lotte replied. "And I can take care of the sales until we find another solution."

Dark clouds seemed to have gathered over the dining room. The Blumenthals and the Fischs sang traditional songs, exchanged smiles, and offered each other support with only a few words. It grew late and they parted warmly. Paul and Clara found it hard to say good night. There were still ten days to go before they left for Kiel and Rostock.

On Sunday morning, Paul and his mother intended to go to Lübeck to visit their family, while Clara and Dr. Fisch were going to spend the day with his older brother. Paul had recently told Uncle Max on the telephone about his and Clara's plans. Paul's fears that his uncle would give him a fierce lecture, calling him irresponsible and ungrateful, proved groundless. His curt remark that they must know what they were doing had surprised Paul.

He kept thinking about it as he and his mother made their way to Lübeck. The bright blue sky was deceptive, and the frozen sidewalk crunched beneath their feet. The overflowing train was filled with the joyful murmur of their festively dressed fellow passengers with their fur hats and muffs. Michael and Robert met them at the station. Paul hadn't seen his cousins for a long while. After their apprenticeships, they had done a year's voluntary military service like their uncles. Robert had a talent for silversmithing, and Uncle Max saw him as a promising successor. Michael, on the other hand, was a good salesman with strong negotiating skills. Now the brothers were back home, planning to continue the family business into the next generation. At least, they had been until recently.

"Now we're jobless because Blumenthal and Sons isn't in a position to take us on," twenty-one-year-old Robert said, his round glasses giving him an intellectual look, Paul thought. In truth, he had passed his exams by the skin of his teeth and preferred to spend his free time canoeing on the Wakenitz River.

"It wouldn't do any good in any case. These days, people are ashamed of buying from the likes of us," his brother Michael added. A year older than Robert, he was bookish and private, only speaking when he deemed it absolutely necessary.

Uncle Max carefully cut the end off a cigar and lit it. "Last week, I had to have the display window replaced because a group of hooligans threw a stone through it. I can understand your decision, Paul." He stood up and moved to the window, where he gazed out in silence over the wonderful view of the Holsten Gate and the old sailing ships at the port on the Lower Trave.

Lotte sat by Martha and placed an arm around her shaking shoulders. "Please don't cry any more, darling. I'm terribly sad about Paul and Clara's choice, but they're grown now, and with everything that's happening, I hope you can understand that it does bring me some solace to think my child will be able to live his life free from abuse. We'll get through these terrible times just as our people always have."

Martha patted Lotte's hand, sniffed loudly, and looked from one to the other. "I guess I can understand that, may the Lord forgive me. Anyway, we have something important we've been wanting to tell you all. Right, Hermann?"

Her husband tucked a lock of hair behind his ear. "That's right, my love." He made sure he had the whole family's attention before continuing. "After thinking long and hard, we've decided to emigrate to Cape Town."

Lotte froze, and Max, who still had his back to them, coughed on cigar smoke.

"Why Cape Town?" Paul asked, stunned.

Martha looked at him gravely. "I suppose because we came to the same conclusion Clara did, Paul. Our people don't have a future here anymore. Robert and Michael can't find work because they're Jews."

Her eyes shone with tears; he had never seen her so emotional. He suddenly felt a lump in his throat. The growing aggression against Jews seemed to be spreading like poison.

"We'll be appreciated in Cape Town. There's a large, flourishing Jewish community there," Michael replied. "We've had enough of insults and threats."

"The noose is tightening around us," Uncle Hermann added. "We have to go now. Can you imagine, that madman Adolf Hitler received considerable support from conservatives in the Thuringia elections last fall. Tell me, what are we to make of that?"

Paul looked at his aunt uneasily. "So you're just leaving? Do you want to sell the business?"

Martha laughed. "They'd like that, wouldn't they?"

Max turned at last and strode back to the table. "There's no chance of that. I'm staying here, and I'll take care of the business. We've survived hard times in the past and come out stronger for it. Blumenthal and Sons is going to weather this storm." He gestured with his head toward the kitchen, where they could hear the clattering of dishes. "I've asked Alma to help me with sales in the shop."

"She's a good housekeeper, but what can she know about our business?" Hermann asked.

"She's a quick learner and she's very practical," Max said forcefully. "And once the situation stabilizes, we'll need to think about finding a skilled silversmith. Do you truly believe the citizens of this country will carry on allowing themselves to be manipulated by the National Socialists? No, our countrymen are better than that. Anyway, I'm convinced the president will soon put an end to this ghastly business." He smiled tightly. "In any case, I'm not cut out to be a globe-trotter. The very thought of a rocking ship makes me ill. But I do confess it will be lonely without you."

Martha threw a napkin at him in mock indignation. "Oh, stop it. Even if Cape Town were right next door, you'd only leave your beloved Lübeck if you were chased out with a riding crop!"

Paul grinned.

Max waved toward the window. "Just look at this glorious city with its gabled houses, sturdy brick buildings, and lovely old town island. Its people with their Hanseatic history and composure. Or think of Thomas Mann, Lübeck's very own literary hero, who recently won the Nobel Prize. What could I hope to find abroad that rivals what I have here?"

Martha shook her head. "You're an incorrigible, sentimental old man."

"That I am," he remarked drily. He turned to Paul. "I presume we're seeing each other for the last time before you two leave to—ahem—further your education?"

"That's right, Uncle Max."

"Then I wish you well, indeed, my dear nephew. And come visit me once you've returned. Seeing your kind face helps me miss your father less."

When Lotte and her son headed for home that afternoon, Paul was in a melancholy mood. His uncle usually clapped him on the shoulder when they parted, but this time he had hugged him in a tight embrace.

"Look after yourselves," Max had whispered in his ear. "I admire your courage."

Chapter 12

Cape Town, Sea Point, April 1931

In Sea Point, which lay in an idyllic location at the foot of Signal Hill on the Atlantic coast, autumn had arrived, transforming the landscape into a sea of red, yellow, and orange hues. In Lotte's homeland, on the other hand, daffodils and forsythia provided the first cheerful hints of spring.

From her small balcony, Lotte had an incredible view of Lion's Head Mountain. But that morning it was shrouded with clouds. Hermann had left the simple two-story house at daybreak. He worked as an assistant in a kosher grocery store on Main Road, looking after the deliveries. His pay could be described as meager at best, but together with the needlework that she and Martha did for a textile firm in the city, it was enough for a modest life. Robert had found a job with a jeweler, and Michael's strong language skills had won him a position managing correspondence for a real estate agent. The brothers shared a tiny apartment in the center of Cape Town and had quickly established a wide circle of friends. Lotte, on the other hand, found it difficult to meet people. There were supposed to be a lot of Germans living on the Cape, but to date she hadn't come into contact with any of them. Since she had next to no English, her contact with the locals was limited to a few polite words.

She remembered as if it were yesterday how her emigration plans had left Paul speechless. The thought that she might never see him again had ignited a fiery pain inside her that had burned ever since. The young couple had moved their wedding forward to before her departure, which had made Lotte very happy. She was amazed at the determination and single-mindedness with which they pursued their goals. Now that she had made her own sea change, her distress over the conversion had eased. And Lotte could not have wished for a better wife for her son. The two seemed destined for one another.

On the day the two of them were married, Clara had looked stunning in her homemade knee-length wedding dress, with a circlet of flowers in her hair. If there was a single image that Lotte would carry in her heart until her last breath, it was the look on Paul's face as he slipped the fine ring he'd wrought onto Clara's finger. With his marriage vows he had formed an eternal bond with Clara—even though it meant untying the one that bound him to her. "You never get anything in life without having to give something else up," she had once told him. She had never imagined it would one day be her from whom he parted.

Despite everything, Lotte did not regret for a second her decision to come to South Africa with Martha and her family. She missed neither the comfort of her former life in Altona, nor the apartment where everything reminded her of Johann. She had observed Paul's astonishment when she pressed his father's diary into his hands before departing. Deep inside she knew that she would never truly get over Johann's death as long as she kept it. It often seemed to her as though his innermost thoughts and feelings came together in a single voice that whispered constantly to her. Here in Cape Town, so far away from everything that had weighed her down in her homeland, she could at last breathe a little. If only she weren't plagued by homesickness and missing Paul, feelings that even pervaded her dreams. Of course she told herself not to cling to him—after all, his last letter had radiated pure joy as he told her they were expecting their first child. Though the news was a balm to her soul, she also felt a twinge of sadness. She wondered whether she would ever hold her grandchild in her arms. Johann's old friends, Gregor and August, also wrote to her regularly. They were both still in touch with Paul and Clara, and although the general situation was worsening, they had assured her that she shouldn't worry. Gregor was only too aware of the difficulties the young couple faced, and on his last visit, he had promised solemnly to support them. *It's so good to know that the children aren't alone,* Lotte thought gratefully.

The rattling of Martha's sewing machine drifted up from the floor below, reminding her not to waste any more time on sentimental thoughts. As she cleared away the breakfast dishes in her small kitchen area, her thoughts turned to Max. Everyone in the family had noticed that something wasn't right, but they had put his sickly appearance down to worries about the business and his unhealthy lifestyle. Unfortunately, they had been mistaken; Max was suffering from chronic heart disease. Dr. Fisch had strongly advised him to cut down on the amount of time he spent working, but Max seemed to shrug off the doctor's words. Lotte knew him better than that, though. Max loved playing the hedonistic businessman, but the truth was that he did not know to whom he could hand over responsibility for the family firm. Paul was an imaginative silversmith, but he lacked the business sense and experience that a commercial enterprise needed.

It's still too soon for him, Max had said three weeks ago in his most recent letter. *I have no choice but to continue running things until I've found a suitable solution.*

Lotte and Martha were anguished at no longer being able to support him. For the first time, they were compelled to entrust the well-being of their family to others. Jakob, the young silversmith he'd hired, was a good man, and she knew he would help Max whenever he could. But was it enough?

Lotte had no sooner gone downstairs than there was a knock at the door.

"Post, ladies," the mailman said, handing her two envelopes.

"Did I hear the door?" Martha stuck her head out of the sewing room, a tape measure looped around her neck.

"Yes. Two letters for you," Lotte replied. As Martha opened the first envelope, Lotte stared at the second, marked "Telegram."

Martha laid the first to one side. "Just a bill." She noticed the telegram. "Who can that be from?" She took the scissors sticking from her overall pocket and opened it.

Your brother is in the hospital. Please call me, Alma Schott.

"Heavens above," Martha exclaimed, swaying slightly.

"What's the matter?" Lotte asked anxiously.

Martha handed her the telegram, and Lotte felt the blood draining from her own face. "Try and remain calm, darling. You stay here while I run to the post office." Without waiting for Martha to reply, she grabbed a cardigan from the coat stand and hurried out. Fortunately, the post office was less than a quarter of an hour's walk. Lotte's heart was racing as she ran through the noisy crowds of Sea Point. When she entered the post office, the clerk who operated the telephone was just arriving. Lotte paced up and down impatiently as she waited for him to open up. What was taking so long? The Afrikaners seemed to have all the time in the world.

At last her call was connected and she heard a deep woman's voice as if from a long way off. "Blumenthal and Sons. How can I help you?"

"This is Lotte Blumenthal. Alma, is that you?"

"Oh, thank God! Yes, it's me. I'm so glad you've called."

"How's Max?"

"They're examining him in the General Hospital as we speak. Your son asked me to contact you. He and his wife are on their way to visit him."

Alma told her how she had found Max half collapsed in the kitchen early that morning. He was unable to speak and fighting for breath, his lips a sickly bluish color. She had called a doctor, who had managed to stabilize him enough to be moved.

Lotte closed her eyes in relief. "Thank you, Alma, from the bottom of my heart. Please give Max, Paul, and Clara my love, and Martha's, too. We'll call again later."

Back at the house, Martha was waiting for her, wild with impatience. After Lotte had told her everything, the two women sat together in silent bewilderment. Even when they managed to turn their attention back to dressmaking, they barely spoke. Their lunch sat on the table untouched, and the afternoon seemed to drag by endlessly. The moment the clock struck five, they set off for the post office to place another call.

The doctors had confirmed that Max had suffered a heart attack. He was now out of danger and sent his love to Martha and Lotte. Paul told them that Max would probably be discharged the following week, provided there were no further complications.

"That's wonderful news," Lotte said.

"It is indeed, Mama. But I'm afraid that's not all. The doctor has forbidden Uncle Max from working and told him that he'll probably need care for the rest of his life. He's devastated."

"How dreadful. Especially for Max, who's always set such great store by his independence. My goodness, how will the poor man cope?"

On hearing this, Martha also pressed her ear to the receiver.

"We'll have to find a suitable nurse for him," she interjected. "Perhaps we'll even have to close our main shop—"

"I'm glad to say we've found a solution," Paul said. "Alma would like to look after him."

"That woman idolizes him," Lotte said softly. "I suppose she always has, and he just can't see it."

"I think you're right, Mama. Max sees Alma as little more than someone who makes sure he's comfortable."

"But what's going to happen to the business?" Martha repeated.

"We'll manage," Paul said. "Next week I'll familiarize myself with the Lübeck accounts. Clara will help Karl in the Altona shop. Of course I can't replace Uncle Max, but I'll do my best to make him proud. At least I can always ask his advice."

Lotte couldn't help thinking of her brother-in-law's last letter. "Thank you, my son," she replied softly. "You'll be up to the job, I'm sure. If only I could be there with you to help."

"Don't be upset, Mama. We'll manage."

"Clara shouldn't be taking on too much," Martha put in firmly.

"She's doing fine, Aunt Martha. I'm keeping a close eye on her, you can be sure of that."

"And so you should, my boy," Lotte replied. "I'll call again tomorrow."

"Yes, Mama. Give Hermann and everyone my love."

A little while later, Lotte was standing on the balcony, watching the magical daily show of the sun going down in a blaze of red over the Atlantic. But she hardly saw the spectacle through the tears running down her face.

Chapter 13

Altona, 1931–1933

It was a demanding time for Paul. He would sit in the office of Blumenthal & Sons in Lübeck and try with growing despair to recall everything he'd learned in Kiel about bookkeeping. His pride wouldn't allow him to trouble Uncle Max about it, so he leafed through legal commentaries and textbooks until he found out what he needed to know. One evening, Paul sat staring at the accounts in greater distress than usual. He had to do something if they were going to prevent the business from going under in the next six months. But what?

That summer night in 1931, he forged a risky plan, which he disclosed to his uncle the next morning. Paul wanted to use part of the family savings to modernize the main shop and appoint Jakob, who was by now an experienced employee, as manager. And last but not least, Blumenthal & Sons needed a new name—one that wasn't "tainted" by Jewishness. No one who sympathized with Hitler's thinking came near the place now. But they might be able to attract the interest of the numerous visitors to the city and those who had recently moved there. Paul sweet-talked his uncle until he gave in. A few weeks later, Holsten Jewelers was unveiled. They held a celebratory opening event with Gregor, August, and their most loyal customers gathering in Lübeck for the occasion. Clara's friend, Hilde Wilhelm, also came. The young dressmaker had converted at the same time Clara had, and the two got together from time to time.

Paul's plan seemed to work. Curious to see what the new shop had to offer, people came in, praising the wares and the welcoming atmosphere. But this success left a bitter aftertaste in Paul's mouth. He found it depressing that customers suddenly trusted them again merely on the basis of a new name, a coat of paint, and a few new chairs. Even fearful Alfons began to pay them brief visits again, inquiring after the family.

One sunny October morning a few months later, as Clara lay beside him, sleepily rubbing her swollen belly, Paul shared his real dream for the shop. The next year, he intended to debut a collection in the Art Deco style. He was working to create a truly distinctive line of matching rings, cuff links, pendants, and earrings. He wanted people to know at first glance that they were made in this workshop. Paul floated on a cloud of elation, and would return home after a day's work with a smile lighting up his face.

Paul and Clara had taken over Lotte's apartment. Unlike his mother, he loved all the little reminders of his parents' past. There was something else, too. The kitchen in Lotte's apartment was kosher, and Paul and Clara secretly continued to cook kosher food. But since so many Jews were seeking safety abroad, it was becoming ever more difficult to find kosher groceries. When the last Jewish store in the neighborhood closed, they reluctantly relinquished one of the last ties to their traditions.

In November, Clara gave birth to a healthy daughter, and Paul was sure that no family could be happier. They baptized the baby, who had inherited her mother's gray eyes and chestnut hair, calling her Margarethe. Sometimes his happiness was so palpable he felt he could actually hold it in his hands.

They attended mass regularly on Sundays and were soon seen as exemplary Catholics. Some of the men were friendly toward Paul, openly expressing their delight that a Jewish couple had been taken into the bosom of the Church. Clara, on the other hand, was met with silent contempt—both from the Catholic women and from her old community. When Paul asked her if she was bothered by it, she would merely laugh and kiss his concerns away.

Paul was still very worried about his uncle. Since his heart attack, he had become a shadow of his former self. He refused to accept his fate and cursed his illness that made climbing stairs so difficult that he rarely left the house. The affable man gradually turned into a grouchy, taciturn recluse. Even Alma was on the receiving end of his moods. Whenever things got too bad and she threatened to look for another job, Max would quickly back down.

Five months later, in April 1932, Paul was able to record positive figures once again for Holsten Jewelers, and he used the capital to modernize the newly renamed Altona Market Jewelers.

With the help of their capable young managers, Karl and Jakob, their excellent reputation spread. And in the period before Christmas, Paul's Art Deco jewelry line, exclusive to them, attracted a lot of attention.

During their regular telephone conversations about the business, Paul noticed that Uncle Max was asking his opinion more frequently. When Paul pointed this out, his uncle replied, "I have to admit that at first I feared you weren't ready for the responsibility. But I was wrong. You've grown into a savvy businessman, and I was right to hand over the reins to you. You combine good business sense with the courage of the young. I'm proud of you, boy."

Words failed Paul. He'd never expected to hear such praise from his uncle. As he'd straightened his tie and examined himself in the mirror that morning, he'd seen the shy, self-doubting boy still in the shadow of the two men who had shaped his life: Max and Johann Blumenthal. But when he looked again that evening, all hint of childishness had left his features. If he were able to see himself as others did, he would be struck by his straight back and the fighting spirit that sparkled in his eyes. But it was enough for Paul to know that he had stepped out of Max and Johann's shadow and steered the family firm safely through rocky waters. He was now a husband, father, silversmith, and business proprietor—more than he'd ever dreamed. Before going home to Clara and Margarethe, he gave himself a cheerful wink in the mirror.

He had been pleased to hear that his mother had by now begun to make friends in Sea Point and was busy learning English and Afrikaans. She seemed to be blossoming in the South African sun.

Clara's dream had also come true: she had passed her training and become a full-fledged kindergarten teacher. Since then she had been working in the Fröbel kindergarten in the Rotherbaum district, taking little Margarethe with her. The gleam in Clara's eyes as she recounted her days confirmed to Paul that their sacrifice had been worth it.

But as soon as they stepped out of the friendly confines of home and shop and school, it was as though a veil was lifted from their eyes. Since January 1933, the National Socialists' swastika banners were everywhere, and the streets were full of uniformed men. A merciless wind was blowing through Germany, awaking in the young couple a profound unease.

One sunny afternoon in April of that year, Paul and Clara took their little daughter to visit the zoo. But they had no sooner reached the center of Hamburg than they noticed official anti-Jewish placards on many of the shop windows. They saw Jewish shopkeepers whose faces were clouded with horror as a cursing mob threw raw eggs at the windows. Brownshirts were patrolling the sidewalk in front of the shops, ordering anyone who passed nearby to stay away from Jews. Paul and Clara crossed to the other side of the street. "Thank goodness we converted," he whispered as he squeezed her hand.

The next Monday, Paul went to the shop early to catch up with the accounts. Gritting his teeth, he set to work before taking a break and opening up the *Altonaer Tageblatt* newspaper.

"Law for the Restoration of the Professional Civil Service of April 7, 1933," the headline said. Paul skimmed the text, then stared at the paper in disbelief. The telephone rang.

"Have you seen the paper?" Uncle Max asked.

"They're firing all Jewish civil servants!" Paul was incredulous. "It has to be a sick prank! For heaven's sake, just think of all our customers and neighbors who are going to be out of a job. Hitler can't do this! If they dismiss all Jewish civil servants, how will they get their work done? Thank goodness we don't work for the government."

"Well, it wouldn't affect you and Clara anyway," Uncle Max said. "But have you read the rest?"

"No."

"They're making an exception for those who fought in the World War or—listen to this—those whose fathers or sons were killed in the war."

Paul was silent for a moment as he took this in. *Papa, you didn't die for your country in vain,* he thought. *They think of you as a German.* Out loud, he said, "So at least my father and all the other Jewish soldiers are being given some respect at last."

"Yes. We have President Hindenburg to thank for that. A few brave Jewish war veterans appealed to him for help, and he told Hitler in no uncertain terms that if the Jews were good enough to fight and shed their blood for the German Reich, they had the right to serve their country as professionals."

"That's something, at least." Paul's voice was shaky. "Father's Iron Cross still means something—it isn't just gathering dust in the cupboard."

"You understand, then," Uncle Max continued, "that Mr. Hindenburg is personally guaranteeing protection for the families of fallen Jewish soldiers. I fear deeply for our friends and neighbors, but we ourselves have nothing to fear."

"What a relief!" Paul looked out of the window. Despite Max's optimism, the rain he saw outside mirrored his growing foreboding.

Chapter 14

During the weeks that followed, Paul and Clara observed the developments with dismay, as their former community members were fired from their jobs and their children thrown out of the schools. The poverty and despair of the Jewish population grew daily.

In quiet moments, when the young couple talked about the prejudice that Jewish citizens were facing, they sometimes felt like turncoats, like traitors.

"Have you noticed the looks people give us? They despise us," Clara said as she rocked Margarethe in her arms. "I'd hoped it would eventually stop."

"It will, darling," Paul replied. "You've been strong for so long. Don't let it upset you. We're safe, and that's what matters."

"You're right," Clara sighed. "But it's so hard to watch the way they're treating people we've known since childhood, while we can enjoy a good life."

Paul put his arm around her. "You and Hilde do what you can for those in the community who are really struggling."

She nodded. "Hilde confided in me recently that she's had a boyfriend for a few months now, and she's very much in love. He's a Jew called Ezra, and he's a printer in his father's business."

"I'm pleased for her. Give her my best wishes. Though the times look hard for a couple like them." He studied her intently. "There's something else worrying you."

Clara leaned her head on his shoulder. "There is. My manager at school gave me a form to fill out—it's required by a new law. I have to prove my Aryan descent."

"What do they mean, 'Aryan descent'?" he said indignantly. "It's none of their business what our descent is! We're respectable Christians who've never done anything wrong. That's enough."

"It's all about blood for them," Clara countered quietly. "Herr Schuld told me I'm obliged to fill out the form, or else I'll be threatened with legal consequences."

Paul kissed her gently. "Don't worry, darling. What do we have to fear? You're a Christian employee, not a civil servant, and on top of that, a Blumenthal, legally protected by our president. The schoolchildren and your colleagues love you. Herr Schuld can't praise you highly enough. He's probably as unhappy about the form as anyone and just has to go along with it. It'll be fine. Fill out the stupid thing so they can't hold anything against you."

"Yes, I'm sure it's nothing," Clara said, and reached for a pen.

One rainy morning toward the end of April 1933, when only a few customers had wandered into the shop, Paul was watching Karl artfully arrange the latest Art Deco bracelets in one of the display cases.

Paul had recently received a lucrative commission from an affluent landowner, Marquardt, to design a necklace and matching earrings for his wife. They were to be unique originals, and he had stressed that price wasn't an issue.

Marquardt was a man with a pronounced penchant for luxury. Paul thought of the grandiose silver chandelier he had commissioned a few years ago. The man wanted something truly special, so Paul had designed a sensational gold necklace set with tourmalines, plus matching earrings, and Marquardt had made an appointment to come and see the design that day. On the phone, he had congratulated Paul on the shop's renovation and stated his intent to place further orders. Fortunately, there were still some well-heeled people who were not taken in by the National Socialists with their contemptuous, barbaric machinations, Paul thought gloomily.

A little later, the landowner entered the shop. His brown uniform was meticulously neat, his black, knee-high boots shining. He sported a narrow mustache on his upper lip. Paul turned cold. He had clearly misjudged the man. When he saw the row of medals on Marquardt's breast, among them the Iron Cross, he could hardly believe his eyes.

"Surprised?" the landowner asked. "These days, I'm glad to say medals are only awarded to brave Aryans."

Paul didn't flinch from the man's disparaging scrutiny. What was his father's Iron Cross worth if the medal could be awarded to a pompous, bigoted man such as this?

Regarding him impenetrably, Marquardt asked to see the designs.

He'll be as delighted as ever with them, Paul told himself. *Even he has to see how unique they are.* "Here you are," he said to his customer with forced cheer. "I've based them on some exclusive pieces from the Baroque period. The tourmalines will look wonderful on your wife's neck. These pieces will be the perfect accompaniment to any attire."

"Very good," the man replied stiffly. "What do you want for your efforts?"

Paul looked up, confused. "I'm sorry?"

Marquardt waved his leather gloves in the air. "Don't worry, of course I'll pay you for the designs."

"Is my work not as you'd hoped? What is it that you don't like?" Paul asked, but Marquardt refused to answer and began to drum on the counter menacingly. After a few tense moments, Paul gave in and stated a price.

Unperturbed, the customer sprinkled some Reichsmark bills on the counter. "On the contrary, I like the designs very much. But I really must insist on the jewelry being made by an Aryan jeweler. I wish you good day." He picked up the drawings and swept out of the store.

Paul's spirits sank to his boots. Never before had he encountered such a brazen insult.

"What was that about?" Karl asked in horror.

"Sheer impudence, that's what it was," Paul replied as he struggled to grasp the situation. "The swine used me. But if I'd refused to hand over the designs, it would have meant my work was completely in vain."

Shaking his head, Paul hurried into the workshop. Distraction was the only answer.

Paul was working on the details of a golden cake dish when Karl stuck his head around the door. "Telephone for you."

Paul picked up.

"Willibald Schuld of the Rotherbaum Fröbelhaus speaking," said the sonorous voice on the other end of the line. "Hello, Herr Blumenthal."

Paul started and looked at his watch. It was only half past eleven. "Hello, Herr Schuld. Is something the matter with my wife?"

"Can you please come and fetch her immediately?" Clara's boss said stiffly.

"Has she been injured? Is she ill?"

"No. I'll explain when I see you. I'll expect you here in half an hour." He hung up.

Paul waved Karl over. "Will you be OK on your own for a while?"

"Of course."

As Paul left, he felt Karl's inquiring gaze follow him. Although he ran, he scarcely managed to catch the tram, and only just arrived at the kindergarten in time.

He found Clara in the playroom. Her lips pinched tight, her face pale, she was overseeing the infants. Margarethe sat among them, whining. Clara absently placed a teething ring in her daughter's little hands.

Paul looked at her with concern. As she turned slowly to face him, Clara looked like a volcano about to erupt. "What's happened?" He looked around. Her colleagues, Frieda and Gertrud, bustled about, tossing him disparaging glances.

"They won't say a word," Clara exclaimed angrily. "I . . . I've been dismissed. I even have it in writing already." She waved toward the pocket in her dress.

"I beg your pardon?" Paul said. Clara's colleagues deliberately turned away from them. Why were they suddenly treating them like lepers? The teachers had always worked happily together before.

Herr Schuld came hurrying in. "Herr Blumenthal. Can you please persuade your wife to leave the premises immediately? She's refusing to go. I must insist, or else I'll be forced to call the police."

Clara shook her head. "I'll go at the end of the day. Not a moment sooner."

Paul could hardly believe his ears.

"We've noticed for a long time that you never join in the conversations about our government's reforms," Frieda sneered.

"Now we know why!" Gertrud cried. "How dare you deceive us like that! To think we entrusted the care of our innocent Aryan children to a Jew like you!"

"I'm a Christian. Why can't you understand that?" Clara insisted, her voice quivering.

Gertrud's words spread like poison through Paul's veins. *A Jew like you.*

"Please calm down, ladies. Don't forget that you're still at work," Herr Schuld said. Once the women were out of earshot, he stepped forward. "So, do I have to call the police, or will you leave the premises of your own free will?"

Paul could sense Clara's rage. He picked Margarethe up and placed an arm around his wife's shoulders. "Let's go. There's no point in staying."

She reluctantly allowed him to take her home. In the living room he pressed her firmly down onto the sofa, poured her a glass of water, and sat down with Margarethe on his lap.

Clara wiped her eyes repeatedly, but new tears kept coming. "I was just finishing a castle of building bricks with the infants when Herr Schuld came and gave me my notice," she said finally in a small, almost inaudible voice. She handed him the letter.

For the attention of Clara Blumenthal, née Fisch, he read.

> *Those who were not born of Aryan parents do not count as Aryan. This criterion is met if one parent or grandparent is not Aryan. This is particularly pertinent if a parent or grandparent belongs to the Jewish religion. For this reason, you are dismissed with immediate effect from your position at the Rotherbaum Fröbelhaus. As a non-Aryan, you are unsuitable for the education and care of German children and young people, as you are not sufficiently trustworthy.*
>
> *Signed, The City Councilor for the District of Hamburg-Eimsbüttel*

Paul lowered the letter.

"I don't understand," he said. "The children love you. Doesn't that count for anything?" He recalled Hindenburg's promise to exclude the families of Jewish war veterans from dismissal. His initial anticipation of somehow being able to fight the dismissal gave way to sudden disillusionment. Clara had "only" married into the family and her own father was not a veteran. Besides, the promise only covered civil service posts. Paul pressed his lips together to stop himself from swearing.

"Nothing counts anymore to them," Clara moaned. The pain in her eyes sliced through him. He took her face in his hands and gazed at her beloved features.

She took a deep breath and drew out a second envelope. "Herr Schuld gave me a written assessment of my work two months ago. He said he was sorry that he couldn't do anything to prevent the dismissal."

Paul skimmed the page.

> *Frau Blumenthal is a woman of impeccable character who handles the children kindly and with motherly care. She doesn't look Jewish. The relationship between Frau Blumenthal and her charges is always impeccable. Her financial situation also seems to be perfectly in order.*
>
> *Signed, Willibald Schuld, Head of the Rotherbaum Fröbelhaus,*
>
> *February 22, 1933*

Paul looked up. His blood ran cold. "Do you know what this means? They've been spying on you for a long time."

"Exactly," she replied, thin-lipped. "I also have a good idea who helped them. I've told you about Adele Petermann, who works for us part-time."

Paul nodded. "The young woman with the one-year-old."

"That's right. She was very open, and told me a bit about her life. Because I liked her, I probably let slip one or two things about my own private life. Nothing too dramatic, but she knows your family owns two jewelry stores."

Paul waved away her concerns. "I can't see how that's a problem. We haven't done anything wrong."

"But I can't believe I was so naive," she replied bitterly. "I bet they even dangled the prospect of my full-time position in front of Adele if she helped them get rid of me."

This idea came as a shock to Paul, but he couldn't think of an argument to refute Clara's suspicion.

"The fact that they think I'm not suitable to look after children really hurts." The gleam in Clara's expressive eyes had been extinguished. "It was all in vain, Paul. Our months of separation, the conversion, all the pain we caused our parents and neighbors, the disputes with them, the extra schooling."

Paul drew her close. "Nothing we learn or experience is ever in vain. No one could have imagined how underhanded they'd be. But one thing I do know: those children had a wonderful, loving teacher in you." His words sounded banal even to his own ears. But there was no comfort to be had for what they had done to his wife—and no understanding of it.

"So you say."

Clara released herself from his embrace. Margarethe had fallen asleep in Paul's arms, and her little head lay against his breast. He stood, took the baby to her bed, and gently tucked her in.

"I should go back to work," he said.

Clara sniffed and looked at him, her eyes rimmed with red. "I know. I'll be fine."

Chapter 15

The bright rays of the morning sun fell on the workbench, painfully dazzling Paul's overtired eyes. After the renovations, he had returned the music box to its usual place. Knowing it was close by meant a lot to him, especially when—as now—he was feeling low. He had tried everything to cheer Clara up, even taking her out for dinner and making her a lovely heart-shaped pendant. But the sadness in her eyes remained. If only he knew how to conjure a smile back onto her face.

For the next few hours he worked feverishly on a design for a signet ring, and all his worries sank temporarily into the background. At lunchtime, unsatisfied with his sketches, he decided to seek inspiration in a book on antique jewelry they kept in a cupboard by the till.

Two men had their backs to the counter as they examined a display case. They wore brown shirts with black ties, black caps, and heavy boots, completed by the swastika armbands of the SS. Every time Paul saw uniformed Nazis, he was filled with trepidation.

Karl indicated the men with his head. "They didn't take the trouble to greet me. Let them wait a moment. How's your wife?"

Since Karl was loyal and discreet, Paul had taken him into his confidence. "I've never seen her so sad."

Karl shook his head anxiously. "She didn't deserve to be treated like that."

The customers turned and Paul froze. They were the roofers, Walter and Richard Sattler. He had known the brothers since kindergarten, and his father had done work for them frequently. Paul and his family had even enjoyed one or two lively parties in their company, but he hadn't seen them for quite a while.

"Hello, Paul." Walter Sattler's thick eyebrows drew together. "Is there any service in this dump or should we stand around growing roots? This is unacceptable!"

"I'm sorry," Paul said as politely as he could. "What can I do for you?"

"You Jews simply can't be beaten for audacity," Richard muttered, pressing his index finger into Paul's chest.

Paul took a step back. "What's that supposed to mean?"

"Do you think we haven't been watching you all this time?" Walter said with disgust. "The esteemed Blumenthals. Don't make me laugh! You always thought you were a cut above the rest. What did we simple tradesmen matter compared to you refined artists!" He lowered his voice. "But that's not all that counts, is it? When things started getting hot for you, you started pretending to be something you're not." He stepped so close that Paul could see the pulse in his throat. "I'm warning you to get the facts out in the open. If you think that you'll be spared just because you got yourself baptized, you're very much mistaken. You'll be exposed for what you are! Lying, deceitful rabble!"

"Come on, let's go to the Aryan jeweler on Ehrenbergstrasse," Richard hissed, grabbing a fistful of Paul's coat and spitting on his feet. Then the two men left the shop, whistling.

Paul suddenly recalled his mother talking about the war fever and sudden hatred for the French back in his father's day. When had Richard and Walter begun to see his family as their new enemy?

He was stirred from his paralysis by Karl handing him a damp cloth for his shoes. Paul looked out the window and the hairs at the back of his neck stood on end as he took in the swastikas hanging from the buildings up and down his street.

It made him all the more anxious to retreat to his workshop. He stared at the music box in its glass case and had a silent conversation with his father. But this time it held no comfort.

Working with children had been Clara's dream, a dream for which she had fought, taken huge risks, and made enormous sacrifices. Paul could sense something dying inside her, like a light gradually fading. When eating, she would push her food listlessly around the plate, and she tossed and turned at night. He decided to keep the unpleasant encounter with Richard and Walter to himself.

When Gregor and August appeared in the store one sunny day in mid-May, inviting Clara and Margarethe for an afternoon out in the countryside, Paul was delighted. "It's really kind of you to call on us. My wife could do with a little distraction."

His father's friends were horrified to learn about Clara's callous dismissal and the impugning of her character.

"It looks like we came at exactly the right time," August said with a wink.

A little later, Paul saw them off, little Margarethe giggling as August pushed her pram. When they returned that evening, Clara was smiling for the first time in a long while.

In the middle of the night, the urgent ringing of the doorbell tore the young couple from their sleep. Margarethe awoke and started crying. Paul jumped out of bed.

"I'll go," he said to Clara, who quickly threw on a dressing gown and went to see to their daughter.

Clara's father was at the door, pale and upset.

"I'm sorry to disturb you," he stammered as Paul ushered him in.

"What's the matter, Papa?" Clara asked as she entered with the baby in her arms.

"I . . . I just made a house call on the old pharmacist on Kaiser-Friedrich-Ufer," the doctor began.

"Herr Lindemann, who won't be treated by anyone but you?" she asked cautiously.

"That's right. He had an attack of lumbago and couldn't stand." The doctor stared into the darkness beyond the window. "I was about to leave when I suddenly heard a racket outside. They were . . . they were burning books, our literature! All the great works—Kafka, Brecht, Tucholsky, Mann. Our people's legacy!" His voice faltered in disbelief. "The flames leapt into the night sky. They said they were going to burn those books all over the Reich. God almighty, what are they doing?"

"Papa," Clara shook him gently. "Who was burning the books?"

"The student division of the SA from the university and a few others, my girl," the doctor replied. "And believe me, there was no mistaking what they said. It's supposed to be a campaign against the 'un-German spirit,' or so the speaker was yelling into the megaphone. 'We're bringing an end to the corrupting influence of un-German literature here and now.'"

No one spoke. Neither Paul nor Clara could fathom this senseless destruction of the works of generations of thinkers and poets.

Once Margarethe had fallen asleep in her mother's arms and had been put back to bed, Clara made them a pot of tea.

Dr. Fisch's hands were shaking as he held out his cup for her to pour.

She laid a hand on his arm. "I'll do it."

"I'm afraid that's not all," her father said once she had filled the cups. Clumsily, he fished in the inside pocket of his jacket, drew out an envelope, and laid it on the table.

For the personal attention of Doctor Nathan Fisch. In accordance with the Law on the Registration of Doctors for Health Care Funds of April 22, 1933, your authorization as a National Insurance Plan doctor is hereby withdrawn.

Clara's face froze. She jumped up. "So you aren't considered suitable to practice your profession either."

Her father's face looked carved from stone. The cup in his hands was shaking so violently that Paul took it from him.

"I've been practicing medicine for almost twenty years," Dr. Fisch said, as if to himself. "My patients come from far and wide to be treated by me. And now this."

The three of them stared at the letter.

"The professional designation has also been removed from the nameplate of the lawyer around the corner," Fisch continued.

Clara was pacing up and down in agitation. "Papa, this is terrible! If . . . if they take away your license—"

"I won't be able to treat any more National Insurance patients! What will become of them then? Most can't afford to pay me privately. Clara, think of blind Levi. Aviel with his diabetes or Jochebed with the leg wound that won't heal. Who's going to look after them?"

"If I know you, you'll continue to treat them free of charge."

"You can depend on that. I won't abandon my patients. No matter what the Nazis say."

Chapter 16

Margarethe

1934–1935

If Paul and Clara had hoped that the withdrawal of Dr. Fisch's National Insurance Plan license was the end of his troubles, they soon found they were mistaken. By October 1934, he was forbidden from practicing altogether. Clara's father had always been a self-controlled, circumspect man, but on the day that he handed the keys to his practice over to a colleague who later turned out to be an active member of the SA, he wept inconsolably.

"Why don't you come and live with us, Papa?" Clara asked.

"We'd love to have you here," Paul added.

"No, you can get that idea out of your heads," the doctor said, leaning forward to add in a whisper, "Those wretched criminals want to bring me to my knees. But they won't break me! Do you think that esteemed gentleman who's stolen my practice will bring himself to treat a single Jew?"

Paul looked at his father-in-law in consternation. "I'm sure he won't, but I don't think you should get involved. If they catch you treating your patients, they could arrest you."

"Paul's right, Papa." Clara hugged her father. "Don't put yourself in danger."

Dr. Fisch gazed at her thoughtfully, but gave no answer to their proposal. From that day on, he never mentioned the subject again. If he treated his patients in secret, he never let on.

A little later, Uncle Max called the Altona shop, asking for a face-to-face meeting. When Paul arrived in Lübeck the next Sunday, he found his uncle sitting wearily in an armchair, his legs under a blanket.

They talked about Dr. Fisch's expulsion from his profession, and the visit from the Sattler brothers, which Paul had kept to himself until then.

An ominous feeling hung over them, heavy as a storm cloud.

When Paul asked after his health, Uncle Max waved dismissively. "It's the blasted Nazis that are grinding me down, not my heart. Where's it going to end? Now they're getting rid of our most intelligent people, while others, thick as planks like the Sattlers, are gaining influence and stirring people up against us. There's even been rioting here." His expression darkened. "You know Fritz Lissauer, don't you? He's a member of the Lübeck Jewish Community Council."

Paul thought for a moment. "Of course. A kind man with a good social conscience. Textile import/export, right? What happened to him?"

"A rowdy gang dragged him out of his office and drove him through the city streets. He was accused of requiring his Aryan employees to work too much overtime. They hung a sign around his neck, which said: 'I'm a vampire and suck the blood of my German workforce'!"

"That's unbelievable! And I can't imagine he'd overwork anyone."

"Neither can I, my boy. People have always been happy working for him. Imagine this: they were singing Nazi songs as they dragged the poor fellow, along with his brother and his son, to a police station, where they were taken into custody on some trumped-up charges. Who knows what they'll do to them there."

Paul shuddered.

Alma served them refreshments and set a little dish of pills before Uncle Max. To Paul's horror, he washed them down with a shot of kirsch liqueur. Then Max told him how, almost every morning, Jakob had to remove posters saying "Jews Not Wanted" from their shop window, and described how would-be customers were regularly deterred by thugs blocking the door. Meanwhile, street brawls had become the order of the day, and every time Alma went out for groceries, she felt like she was running the gauntlet. She was cursed and threatened with being reported to the police for working for a Jew. Some people had even accused her of having an affair with her employer.

"Alma says she can handle the threats," Max continued, "but most of the shopkeepers throw her out, and the kosher store owners have emigrated."

"They all left Altona some time ago. But if those thugs won't let your customers in, how's the business surviving?"

"In the last two months we've just about made enough to cover our overhead costs," his uncle replied. "But there's no hope of a profit."

"My shop's down, too, but fortunately not by as much," Paul said.

His uncle's face, once so youthful, was now lined with deep creases. At fifty-six he should have been in the prime of his life.

"Now listen to me," Paul said in a tone that brooked no argument. "We have to close the business as soon as possible and emigrate."

The older man began to protest, but Paul silenced him with a wave of his hand. "I'm not going to argue, Uncle Max. I know you've put your whole life into this business. But I won't allow them to destroy us. We've fought for it for too long to let that happen."

Max Blumenthal was about to pour himself another drink, but Paul grabbed the half-empty bottle and took it to Alma in the kitchen. When he returned to the living room, his uncle was lost in thought.

"You'll ruin your health," Paul said gently.

His uncle turned his head slowly. "Give up my shop? Just like that?"

"It's for the best."

Max Blumenthal brought the flat of his hand down on the arm of the chair.

"Never! Johann didn't sacrifice his life for this country in vain. Hindenburg has promised to protect veterans' families. We must trust him. He'll put Hitler in his place."

Paul knew he had to tread carefully to avoid overexciting his uncle. "Our people have always been persecuted, have they not? And when things got bad, they moved on. It's time for us to do the same."

Uncle Max leaned forward. "We're not going to surrender that easily, my boy. We can use our private savings to keep the business afloat a while longer. We'll set ourselves a deadline of fall next year. If the situation hasn't improved by then, we'll fold. That's my final word." Max Blumenthal stretched. "But let me make one thing clear: Business or no, I'm not going anywhere—not to Cape Town, not to Timbuktu. I'm staying here and that's that."

"We're living in difficult times and we have to weigh all our options," Paul said cautiously. "Maybe we should think about selling this building." He was saying out loud what he'd been thinking for a long while. "Your neighbor, Herr Schuster, told us a while ago that he was wanting to expand his textile business—"

"Are you out of your mind?" Uncle Max boomed. "You're talking about our family home. I won't hear of it!"

Paul regarded him intently. "I'm just asking you to think about it. I'm sure Herr Schuster would offer us a fair price. Please don't think it's a suggestion I'd make lightly."

"But apparently you would!" his uncle flung back at him. "Who are you to say, anyway? You've never lived between these four walls—your father's home, your grandfather's. And we both know how willing you are to, well, give up your heritage when it suits you. Now, will you just leave me in peace. My offer about next year stands. But as far as selling the house is concerned, you'll only get me out of here in a coffin. That's the end of the conversation."

His uncle's anger left Paul momentarily speechless.

Alma broke the painful silence by arriving with coffee and cakes. Paul gave her a grateful smile, but his uncle barely seemed to notice.

"It's quite a long time until next fall," Paul ventured after she had left the room. "Do you think that's wise, given the way things are?"

"When else would you suggest? We need time to sell off our goods at a reasonable price. Since the other half of our clan is off sunning themselves in South Africa, it's up to us to run the shops ourselves. Or had you forgotten that?"

Paul smiled sadly at Max. His uncle's grinding jaw betrayed his inner turmoil. "Of course not," he said. "But our savings are already dwindling. The sooner we bring this sorry chapter to an end, the better it will be for us all."

The terrible discussion rumbled on for another hour. Paul had to restrain himself as his patience was sorely tried. He finally gave in, knowing that if he pushed too hard, Max would dig his heels in completely.

When they spoke over the following weeks, Max remained unmovable, referring to other difficult trials they had come through successfully. Paul did at least manage to convince him to run their stock down and hold a sale for their current jewelry lines, while continuing to offer the exclusive pieces to select regular customers.

They enjoyed some success; not three months later the majority of their collection had been sold. During one of their weekly telephone conversations, his mother and Aunt Martha advised him to deposit the profits in a safe place. But where? Clara and Paul gave it some thought and decided to call on a friend.

One afternoon, Paul made his way to the venerable bank building in Altona's old town. Once there, he looked around for a tall man with white hair.

Gregor approached, giving the Nazi salute with which he greeted all his customers. He looked elegant in his gray suit and snow-white shirt.

Then he looked around surreptitiously and said, "I'd rather have spared us the salute, but you know what people are like. It's good to see you. What brings you here?"

Paul lowered his voice to a whisper. "I need to speak to you urgently. What time do you finish work?"

"In a little under an hour."

"I'll wait for you in the reading room at the Hermann Tietz department store. No one should see that we know each other."

"Of course. I'll see you there. But you're worrying me."

"Thank you. I'll explain everything later." Paul left the bank and headed for the department store.

He became increasingly nervous as he crossed the clothing department with its opulent stucco ceiling. The second floor of the Art Nouveau building housed the hat department. Paul hurried past ornate cosmetics counters and stands displaying elaborate hats and matching purses. On the third floor, the walls of the art department were hung with valuable paintings, and the evening light shone down on the geometric patterns of the parquet floor.

He finally reached the reading room on the fourth floor. The plush carpet swallowed his steps as he slipped past the rows of bookshelves. Fortunately the room was busy. He selected a book, taking no notice of the title, sat down on a sofa, and feigned absorption. What had things come to, having to meet friends in secret? He felt like a criminal. He stole a glance at the hands of the designer clock above the door, but they seemed to be standing still.

When he finally glimpsed Gregor from the corner of his eye, he lowered his head over his book. A young waitress asked if he wanted anything, but Paul's hands shook so hard he couldn't lift a glass to his lips without spilling the contents.

Gregor sat down beside him, a fashion magazine in hand.

"Fashion?" Paul suppressed a smile.

"It was the first thing I saw. What's the matter?"

Paul looked around, but no one was taking any notice of them. "I need your help."

Paul outlined the situation for the older man, who promised the strictest secrecy and agreed to keep their profits in a safe-deposit box.

"I'm sorry to say, not even your wife should know about it." Paul took a notebook from his pocket, in which he had hidden a plain envelope, and pretended to make notes in it about the book he was reading. "I don't want to cause trouble for you."

"I know."

Paul passed him the notebook.

"I'll take care of everything," Gregor said. "Don't worry."

"We're fully aware of what we're asking of you. But we can't see any other way."

"On the contrary," Gregor murmured. "I'm only too pleased to be able to do something for you. I pray for your father and for you every day. Thank you for trusting me."

"I'm the one who should be thanking you. I'll see you soon." Paul put the book back on the shelf and left the reading room.

That night, Paul and Clara breathed a sigh of relief.

Margarethe, who had by now grown into a four-year-old with copper-colored braids, would fling her play-warmed body into Paul's embrace the moment he returned home. One summer evening, he hugged her to him affectionately and kissed her cheek, which tasted of Ahoj sherbet and Delial sun cream.

"You've been working late today, Papa. Please can I see the music box?" she begged, looking up at him hopefully.

"Later, Margarethe," he told her, sitting her on his hip and drawing Clara into his arms.

Margarethe wriggled until her father put her down. Her face set in determination, she tugged at his trouser leg. "The music box, Papa. Please. Please."

He exchanged a knowing look with Clara.

"I'll be very careful."

Paul bent down to her. "It's a deal." He opened the bureau drawer where the silver box now lived and gave it to his little rascal. "Be good."

Holding one another tight, they watched their little girl, radiant with joy, toddle off on her chubby legs to the room that had once been his, and close the door loudly behind her. The room was suddenly still.

"It's amazing how attached she is to that music box," Clara said. "What does that old thing have that all her toys don't?"

"Good thing I moved it up here or she'd be making me run back to the shop all the time."

Paul kissed his wife and settled down on the sofa. He loved this spot, loved that he could watch his wife preparing supper. He gently stroked the soft fabric. As a young boy he had sat here with his parents. And later, with his mother as she read his father's diary. His eyes were drawn to the bureau, in which he kept the little leather case. How often had he weighed first the medal, then the diary in his hands, silently debating whether to read it? But he never had, too afraid the diary might alter or even destroy the childish image of a heroic father that he'd built up in his imagination.

Deep in thought, he went to the bureau and took the book from its little case, running his fingers over the cover. He paused on the stains. That was Father's blood, clinging to it like the warning of a silent witness. Paul's mouth went dry. But he was grown up now. It was time to meet his father as an adult.

He opened the book. The unfussy handwriting perfectly matched his memory of the slim man in his spotless suit. On the first page, he saw sketches of men in uniform playing cards. Paul was thrilled by the quality of the drawings. But why should he be surprised? His father's old jewelry sketches were beautiful. Paul found the first entry.

> *November 3, 1914, Ypres by the Yser*
> *Oh man, what are you capable of? This has been on my mind ever since I saw Herbert, his face a picture of hatred, shooting at the enemy, and how eagerly the lads nodded their assent today when Brandt said we could destroy the French within a week. Their faces shone as if with fever, a repulsive sight. The heavy artillery shakes the ground. Day and night I hear the cries of pain from wounded men, and smell their rotting bodies. The stink clings to my uniform, my hair, and lies like a film on my skin. I breathe it in with every breath. I'll never be free of it.*

Margarethe burst into the room, giving Paul just enough time to put the precious book back in its place. Snuggling up to him, she examined the base of the music box. "Tell me what it says, Papa."

As Paul repeated the familiar inscription, his daughter activated the mechanism and gave a cry of pleasure as the little bird sprang out twittering.

Just as quickly, she turned serious. She looked up at him with trusting eyes. "Your papa gave this to you, and you're looking after it until I'm old enough, right?"

"That's right, darling," Paul replied softly.

"Give it to me, Papa," she said with deep conviction. "I love it so much. I'm old enough now."

Paul looked affectionately at Margarethe's snub nose, her rosy cheeks, and the pleading in her wide eyes.

"I understand, but you're still too small," he said gently.

The little girl pouted. "How old were you?"

"When your grandpa gave me the music box? Four."

Margarethe clapped her hands. "You see! I'm nearly four, too. And I haven't ever hurt it even the tiniest bit."

Her victorious grin brought a smile to his face. "I can see I'm running out of arguments."

The little girl wrinkled her nose. "What do you mean?"

"It doesn't matter." Paul stroked her thick, wavy hair. "Very well, you've convinced me. But you have to look after the music box like a treasure. Your grandpa worked very hard to make it so beautiful. It means you now have a big responsibility. Can I depend on you?"

Margarethe nodded enthusiastically. "I won't take it outside, so no one can ever take it away from me."

"You're a clever girl." Paul stared at the silver memento, which she hugged tightly to her chest. "Treat it well, so that you can pass it on to your children in the future."

Margarethe lifted three fingers, as she had seen Alma do. "Yes, Papa, I promise."

"Good, then it's yours."

Chapter 17

The Blumenthals watched anxiously as the business stagnated. One Friday, Max insisted on ignoring his doctor's warnings and came to visit them in Altona.

While Paul and Karl were busy with customers, Uncle Max sat in the workshop with a pot of tea, poring over the accounts and the newspaper.

When Paul went to sit with him that afternoon, his uncle pointed to the latest edition of the *Hamburger Fremdenblatt*. "Have you seen this filth?" he asked angrily.

"Yes, Clara read it to me this morning."

"Outlawing marriages between Jews and Aryans! Nullifying the ones that already exist. They're calling it 'racial defilement' and saying they'll throw people in jail for fifteen years—for getting married!" Uncle Max howled.

"'Any extramarital relations between Jews and Aryans are also forbidden with immediate effect.' That's totally crazy," Paul replied. "How can the National Socialists have the nerve to dictate whom people can love! When will Hitler finally be brought down? This stuff is sick!"

Max cursed. "They won't get away with it—you mark my words! The German people won't stand for it."

Paul pictured the Sattler brothers and Clara's spiteful coworkers, and frowned doubtfully. "Have you read the rest, Uncle Max?"

"Are you talking about domestic servants?"

"Yes, precisely. What's to become of Alma?" Paul asked.

According to the "blood protection law," Jews were forbidden from employing women of German or Aryan blood under the age of forty-five.

"Nothing. We'll ignore it, of course," his uncle shouted. He scowled at his teacup, and Paul thought how he would probably have preferred a nip of rum in there. "And what's more, I've been banned from my local bar! 'Jews and non-Aryans are no longer welcome here. No exceptions,' Fiedler's son said when he took over." Uncle Max snorted disdainfully. "His father would never have thrown me out."

He paused for a moment, and Paul thought he would change the subject.

But his uncle looked at him and exclaimed: "After fifty-six years in this country, I'm told that a Jew isn't a German citizen anymore, that I'm politically irrelevant and inferior. What have we ever done to them, apart from being born Jewish? But there's one thing the bastards can't take away from me: I'm proud of being a German Jew and I love my homeland."

When Paul told him that Clara and Margarethe had been forbidden access to the lake in the park, the ailing man nearly fell from his seat.

"These Nuremberg Laws will be the death of us!"

"And we're exactly the same to them, even though we're baptized Christians." Paul sighed. "Has Herr Schuster given you a response to your offer yet?"

"He's offering no more than half of what the building is worth," his uncle grumbled. "He said no one would pay a Jew such a high sum. But I won't let it go for a pittance. Especially not to that jumped-up idiot, who's been treating us like dirt recently. Us—a family of long-established, well-regarded merchants. When his store has only been around for a few years, a fact he's conveniently forgotten!"

Paul thought it wise to keep his opinion to himself so as not to wind his uncle up any further. "What a pity. But I still think we ought to close the main shop as soon as possible. You can live without worries for quite a while on savings, if you're very careful."

"We'll close the shop when we're ready, and not a day sooner," Uncle Max said dismissively. "And as for what you're implying, how could I waste money when I can't even set foot in my local bar? The good old days are long gone. Now even my nephew's ripping the bottle from my hand."

Uncle Max was obviously doing his best to joke, but the bitterness was unmistakable. Paul tried to imagine what his evenings were like, alone in his apartment with no one but Alma for company. He couldn't help wondering how he would cope if a new business opened on the ground floor. And that raised another question: How would the new proprietors treat a Jewish landlord? The specter of never-ending conflict with his Christian neighbors renewed Paul's feelings of despair.

"I know you don't want to leave your home, Uncle Max. But have you thought how sad it will be to see strangers coming and going in your shop, day in, day out?"

His uncle took a deep breath. "And where do you think I should live, boy? In Jerusalem or Cape Town, perhaps?"

"The climate would certainly do you good," Paul said defensively. "But let's drop the subject for now. I don't know how to convince you. This place is more nightmarish every day, Uncle Max. No one wants anything to do with us, and the Nazis keep getting more violent. I'm worried about you. I'd be happier if you'd at least look for a new apartment somewhere safer."

His uncle's harsh laughter echoed in Paul's ears. "You think you're so grown-up, don't you? But you're so naive. Who do you imagine would rent me an apartment?"

Paul gasped painfully. "Other Jews?"

"The terrified ones about to sell to their neighbors for nothing, too? No, no. I will not be forced from my home," Uncle Max said, struggling to his feet. "Can you please ask Karl to walk me to the station?"

"Of course." Paul went to the front of the shop. "You can head home from there," he told Karl. "I'll close up tonight."

A short time later, Paul watched his uncle making his slow way out.

Later, he couldn't recall how long he stood there, motionless, Uncle Max's words spinning around in his head. After a while, he got a strange feeling that he was being watched. Four SA men had stopped in front of the shop. One was peering through the glass, while the others were affixing a huge poster to the window. Paul narrowed his eyes to make out the words.

"Germans! Defend Yourselves! Don't Buy from Jews!"

Paul froze, his pulse racing, as the SA troopers stormed into the shop. One of them raised his baton and casually struck the display case to the right of the entrance. Glass rained down in a thousand shards. The other three surrounded Paul. The tallest, a man of over six feet, grabbed him in a headlock. "Blumenthal, isn't it?"

"I am. Let me go, if you don't mind." Paul pushed the man away with all his might, only to be rammed against the counter. "What do you want with me? As a Christian I demand that you remove that poster!"

Paul had no idea where he got the courage to utter the words, which crossed his lips as if unbidden.

"So, you claim to be a Christian?" The SA giant stared him in the face. "Parasites! Stinking, filthy worms! We'll get you all; you can count on that."

He pushed Paul away and whirled around, knocking the till to the floor before marching out behind the others. Paul sank onto a stool, took out a handkerchief with shaking hands, and wiped his face.

"What's happened, darling? And where's Uncle Max?" He became aware of Clara's breathless voice.

"He left."

With her hair neatly tied and an apron around her waist, she rushed into the shop and let out a cry as she saw the smashed display case and the state of her husband. She cupped his face in her hands and examined him anxiously.

"I'm all in one piece."

Paul tried to keep his voice steady as he told her briefly what had happened. "Go upstairs to Margarethe. I'll clean up this mess."

Later that evening, Clara came to sit by him on the sofa.

"I've kept my thoughts to myself until now. But this has brought things to a head . . . What if something happens to our little girl? Margarethe heard the noise earlier and was horribly afraid. Just look at yourself! You're nervous and jumpy all the time. Do you think I haven't noticed? Do you remember that day when those brutes outside the shop cursed me and called me a Jewish slut? They hit you in the face. Since then it's got worse every day. We're living in constant fear!"

"I know," he replied quietly.

Clara looked him in the eye. "I can't and won't go on like this. Your uncle's behaving like a spoiled child. We have to do something."

"I'll talk to him," Paul said, drawing her close. As he stroked her hair in an attempt to calm them both, he recalled the words of the SA trooper.

Parasites! Stinking, filthy worms! We'll get you all.

All that night they lay entwined, neither of them able to sleep.

Chapter 18

As Paul entered the store the next morning, he found Karl standing by the missing display case.

"Herr Blumenthal, what happened here?"

"Good morning, Karl. Let's just say we have an SA trooper's baton to thank for this."

The manager looked past him to the window. "What kind of a world are we living in? These people should be ashamed of themselves."

"Thank you for standing by us," Paul replied. "Karl, are you . . . are you getting any trouble because you work here?"

"Oh, don't worry about it." Karl smiled, thin-lipped. "I can look after myself." He indicated the poster on the window. "This, though. I've tried everything, but I can't get the damn thing off."

"Don't worry."

Working together, they moved furniture to fill the gap where the display case had been. Paul looked out and his breath caught in his throat. It was ten o'clock in the morning; by that time the stream of people on their way to work had normally died down. But today, a small crowd of curious onlookers had gathered outside the store, watching them intently. Some seemed calm; others were shaking their heads or looking distraught.

The two men looked at one another.

"What's going on?" Karl murmured.

The crowd grew denser, pushing in the direction of the jewelry store. Then an elderly lady in an elegant, wide-brimmed hat stepped forward from the throng. She held something up and waved.

Paul blinked. It was the owner of the Herbartz shoe store on the Rathausplatz—a pleasant, lively woman of around sixty. The urgency in her eyes made Paul open the door.

"My dear Frau Herbartz. What—?"

She took his hands and squeezed them.

"What do these people want?" Paul asked. His skin prickled under the gaze of fifty pairs of eyes.

Frau Herbartz handed him the *Völkischer Beobachter*, the Nazi Party newspaper.

"Good morning, Herr Blumenthal," she said at last, indicating the people behind her. "Look at this gawping crowd. They look on without raising a finger at what they're doing to you. Have you seen their unfeeling faces? It's shameful, the way you and your people are being treated." She paused for a moment, and each word penetrated to his heart. "Paul—may I call you that? I've known you since you were a two-year-old whippersnapper. You sometimes used to play with our Gislind."

"I remember, Frau Herbartz." His voice came out as a whisper, and he hoped she could hear him above the strong wind. He didn't feel the fine drizzle, or hear the rattling of a nearby tram.

Her eyes misted over. "You know, your late father meant a lot to me. He was a true artist and a fine man who had a friendly word for everyone and loved his family above all else. Whenever I visited the store, we always liked to talk. I admired him."

Uniformed men in long brown coats now appeared in front of the crowd, and all eyes turned to them. Paul thought he saw guns on their shoulders.

Frau Herbartz lowered her voice. "We have to be careful. I just want to tell you how incredibly sorry we are about what's happening here.

Please rest assured that my family and I disapprove of the government's actions. Please read the paper carefully. I can't say any more about it. I wish you and your family all the best. May God watch over you."

She squeezed his hand one last time before turning on her heel, ignoring the severe expressions of the SA troopers, and leaving Paul shaken to the quick. He hurried back into the shop, although he felt the eyes of the rubberneckers stab into his back like knives.

With a nod of his head, Paul asked Karl to join him at the counter. The front page of the *Völkischer Beobachter* bore an announcement in large letters. They were calling for a boycott: no Aryan was to so much as enter a Jewish store. Paul's head swam as he imagined people fighting to keep their businesses afloat with not one Aryan customer. He closed his eyes and took a deep breath. When he opened them, he saw that they'd included a list of Jewish businesses in Altona and Hamburg to avoid. Paul skimmed the list of names.

Herbert Fleischmann, haberdashery, Behnstrasse
August Löwenberg, wool store, Mörkenstrasse
Hermann Rotmensz, dressmaker and tailor, Adolphstrasse
Hermann Tietz, department store, Jungfernstieg
Altona Market Jewelers, Paul and Max Blumenthal, Königstrasse

"For God's sake!" Karl exclaimed.

Paul closed his eyes, then slowly opened them. But the hope that he had been mistaken was dashed as he scanned the list once more.

Altona Market Jewelers.

Paul pushed the newspaper away as though it burned his fingers. "We're finished."

"Surely our regular customers will stay loyal."

"'Anyone who acts in defiance of this notice is a rogue and a traitor to the German people,'" Paul quoted from the article. A paralyzing weakness suddenly overcame him. The list even included the Tietz department store, with its chic French hats, books, and quality carpets. He suddenly recalled his meeting with Gregor in the same store's reading room. Then he felt a hand on his shoulder.

"What will you do now, Herr Blumenthal?"

Paul's chest tightened. "I don't know. You go home. I have to talk to my family. Look after yourself. Emotions are running high outside. You'd best leave through the back. I'll open it for you."

Karl nodded grimly. "Thank you."

When Paul was alone, he moved stiffly to the display window, where a few of the little Hitler Youth had their noses pressed flat to the glass, and moved to lower the blind. A split second later the glass shattered with a deafening crash, merging with the sneering laughter of bystanders. A stone the size of a fist just missed his shoulder. More stones flew. One hit Paul's ear. He pressed his hand to the bloody wound and was about to hurl himself toward the stairs when hands grabbed him from behind, threw him to the floor, and turned him over. He looked up in terror into the distorted faces of two brownshirts. One of them aimed a boot into his stomach. Paul gasped for breath. The second kick landed on his chest. He groaned and involuntarily curled into a ball. But the men showed no mercy. With the metallic taste of blood in his mouth, he fought to stay conscious.

"Revolting vermin," he heard. "Come on, let's piss on him."

The next moment, as if through a fog, he saw them opening their flies. Paul didn't know how he mustered the strength to leap to his feet, but he still felt a stream of urine on his back. The thugs laughed.

When they had gone, he grasped the edge of the counter with his fingers. He was overcome by dizziness. Clara mustn't see him like this. No one should see him like this. *The washbasin in the workshop,* he thought. He managed to stagger to it, threw off his coat in disgust, and washed himself as well as he could. His body was burning with pain. Paul struggled to steady his breathing. He needed a few minutes before he could face Clara. Despite himself, he felt tears of shame rolling down his cheeks. When his dizziness had subsided, he took his torn coat by his fingertips and threw it in the trash, then stumbled up the stairs. Clara was waiting for him, her eyes wide with fright.

Margarethe ran toward him.

"Papa!" She stopped short. "You're hurt!"

"Just a few scratches, darling," Paul managed to say.

Clara sent their daughter to her room to play.

"Take your clothes off and let me have a look." She gave a cry of horror as she examined his body. "For heaven's sake, who could have done this?"

"Three guesses," Paul gasped as she dabbed at his bleeding ear. Fortunately the stone had only grazed him. He gave her a halting account of what had happened.

Clara listened as she felt his stomach and back. He winced and suppressed a groan.

"Papa should take a look at this," she whispered. "You've got some serious bruising."

"No, I'm fine," he replied firmly.

She sighed. "You know best. Where did you leave your coat?"

"They tore it. I threw it away."

"I'll mend it," she said. "I'll just go and fetch it."

"No!" He held her back in an iron grip as the sudden sound of crashing and banging from the shop reached them.

He jumped up from the kitchen chair. "They're looting the store! I . . . I have to get as much of our stock as I can to safety."

"And allow them to beat you to death?" Clara shook her head forcefully.

Paul said nothing. He sat and listened, tasting the blood in his mouth. "When it's all calmed down, I'll go and set things right."

Clara wiped tears from her eyes. "Very well. But be careful."

When Königstrasse was dark but for a few streetlights and all the noise had died down, Paul gritted his teeth and crept downstairs with a flashlight. Every movement hurt. His eyes roamed over the smashed chairs, the light patch on the floorboards where a Persian rug had lain, the damp urine stain, and the shards of glass from the crystal chandelier. The vandals had been satisfied with removing the jewelry on display; most of the cases themselves were still intact. Paul swept shards of glass and splintered timber together and placed the wrecked furniture in a chest. He ran his hand over the deep dents in the solid wood counter. It had been too heavy for the looters, so they'd merely damaged it in their madness.

He made his way painfully into the workshop, where a curtain concealed a niche containing an old, inconspicuous cupboard.

His lips curled into a grim smile as he remembered his father's words. No one had any idea about this secret that he shared with his father—not even Clara. Johann Blumenthal's advice had been clear: *Make duplicates of valuable pieces.* And Paul had taken the advice to heart even before he converted to the Christian faith. The glass cases out front had contained only cheap display copies, while the originals were kept in a secret compartment in this cupboard. Paul had always told his customers that he would fetch the piece they wanted from stock. He suspected his father had done the same. The sight of the carefully packed silver and gold treasures filled him with one last glimmer of hope.

"I pray you've been taking similar precautions, Uncle Max," he whispered into the darkness. Paul took a deep breath and locked the cupboard. "My business may be in ruins, but the money I need for my family's last chance at safety is right here before my eyes."

Chapter 19

To Paul's surprise, he found Karl standing outside the door the next morning.

"I came to ask what we're going to do. Oh, no! You're hurt!"

Leaning heavily against the door, Paul recounted the previous day's events.

Karl clapped his hands to his head. "My God. I'm so sorry. Can I help you clean up?"

"That would be good, thank you. To be honest, you've come at exactly the right time," Paul replied with relief. He called up, "Clara, I'm downstairs with Karl." Paul ushered him past the counter and into the workshop.

Karl looked at him inquiringly. "I don't understand. There's no cleaning up to do in here."

"I know, but I need to ask a favor." Paul moistened his swollen lip. "It's a small but incredibly important errand."

"I'd be happy to help. What do you need me to do?"

Paul looked at his watch. Shortly before eight. "I've got a few things to do in the workshop first. Can you give me a few minutes?" Paul took a deep breath. "And can you watch over the shop? Let me know if anyone comes?"

Karl's eyes widened. "You want me to keep lookout?"

"Yes, you could say that."

"Understood. But hurry, please."

In the workshop, Paul laid the real jewelry in an old leather bag and hid it in a wooden shed in the backyard. When he returned to Karl, holding his side where it hurt, he handed him a letter. "Could you please deliver this into the hands of the person it's addressed to? It's personal."

"Of course." Karl set his hat on his head and walked down Königstrasse.

Paul said a quick prayer for his plan to work. His eyes glued to his watch, he counted the minutes, which seemed to stretch away into eternity. Neighbors and former business associates stared through the broken window, some with sympathy, others calling out comments that the wind mercifully whipped away. He caught sight of Egon Schilling, their new neighbor to the left, surrounded by his wife and four children—the Steinfelds, their old neighbors, had moved out a year ago. When the Schillings noticed him, they crossed to the other side of the street.

Paul was a bundle of nerves by the time Karl returned a few minutes later. "He sends his greetings and I'm to let you know he'll come at about five."

"Thank you so much, Karl. I'll be in touch."

After shaking Karl's hand warmly, Paul was alone again. He stared at the telephone. No call had ever seemed so difficult as the one he now had to make.

Max Blumenthal gasped in alarm when he heard Paul's brief account. *I hope he isn't alone in the house,* Paul thought. He couldn't bear to think that his uncle's heart might not be up to the news. "Is Alma there?"

"She's right here. The good lady's brought me freshly baked cakes," his uncle replied absently.

"Good. Please listen carefully. You have to get everything to a safe place immediately. Do you understand?"

"Yes, of course, I'm not senile," Uncle Max muttered.

"Good. Close the shop, before it happens there, too. Promise me."

"There's not much left here anyway," the older man said after a brief pause.

Paul was flooded with relief. "Thank you. We'll come to see you as soon as we can. We'll talk more about everything then. I'll call Mama later."

"Break it to her gently," Uncle Max said. "I know what it's like to watch helplessly as events unfold."

"You can depend on me."

As Paul ended the call he felt more exhausted than he ever had before. He would call his mother like he did every Thursday. It wouldn't do anyone any good if he alarmed her by sending a telegram. Ignoring the group of brown-coated men patrolling the street in front of the shop, he returned to his family.

But he couldn't resist going back into the shop for long. Paul's hands were clammy with anxiety. He was freezing despite the warm summer breeze. *Please let everything go smoothly.*

Paul positioned the only intact chair so that he had a good view of the back door and the locked shed, then sank onto it. From the street that ran parallel to theirs, there was a narrow, barely noticeable passage leading directly to their yard. Only a very few neighbors knew of it. His plan was risky, but he wouldn't be his father's son if he didn't make some attempt to safeguard their existence. From above he heard Margarethe's happy laughter and the rapid pattering of her small feet.

Dr. Fisch suddenly burst through the front door, white as a sheet. "My God! Why didn't you tell me?"

"We didn't want to disturb you yesterday evening." Ten minutes to five. Beads of sweat were forming on the back of Paul's neck. He peered at the door, his pulse racing.

Dr. Fisch laid a hand on his shoulder. "We'll talk later, when Margarethe's asleep. Are your girls at home?"

"Yes. They're upstairs."

"I'll go up and play with the little one." Dr. Fisch indicated his shoulder bag. "I brought her a jigsaw puzzle."

"I'll be up soon." As he heard his father-in-law's footsteps echoing up the stairs, Paul sighed with relief. Five minutes to five.

A white-haired figure in a dark coat came down the passageway. Paul was relieved to see Gregor, but stiffened again as Herr Schilling came outside to play with his children next door. Gregor noticed the family, too, and pressed himself against a wall of the shed as Paul looked on anxiously.

It felt like forever before Schilling called his children together and sent them indoors to wash their hands. Gregor remained as motionless as Paul while Schilling lifted his youngest, who refused to obey, into his arms. When the backyard was finally silent, the two men exchanged a glance. The padlock was in place but unlocked, and Gregor slipped into the shed. Paul trembled. Gregor slipped out with the leather bag and hung the padlock back in place. He gave the slightest nod in Paul's direction before disappearing between the overhanging branches of the fruit trees.

Once he was sure Gregor was gone, Paul hurried out to the deserted yard. In the shed he looked around, paused, then found the scrap of paper fixed to a wooden slat.

50 A. + 50 G. Destroy message. G.

A soft sound of surprise escaped Paul's throat.

He understood. August would take half the jewelry into safekeeping, Gregor the other half. If everything went as planned, they would sell it and place the money in the secret safe-deposit box.

Paul sank back against the wooden wall in relief. Once he had calmed down a little, he placed the scrap of paper in an old clay flowerpot and held a match to it. A split second later the paper went up in flames.

He headed back into the shop.

"Are you coming?" Dr. Fisch suddenly called down through the floorboards, making Paul jump. "Clara's made waffles."

Paul's knees felt like jelly beneath him. He could only hope that Clara and his father-in-law had seen nothing of his clandestine activities.

"I'll be right up," he called, praying he had made the right decision.

Chapter 20

Cape Town, Sea Point

If only I could do something. After Lotte's long conversation with Paul and Clara, she'd gone with Martha to a restaurant near their house. It was impossible to concentrate on sewing right now. The calming mountain views from the panoramic terrace at the Blue View Restaurant drew the locals back again and again, and offered travelers a welcome place to relax after their hikes. It was also close to the kosher grocery store where Hermann worked.

The two women found a quiet table in the corner where Lotte could tell Martha what had happened.

"Close the business! I never thought Max would give in," Martha said.

"He has no choice," Lotte explained. "Paul told me that suppliers are no longer allowed to work with Jewish businesses. The tax office is after them, too, and Christians aren't allowed to shop there! Can you imagine? But I'm afraid that's not all." She paused.

Martha looked at her attentively. "My God, Lotte, what happened? Is someone hurt?"

"Well, Paul's been beaten and kicked by SA troopers. Martha, the Altona shop was looted." She took a deep breath, trying to gather her nerves. "A few days later, Clara saw a picture of her friend Hilde

Wilhelm in the *Altonaer Tageblatt*. She and her boyfriend hanged themselves in their own doorway."

Martha pressed a hand to her mouth.

"The young man had a sign around his neck: 'I'm a Jew and I love a Christian.' Her sign read: 'You won't divide us!' Clara could hardly bear to see it. She immediately went to the church to pray, but the priest banned her from entering."

"What did you say?" Martha spat. "I can't have heard you right. If a church is no longer a place of refuge, what's the point of it?"

"The priest is a member of the Nazi Party." Lotte turned away to conceal her welling tears. "They're not welcome anywhere anymore. Clara was floored. They intend to move. They have to move." At that moment, heavy clouds moved across the sun as if to emphasize her words, and Lotte shivered, drawing her light shawl more tightly around her. "When I think of all the plans Paul and Clara made—all in vain. What's to become of them?"

"We must trust in the Almighty," Martha said resolutely.

"Is that all you can say?" Lotte asked, more harshly than she had intended.

Her sister-in-law leaned across the table. "Darling, I understand your worries only too well. I feel the same, of course I do. But you and I are thousands of miles away. It won't help anyone if you cry in your sleep and can't concentrate during the day."

The words were sympathetic, but Lotte thought she sensed an edge to her voice.

"You can talk," she heard herself say. "You have Hermann and the boys here with you. Your family is safe!"

The hard lines around Martha's mouth vanished. "Forgive me, Lotte. Of course you're right. I sometimes forget how lucky I am. But Paul and Clara are smart. Trust them; they'll do the right thing. The one I'm most worried about is Max."

"Oh, Max," Lotte said. "He's like an ancient tree that's too old to uproot. What will he do without the business? Without a purpose in life? Poor Alma."

A well-built, tanned man in an apron came over to their table. Dark-brown eyes looked down at them from behind glasses.

What eyes with that flaxen-blond hair! Lotte thought.

"Shalom, ladies. I'm sorry to have kept you waiting. My name is Antoon Kuipers, and I'm the owner here. The waitress has run off with a guy half her age, leaving me to take her place." He grimaced comically, making Lotte laugh. "What can I get you? I have a wonderful white wine from the Stellenbosch Farmers' Winery. Served chilled, it's an absolute delight at this time of year." He spoke English with a Dutch accent, which Lotte found charming.

They gladly accepted Kuipers's recommendation.

Martha watched him go. "What an interesting man. He seems to have a good sense of humor."

"Yes," Lotte said, her gaze wandering to the view of Table Mountain. Paul had told her they were considering an auction at the Lübeck premises. He didn't believe they would be able to sell any more of their stock now. This place was so beautiful, and she so badly wanted to take Martha's advice and trust that her family would find their way. But would they? How grave was the danger?

"Lotte? Were you listening to Herr Kuipers?"

Embarrassed, she turned her head to the handsome proprietor. "I'm sorry. Did you say something?"

A light smile played on his lips. "I did. First of all, I wanted to ask if there was anything else you wanted?"

Lotte waved her hand. "No, thank you, not for me."

Kuipers glanced around to see if anyone else was waiting for him. "Can I sit with you for a moment?"

Lotte did her best to hide her astonishment.

"Yes, of course," Martha replied for her.

"You're from north Germany, aren't you?" Kuipers asked once he had taken a seat.

"We're from Altona," Lotte said.

He nodded. "I thought so. I worked for a few years in Hamburg in the twenties. I love hearing that accent again. I hope I'm not being too forward?"

His obvious pleasure had a disarming effect. "No, not at all," Lotte replied quickly, catching a meaningful look from Martha.

"You're fairly new here on the Cape, aren't you?"

"How can you tell?" Martha asked with a grin.

"I've seen you in here a few times and couldn't help noticing you have that slightly lost look," Kuipers said. "I was just the same ten years ago. Cape Town is wonderful, but we all find it hard to leave our homeland. Am I right in thinking you're also Jewish?"

"We are," Lotte said nervously.

"Most immigrants now are Jewish. It's no wonder given the dreadful things happening back in Germany." Kuipers looked at Lotte frankly. "May I invite you and your families to Shabbat dinner tomorrow? Please be my guests. I'm expecting quite a number of people from the Jewish community and I'd like to introduce you. It's not a good thing to be alone in a foreign country."

Lotte lowered her wineglass and Martha nodded encouragingly. "Yes, we'd like that. Thank you, Herr Kuipers."

He clapped his hands. "Wonderful. I'll see you here on Friday." He gave them a brief bow before crossing to another table to take their order.

Lotte looked at his broad back thoughtfully.

"He likes you! Did you see that sparkle in his eyes?" Martha gushed.

"Really? I didn't notice a thing."

Martha shook her head in mock seriousness. "Ever since Johann's death you've walked around with blinkers on your eyes. All these years,

I've noticed the way men look at you, but you never see it. I could almost confess to being a little jealous."

"I beg your pardon," Lotte replied. "What do you mean?"

"You're still a pretty, desirable woman. No one's ever looked at me that way. I think men find me too independent and forceful."

"But you have Hermann."

"Oh, I do, and I thank the Lord for that." Martha's face turned serious. "Lotte, you don't think you'd be betraying Johann if you went out with another man, do you?"

"I'm sorry. If you're referring to Herr Kuipers, I don't know the first thing about him."

Martha raised her glass. "That's true. But, please, open your eyes a little. Look to the future; make a new start here. Or do you want to be unhappy for the rest of your life, and what's more, to spend your old age alone?"

It was a long time since she had worn her best dress. Lotte examined herself critically in the mirror late that Friday afternoon. As the silky, deep-red material now hung too loosely around her figure, she had quickly sewn herself a fabric belt. Her shoulder-length hair was still a shimmering deep brown, just a few traces grayer than it used to be. But the sorrow of recent years had left its marks on her face. Ever since Herr Kuipers had extended the invitation she had toyed with the idea of declining it. But she did not want to be impolite, and knew that Hermann and Martha were looking forward to it.

Lotte's doubts vanished as she reached the door of the Blue View Restaurant and was met by the sound of Jewish folk songs.

Antoon Kuipers lost no time in introducing Lotte, Martha, and Hermann to his other guests. The Hönisch family of ten was originally from Westphalia and had lived in Cape Town since the late 1920s. Seligman Hönisch, the father, said they were lucky to have left Germany at the right time. Aaron and Sonja Löbinger were of Romanian origin and had lived for a long while just outside Berlin. They had emigrated a year before Hitler came to power, and Aaron was now working for a construction company outside Cape Town. Lotte was enchanted by their one-year-old, Felix, who hopped around boisterously to the music. The Eppsteins, a cheerful couple in their eighties, had left Frankfurt when they were evicted from the apartment where they'd lived for over fifty years. Their daughter, who had married a businessman from Cape Town, invited them to come and live with her. Hermann and Martha were soon drawn into a lively conversation with the Hönisch family, but Lotte hung back. She was seated opposite a dainty woman around Paul's age, who made little contribution to the conversations going on around her. She could almost be described as pretty, apart from prominent cheekbones that lent her face a certain severity. Lotte noticed she was clutching something in her hands.

The woman raised her head and gave Lotte an absent smile. Her attention then returned to little Felix, whose antics she followed intently.

Meanwhile, Herr Kuipers offered drinks to his guests. After pouring a glass of wine for Lotte, he followed her gaze.

"That's Ewa Tulinski," he whispered. "She's only been on the Cape for a few weeks. Her fiancé has a shop in Göttingen. When the government forbade relationships between Aryans and Jews, he bought her passage on a ship here, so she would be safe."

"How sad," Lotte whispered back. "She doesn't let little Felix out of her sight."

"Yes. Ewa was pregnant when she left Germany, but the voyage was difficult and, well . . . The poor thing always carries the doll she made for her unborn child."

Moved, she met Antoon Kuipers's dark eyes. "So many dreadful stories," she whispered. "And so few are willing to stand by us. Why are we being treated like this? It seems as though we'll never know peace."

"I ask myself the same thing. That's why I'm so eager to make sure you feel welcome here, Frau Blumenthal. If I may speak openly, you caught my eye straightaway. Have you had a chance to get to know Cape Town?"

Lotte shook her head regretfully. "There's so much work to do and, honestly, I haven't felt confident enough to venture beyond the neighborhood. You should know that I'm not very adventurous."

"I don't believe that. All you need is a little push." He put on an innocent expression. "People say I'm a good tour guide. So if you have the time and inclination, I'll gladly show you around. I'd especially like to show you the local vineyards. The landscape out there is incredible."

"Maybe I'll take you up on your offer one day." Lotte had no intention of doing so but didn't know how to get out of the situation politely.

"Just let me know," Antoon said before turning his attention to his other guests.

Over dinner, Lotte noticed Ewa repeatedly making eye contact with her, so after the meal she went to sit by her while the others stood around casually in groups. Carefully, she drew the young woman into a conversation. Ewa was reticent, but warmed up as Lotte recounted her own journey. And Lotte soon discovered that Ewa had not only traveled to South Africa on her own, but, to Lotte's amazement, was all alone here, fending for herself. She was grateful to be invited to events like this, but she felt ill at ease with the Jewish community here.

"Why's that?" Lotte asked gently.

Ewa lowered her head. "They've all got someone, or they're waiting for relatives who are going to follow. Wherever I go, I'm an outsider." She stood abruptly and ran out without another word.

Lotte watched her, feeling awkward and ashamed. *I should count myself lucky that I've got Martha and Hermann with me,* she thought. She recalled Antoon Kuipers's words. *It's not a good thing to be alone in a foreign country.*

Lotte's chest tightened. To give herself time and space to think, she escaped out to the terrace and sucked in deep lungfuls of the salty Atlantic air. Martha's words about opening her eyes had shaken her. *My darling Johann,* she asked him silently. *What would you advise me to do if you were here?* She stood motionless for a long while, gazing out over the ocean with its waves breaking onto the rocky shore. Finally, she stretched and turned back to the restaurant.

As the first guests began to leave, Lotte made her way to the bar.

Antoon looked up and smiled. "Frau Blumenthal, what can I do for you? Another glass of wine, perhaps?"

"No, thank you. I've drunk enough." Lotte stared at her feet. After a long moment, she looked up. "But I would like to get to know the city. May I take you up on your offer of a guided tour?"

Chapter 21

Altona, October 1935

One sunny Sunday in October, Clara and Paul were sitting in Max's living room in Lübeck, enshrouded in a bitter silence. Uncle Max stared into space, his stiff bearing reminding Paul of a wax figure. Margarethe had withdrawn into a corner, where she leafed through a picture book before searching for something in her little bag. *Little rascal,* he thought as he caught a glimpse of the music box, which she must have packed away secretly that morning. She approached the table, looking inquiringly from her father to her great-uncle.

"Ilse next door says that when grown-ups aren't talking, it means they're mad at each other. Are you mad at each other?"

Paul folded a napkin into the shape of a bird, surprised by Margarethe's candid question. "No, we simply hold different opinions. Go back to your toys."

"Why do you both have to be so stubborn?" Clara said with a shake of her head. "It won't do us any good if you refuse to talk. We have to come to a decision."

The despair in her voice broke through the wall Paul had built. "Tell that to Uncle Max. He's the one who's not willing to talk."

"You're asking a great deal from an old man," he replied. "At least give me a month longer so I can sell the tools."

"No. We have to hold the auction now. Just look at the bill from the tax office. We've already waited far too long." The full import of his uncle's words suddenly seemed to dawn on him. "The tools? They're the least of our worries. What about the stock, the chandeliers, the carpets, and the goods we still have on our hands?"

"Come with me." Max got up. "Margarethe, Alma's in the kitchen baking a cake. You go see if she needs some help."

The little girl didn't need telling twice.

As Max led them to the door of the shop, Paul saw beads of sweat on his uncle's brow.

"You haven't been in here recently, have you?" Uncle Max asked as he opened up.

Paul and Clara stood rooted to the spot. The window had been secured against prying eyes with sheets. Paul squinted in the semidarkness. The room looked as though it had been swept clean; only lighter patches on the walls, where shelves and display cases used to stand, suggested the better times of the past.

"Feel free to take a look in the workshop," Uncle Max said softly. "It's all been sold except for the tools."

Paul rubbed his eyes. "Now I *am* surprised."

Back in the living room, Uncle Max sat down in his armchair again. His heart was still troubling him, and it took a moment for him to catch his breath. He looked at them. "Did you really believe I'd look on as everything we've built up over the years was auctioned off for nothing? You should know me better than that!"

"No, Uncle Max, of course not," Paul said in a placatory tone. "It's just—the SA won't give us any peace until they've driven us all to ruin."

Max Blumenthal snorted. "You don't say! I'm sure the two of you have every little thing worked out and know just where you intend to live once you've sold the Königstrasse property?"

"Well, I mean, not yet," Paul said evasively.

His uncle harrumphed. "So, do you really want to hear my decision?"

"Of course," Clara and Paul said together.

"Then listen to me well, my dear young things." If Uncle Max's voice had sounded breathless or weak before, it was nothing of the sort now. "You think I'm a pigheaded, stubborn old thing who refuses to accept change. I won't deny it. Nevertheless, I'm telling you"—he tapped his temple—"my mind is still sharp as a wire cutter."

"We never doubted that," Paul said with consternation, exchanging a look with Clara.

Max Blumenthal frowned. "While you were assuming I was wallowing in self-pity, I was busy getting rid of everything I could," he whispered, as though the walls had ears. He drew out a thin leather wallet from his waistcoat pocket and laid it down on the table. "That's for you."

Paul opened it to find a document and a wad of Reichsmark bills. "What's this?"

"Half of the money from the sale of Holsten Jewelers. Herr Hofmann from the laundry at number seventeen came to see me recently. He's horrified by what's going on. He told me he wants to move to smaller premises. Whether or not that's his real reason, it's come at just the right time, and we soon reached an agreement."

Speechless, Paul counted the money. "This is a lot more than that lout Schuster offered," he said, his voice hoarse because of the lump that had come to his throat. "You did well. I can't believe it."

"Oh, believe it, my boy."

Paul suddenly shoved the envelope away. "Keep the money. We'll manage with what we have."

"I don't accept that," the older man replied. "Have you forgotten what the SA did to your shop? And you haven't been able to find a buyer, right? Next thing you know, they'll force you to hand it over to an Aryan, like they did with Clara's father." Anger made Max's voice tremble. "Just like that, an Aryan doctor sitting at Nathan's desk, seeing his patients, acting like he owns the place! You can be sure they won't leave you a thing!"

Clara breathed in sharply and hurried from the room.

"You could have used a little more tact," Paul said. "The situation's hard enough for her as it is."

"It's not my way to beat about the bush. Sorry." He pushed the envelope back toward his nephew. "I can live more than comfortably on half of this. Take the money; you'll need it."

"What for? We're just moving out to the countryside. If we're careful, we can live on very little, not call any attention."

Uncle Max shook his head with a worried frown. "Don't have any illusions that you'll be safe out in some village. If they want to, they'll find you anywhere."

Clara returned, outwardly calm.

Max moved to the sofa next to the two of them and asked them to come closer. He looked at them intently.

"I spoke to your mother a few days ago, Paul. The *Usambara* sails from the port at Bremen for Cape Town on November 19. Then there's the *Watussi* on April 5 next year. You can use the money from the sale of the business to pay the travel costs, the taxes, and that damned Reich Flight Tax." His uncle's features were contorted with rage. "They take twenty-five percent of your assets! That'll swallow up the majority of your share. Anyway, once all the formalities have been completed, you'll receive a clearance certificate from the tax office, and then nothing will stand in the way of you going to South Africa."

"Thank you, Uncle Max, but we don't want to leave the country."

It was not quite true. His mother had practically begged them to join her in Cape Town. Her arguments were perfectly reasonable, but what would become of Dr. Fisch and Uncle Max? There was no way he and Clara could leave them behind. And since the two men refused to abandon their homeland, he and Clara had given up on any thoughts of emigration.

Max Blumenthal's lips tightened to a thin line. "You have to get away from here. You shouldn't waste any more time."

"Only if you two stubborn mules come with us," Paul insisted.

As they were speaking, Clara's gaze moved from one Blumenthal to the other, and he loved her for allowing him to hash it out with his uncle in his own way.

"I'm afraid that's impossible, my boy."

"Why? You can come back to Lübeck when the tensions die down."

Uncle Max looked exhausted. "Nathan tells me I'm too weak for the long sea voyage. It may not look like it, but I'm hanging on by a thread."

Clara's eyes filled with tears.

Paul licked his lips. "Then we're staying."

"I agree. One more reason for us to be here, Uncle Max," she said.

"Ah, now I understand," Max said. "You don't want to leave me alone."

"Nor my father," Clara said.

Max Blumenthal let out such a curse that she winced. "Has it occurred to you both that I might not want your pity?"

Clara and Paul looked at one another in confusion.

"I don't want to stand in your way," Uncle Max said. "And apart from that, I find your attitude pretty selfish."

"Selfish?" Clara said. "What's selfish about sticking together in times like these?"

"That's not what I mean." Max took her hands. "But you're not thinking of Margarethe. Do you want her to grow up in a gray, hate-filled world like this one? I want my great-niece to have a life of freedom—the freedom to choose where she can work and whom she can love. And if that means you have to move to the other side of the world, then it's a price I'm happy to pay."

The living room was so quiet that they could have heard a pin drop. Childish laughter drifted in from the kitchen, taking some of the edge off.

Then the doorbell rang.

"Perfect timing. I'm expecting another visitor," Max continued.

The young couple watched from the sofa as Alma and Margarethe accompanied the new arrival into the room.

"Papa!" Clara exclaimed in surprise. "What are you doing here? Why didn't you take the train with us?"

Max raised a hand. "Shalom, Nathan." He shook the doctor's hand. "Please make yourself comfortable."

Dr. Fisch kissed his daughter and granddaughter and clapped Paul on the shoulder. "Our plan to surprise you obviously worked."

"It certainly did," Paul said.

"If I can explain briefly," Max said, signaling Alma to take Margarethe back to the kitchen. "We want to take this opportunity to make you understand the way we see things."

"That's right," the doctor said. "Max and I are worried about your future."

"It's also *your* future," Clara protested.

The doctor waved away her concerns. "Max and I have different reasons why we want to stay in our homeland. But our decisions are final."

Clara tutted angrily. "You seem to have fixed this all up nicely. But if you're staying here, then so are we, and that's that."

Paul was drumming his fingers on the table. "I agree with Clara. We won't leave you here to deal with the brown-shirted masses alone. There are plenty of small villages between Lübeck and Hamburg where the Nazis won't bother us. We'll find ourselves a nice, modest house—"

"No!" Dr. Fisch's face was deadly earnest. "You're young! You can make a new start anywhere in the world. My patients are too ill to leave, and they have no official medical care here. I've sworn an oath and I'm obliged to keep it."

"I can't leave you behind, Papa."

Paul hugged her to him.

"It won't be forever," Uncle Max said. "We simply have to weather the storm. You can't be held back by two old men."

"Think of Margarethe," Dr. Fisch added urgently.

"Once you've dealt with the formalities," Max said to Paul gravely, "transfer the rest of the money to a bank account in Cape Town. Have someone you trust do it for you." He handed him a piece of paper. "This is Hermann's account. He'll deal with the rest. But I'm warning you! If you're thinking of smuggling any possessions past the authorities, don't. I've been told that they've cast a fine net to catch anyone intending to flee. The Reich records forwarding addresses of Jews and other non-Aryans, and shipping companies will inform the authorities if you try to send anything ahead. You're not allowed to take anything of value or more than ten marks with you. So you need to take precautions. That's all I've got to say." He gave his nephew a meaningful look. "Make your decision soon."

Margarethe rushed into the living room with a cake tin, and Paul got up stiffly. "Thank you. We have a lot to talk about." He put an arm around his daughter. "Come on, we're going home."

He gently steered her and Clara from the room, followed by Dr. Fisch.

On the train ride back, Clara was doggedly silent, while Margarethe hugged her bag to her chest, looking very unsure of herself. Paul found it hard to look at Dr. Fisch's pained expression, which turned gradually to despair with each mile the train traveled toward Hamburg. Clara said goodbye to her father coolly and, once home, she took Margarethe into the garden without a word. Paul watched them from the kitchen window, knowing his beloved wife's heart was breaking.

Late that evening, as she stood kneading dough, Paul went up to her and put his arms around her waist. "We'll get through this together, darling."

She suddenly turned to face him and threw her arms around his neck. Scraps of dough stuck to his shirt, but he didn't care. Sobbing, she buried her face in his shoulder. He was overcome by a feeling of helplessness as he stroked her silky hair, until she looked up and allowed him to brush the tears from her cheek.

"They're both right, though I hate to admit it. There really isn't any other way. We have to emigrate. You know what that means, don't you, Paul? We'll arrive in Cape Town with nothing, a terrible burden on your mother or some local charity."

"No, we won't," he replied confidently. "We'll be able to start a new life there without any financial worries. I promise you."

Her expressive eyes suddenly looked darker. "You're a dreamer. A dreamer, and I love you for it."

Paul kissed the tip of her nose and untied her apron strings, feeling for the zip of her dress.

"My hands are all dirty," she protested between kisses.

He smiled and handed her a cloth, then slowly guided her backward into the bedroom and quietly shut the door.

Chapter 22

They made love tenderly until Clara eventually fell asleep in his arms. It was now past four, and Paul was still staring at the ceiling. By the time the sky was streaked with its first hints of red, his plan had been forged, each step carefully thought through.

After breakfast he left the house under the pretext of wanting to tell August the latest developments. Which was true, in part. The less Clara knew the better.

With his hat drawn down low over his face against the keen wind, he set out. Children with satchels on their backs passed him in a noisy gaggle, and an old man leaning heavily on his stick stepped out of their way. A tram rattled past him, a white sign on its side declaring in black letters: "Jews Not Wanted Here!"

Paul watched the tram pass before turning toward St. Paul's. He suddenly staggered as he was shoved roughly aside.

"Here's our esteemed Blumenthal," sneered Gustav Johansson, the fat butcher from Mörkenstrasse whose family ran a shop near the war memorial. "Why don't you all clear off to Palestine where you belong? We'll gladly help you pack."

"Take your hands off me," Paul hissed. "And what's that supposed to mean? We're all equal before our God."

The butcher stared at him, speechless, for a moment, then grabbed Paul's arm. "'Our God'? Oh yes, you've become Christians in recent years. How could I forget?" His eyes narrowed to slits. "Watch how you speak to me. I can report you to the police and have you thrown in jail any time I like."

Paul tore free, shaken. He and his mother had always been friendly enough with the Johansson family. What was more, they had occasionally given them food during the war. But those former connections, the recollections of a shared past, seemed to have been erased from people's heads. Paul turned onto Wilhelminenstrasse. August was the only man who could help him now. He knocked on the door of the workshop in August's front garden, and it wasn't long before his son, Emil, an adolescent with fuzz on his chin, opened up.

"My father's not here. He's out delivering some furniture. Do you want to wait?"

"Yes, please." Paul watched as Emil hurried back into the little office and began hammering on the keys of his typewriter.

A few minutes later, Johann's old friend came in. His jaw dropped when he saw Paul. "Well, what a surprise! What brings you here?"

"Good morning. I'd like to place an order for a small table, please." Paul's lie was for the benefit of Emil, but the young man seemed absorbed in his typing anyway. He put a finger to his lips and lowered his voice. "Can I speak to you in private? It's important."

August threw his work gloves down on the wooden bench and sent his son out, then took a seat at the desk and stretched out his stiff leg. "What can I do for you, Paul?"

Paul handed him an envelope. "Uncle Max has sold the business in Lübeck and given us half the proceeds. I don't want to visit Gregor at the bank and risk the authorities noticing. Could you please ask him to transfer our assets in separate small amounts, from different accounts, to this one? The bank details are in here."

August opened the envelope, then looked up, nonplussed. "Cape Town? You're going to emigrate?"

"That's right." Paul gave him a brief summary.

"I understand. I'd probably do the same in your shoes. We'll miss you, boy," the carpenter murmured sadly. "I'm seeing Gregor tomorrow evening. I'll discuss it all with him then."

"Thank you. What on earth would we do without you two?"

"We promised your father," Johann's friend said simply, studying Paul's face. "But that's not the only reason you're here, is it?"

Paul nodded. "You know me too well. There is something else. You used to tell me sometimes you had some contacts in the black market. Is that still the case?"

August grinned broadly. "Too right. After all, we're not far from the Reeperbahn district, my boy. How far underground do you want to go? Are you interested in streetwalkers, perhaps, or do you want to arm yourself?"

"Neither of those," Paul replied, fighting to conceal his embarrassment. "I'm looking for a discreet printer."

August looked at him sharply. "What's your plan?"

"Do you know anyone or not?" he said evasively.

August thought for a moment, then rose with a sigh and crossed to a cupboard. "My client file," he muttered as he searched through a thin folder. "This is your man. A shady character. He may have retired by now—I haven't seen him around for a while—but you might as well try your luck." He made a note on a scrap of paper.

When Paul reached out to take it, August shook his head. "Tell me what all this is about first."

"I don't want to get you involved."

"It's far too late for that. So spit it out, or this paper goes in the trash."

Paul knew there was no point in arguing, and took August into his confidence.

August blew out his cheeks. "Forged passports? That's a risky business. If it comes out, your lives will be in danger. It's a huge responsibility you're taking upon yourself. Are you sure you've thought it through?"

"I have." Paul stared into space past the older man.

Would you have acted any differently, Father? he wondered. *What price would you have been prepared to pay to live in freedom?*

"Just be careful." August jolted him back to reality and pinched his cheek as he used to when Paul was a little boy. "And don't you dare keep anything secret from me and Gregor."

"It's a promise. Will you give me the address now?"

August placed the paper on the desk. "Tell the man that I sent you. Otherwise there's no way he'll talk to you. And keep me updated."

Paul hugged him. "Thank you for everything."

The morning was nearly over by the time he returned home. Margarethe was helping her mother chop vegetables, chattering and fidgeting the whole time. Clara looked inquiringly at Paul, wiped her hands on her apron, and sent their daughter out into the garden. "The music box stays here."

"OK, Mama." They heard Margarethe's little feet going down the stairs.

"Sit down," Paul began.

Clara listened attentively, but she stiffened the more she heard. "That's far too dangerous. Why can't we make an official emigration application, like Uncle Max and Papa suggested?"

"So that we arrive in South Africa with no home, no work, and no future? What life will we be taking our child to?"

He made as if to draw her into his arms, but she broke free and began pacing the living room. "There has to be another way."

"Tell me one," Paul countered. "If we're in the authorities' files as potential emigrants, they'll confiscate the profits from the auction, too."

"Thousands upon thousands of emigrants have already been subjected to that," she argued. "We can get through it, too."

The next moment he was beside her, cupping her face in his hands. "The printer showed me his ledger. It's full of months' worth of 'special orders,' as he called them."

Clara shook him off. Her eyes were fiery. "So you've already decided. I can't believe you made the decision without me. You'd rather put me and Margarethe in danger than let the Nazis steal from you?" She fell on him, pummeling his chest with her fists. "The money isn't that important, Paul! Your family in Cape Town wouldn't let us starve. You ought to be ashamed of yourself!"

Paul held her tightly. "I know I should have discussed the plan with you first. I'm sorry. But my mother is working so hard just to support herself. And this business, it's my legacy from my father. I want to know that we can pay for Margarethe's education, give her a secure future! Don't you want that?"

"You know I do," she conceded. "But you deceived me and I'm frightened. Really frightened."

"We mustn't under any circumstances draw attention to ourselves. Once we've got the passports, we'll leave the house as if we were going to come back any moment."

"But we'll need luggage," she interrupted.

"We can buy what we need on the way. We'll take nothing but our papers and the bare essentials."

"Are you crazy? Who'll take care of the house? We can't just leave everything behind."

"We have to," he said passionately. "No one should enter this apartment, not even your father."

"The SA will destroy the place! Our home!"

"We can't worry about that. We have to vanish into thin air."

Clara snorted. "They'll come looking for us."

"Of course they will. And that's why we won't be on the first ship that leaves. We're bound to find some sort of work in the countryside. We'll wait out the winter there, until the roads are clear of ice. Hopefully the Nazi thugs will have called off their search by then."

"What if someone recognizes us?" Her voice was little more than a whisper.

"Trust me, darling."

She looked out of the window. "When's all this going to happen?"

"It'll take about two weeks for the passports to be ready. That gives us enough time to say goodbye to our old life." How lost Clara looked. If only he could spare her all this. He turned her to face him. "One more thing: we mustn't say a word to anyone. Do you understand?"

"What about Margarethe?"

He shook her gently. "Not a word, Clara."

"I don't know if I can do that."

"You can and you must."

That night they lay side by side without moving, each lost in their own thoughts. Paul did not dare to take her in his arms; he understood she'd need time to forgive him for making the decision without her.

When at last he heard Clara breathing deeply and steadily, he tiptoed into the living room, which was lit by faint moonlight. His eyes were drawn to the bureau where he kept his father's diary. He sat by the window with Johann Blumenthal's last thoughts and switched on the side-table reading lamp.

April 20, 1915, Ypres by the Yser

They assured us of a quick victory. How blind they all were! We've been sitting tight in Ypres for 169 days and waiting for orders about the next operation since the day before yesterday. We crouch in the mud like worms, stinking, louse-ridden, and keeping company with rats. Toni has been afflicted by a stammer ever since he got sprayed with the mangled innards of one of our boys during a shell attack. Piet sometimes breaks out in hysterical laughter. We're worried for his sanity. However, despite it all, I'm grateful for every day I live to see the sunrise. But I'm weak—instead of trusting in the Almighty, I'm beginning to doubt His existence. No god in the world could want carnage like this. The things I've experienced in this filthy hell shouldn't be set down in detail. I think of Martha—when I used to have difficulties with my schoolwork, she'd advise me to write it all out. She always used to say it would sink in better that way. She's the wisest of us all. But setting these experiences down is exactly what I want to avoid; it's more than enough that they burn in my head. When I think I can't stand it any longer, I look at the photograph of Martha, Hermann, and the boys, and the one of Lotte and our little Paul, and beg Adonai to keep them safe. Last week the photographs got smeared with dirt, but I managed to clean them. Lotte and Paul look so beautiful and innocent. If there's one thing that keeps me going from day to day, it's the thought of holding them in my arms again. I often wonder if Lotte will still be able to love the man I've become. The war has changed us all. The demons will live on in our hearts. But once I'm back at home, perhaps I'll be able to bury them under the beauty of family, work, normal life. I wonder if my little boy can sense that I tell him a bedtime story every night in my thoughts?

Chapter 23

They left their apartment as the Blumenthal family one afternoon at the end of October 1935. As they set out for the station, Clara made as if to turn and take a last look at their home, but Paul held her back.

"Are we going to see Uncle Max?" Margarethe asked hopefully, her little hand in her mother's.

"No. We . . . we're going on a trip, sweetheart," Clara replied.

A short while later, they boarded the crowded Lübeck train, leaving all trace of the Blumenthals behind in the station. Paul squeezed Clara's ice-cold hand as they neared their destination.

In Lübeck they headed straight for a department store. When Paul told his daughter about the new clothes they were going to buy her, her innocent pleasure caused him a pang of guilt. The clothes had to be simple and practical so they would become invisible in the flow of passersby. Margarethe was delighted—until the moment when her parents told her to throw away her beloved red coat.

"No, Mama," she protested with bitter tears. "It's beautiful and it has a pocket for the music box."

"So does your new coat," her mother replied. "Do as I say."

Margarethe obeyed, though her mouth was set in defiance.

Paul got his hair cut and parted it down the side. The haircut and the plain round glasses made him look older. He swallowed as he watched Clara's long, chestnut hair fall in waves to the floor. She was barely recognizable with short hair. Now they were the spitting image of the people whose faces had been used for the passport photos.

Poor Margarethe was bewildered, and Paul wanted so much to be able to explain it all to her.

He arranged lodgings for them under the name of Dölling in a nondescript boardinghouse on a side street.

The two adults had a hard time fending off Margarethe's questions, and were relieved when she finally fell asleep late that evening. They moved quietly into the dark hallway to talk. The crackly sound of the Comedian Harmonists singing "Ein Freund, ein guter Freund" drifted up to them from the gramophone in the landlady's living room. *A good friend indeed,* Paul thought grimly.

He took a map from his pocket. "Look here. Southwest of Lübeck, there are some settlements, probably farms. We can try our luck there."

"If you like," Clara replied. "I don't care where we go, as long as we can get far enough away from the thugs."

The following morning, they made their way to the tram stop.

"Where are we going now?" Margarethe asked outside the boardinghouse.

Paul crouched down. "We're going to the country." He stroked her copper-colored hair. "Your mama and I have a big secret. Can I trust you to keep it?"

Margarethe's cheeks flushed. "Oh yes, a secret!" She hopped on one leg in delight.

"But it's a secret you mustn't tell *anyone*."

"I won't, Papa."

Paul looked at his daughter, his expression deadly serious. "Swear on your music box."

Without hesitating, Margarethe dug into her coat pocket, kissed the little keepsake, and declared solemnly, "I swear."

"Good. Listen carefully, darling. From this day on, we have new names. I'm Peter, Mama is Charlotte—and you're Emma."

"Emma? But that's not my name."

"It's very important. Do you understand?"

"But I don't like that name." She pouted.

"I don't like mine either, sweetheart," Charlotte said. "But we'll get used to them—you'll see."

Peter could see his wife trying to smile encouragingly. "Shall we go, darling?"

A handful of people were waiting at the tram stop, but took no notice of them.

A hint of frost was hanging on the air, and by the time the tram arrived their ears were icy cold. "No Jews Allowed," Peter read. He guided his wife and daughter firmly onto the tram. An elderly couple sitting opposite looked at them curiously, but he forced himself to meet their gaze impassively. The tram took them past the Mühlentor Gate, and then they saw a classical villa on the right. A little while later, they got off and continued on foot, past neat estates from which they could hear the clucking of chickens and barking of dogs. A landscape of small meadows punctuated by groups of trees extended away to their right.

"Straight ahead," Peter told his family.

They had been walking in near silence for a little under an hour when the suburban houses gave way to more extensive fields where cattle grazed. The sun rose higher and warmed their faces. Emma was whimpering; her feet hurt. At last, a small restaurant and inn came into view, and they decided to rest.

The only customers were a few men in work pants and boots sitting at the counter. The appetizing smell of meat and vegetable stew filled the family's nostrils. They found a place at a corner table and ordered fried potatoes and homemade sausage from the owner.

When the owner came back to serve their food, Peter seized the opportunity. "We're looking for work and clean lodgings. Could you perhaps use some hard-working labor?"

The proprietor's plump face creased into a good-natured smile. "I could have, if you'd arrived two months earlier. But the harvest's all in now, and our guest rooms are newly renovated. I'm sorry, Herr . . . ?"

"Dölling," Peter replied quickly. "That's a pity. Do you happen to know of anyone with work?" From the corner of his eye he noticed his daughter looking at him in confusion. To his relief, she was too shy to intervene.

"I don't know anyone looking for help around here," the man replied after a moment's thought. "But there are some farms farther afield that you could try."

"Thank you." Peter tried not to let his disappointment show.

Once the man had left them alone, Emma said, "Dölling? That's funny, Papa."

"That's what we're all called now," he told her quietly. "Don't worry. I'll explain everything to you when you're older."

Her expression darkened, but she remained silent.

After a quick meal, Peter led the family several miles farther down the road. They were turned away from the next two farms. At the third, a buxom woman regarded them disapprovingly. "I could use the two of you, perhaps. But I can't feed a child as well."

Their hope for a place to stay began to falter.

"It's only early afternoon. We've got plenty of time to find a place before nightfall. Come on," Peter said, kissing them both on the brow.

A little later, by which time Emma's steps had slowed to a crawl, they reached the village of Krummesse. The wind had picked up, and it battered their exhausted bodies. The brave face Emma had been keeping up all day finally failed her, and she cried as the wind began to howl.

Peter noticed a sign half concealed by tall bushes, pointing toward an estate that lay nearby. Charlotte and Emma wouldn't be able to hold out for much longer; they all needed a warm bed and somewhere to wash. He felt his belt, where a leather money pouch hung. Charlotte had a little more of their savings tucked away between her breasts. The remainder was well hidden in a secret compartment in her bag, which they didn't let out of their hands for a second. Without speaking, he gave an encouraging hug to his wife, who had become ever more taciturn as the day wore on. Seeing that his little daughter was pale with exhaustion, he hoisted her onto his shoulders and followed the sign.

A lake came into sight on their left. Startled by their footsteps, a small flock of water birds took to the air, screeching. The view opened up to a vast, beautifully laid-out park, dotted with pairs of beeches and oaks whose branches swayed alarmingly in the gale. Beyond that they could make out meadows and fields of rye, against a backdrop of dark-green forest spreading away into the distance. As they walked on, Peter saw a long, low building to one side of the meadows, which he supposed housed cow stalls or pigsties. Two heavy horses neighed from a field shelter. A kitchen garden completed the idyllic picture of a country estate. The brick façade of a manor house shimmered through the leaves of a circular group of lime trees. Small twigs flew past on the wind, and autumn-hued leaves had formed a thick carpet that rustled beneath their boots.

They stopped at the front door, and Charlotte removed some leaves from Emma's hair.

Peter reached for the wooden door knocker.

A man of around forty, a leather apron over his paunch, opened the door. He stood a head taller than Peter, and his broad shoulders bore testimony to years of backbreaking labor. "Heil Hitler. Can I help you?" Brown eyes studied them intently, coming to rest on Peter.

"My name is Peter Dölling, this is my wife, Charlotte, and our daughter, Emma," he said, his voice raised over the wind. "We're looking for work and somewhere to stay the night."

"I'm Friedrich Lükemeier, the tenant farmer of this estate." He ducked to avoid a couple of twigs blowing toward him. "Damned weather. Come in. Wouldn't leave a dog outside in this."

Peter suppressed a sigh of relief. The man led them into a kitchen containing a table big enough for at least a dozen hungry people. The stove in the hallway radiated a cozy warmth.

Lükemeier called and a young girl appeared. She looked barely fifteen and wore a headscarf from which strands of light-blonde hair escaped. At a word from him, she heated milk in a large pan and sweetened it with honey.

"Thank you, Brigitte. Can you please prepare the room by the kitchen for our guests? Then make us all a good meal. After that, once you've seen to the animals, you can go."

The girl curtsied and hurried off.

The tenant handed them mugs of milk. "This is the best thing when you're frozen through. Have you come far?"

"Yes, we've been on the road for a few days," Peter replied evasively, suddenly turning hot and cold as he remembered that the details on their passports identified them as coming from the Mecklenburg region. It wouldn't take much to betray themselves.

"You rest first, and we can talk later. I've got work to do."

"We're very grateful to you, Herr Lükemeier," Peter said.

"It's no trouble." He shuffled out of the kitchen.

They drank the hot milk in silence. Emma's eyes were already closing as Brigitte appeared and invited them into the guest room. A short time later, the little girl was asleep in bed.

Peter and Charlotte sat together on a bench by the window. Outside, the wind was driving dark clouds across the sky and rattling the shutters so angrily that it took some effort for Peter to close them.

He drew her head against his chest. "The man seems very welcoming."

"Yes, but he doesn't miss a thing," Charlotte said quietly. "Did you see the way he was looking at us?"

"Can you blame him? I'd be just as careful in his position."

A flash of light shot through the cracks in the shutters, and they jumped as it was followed almost immediately by a rumble that shook the air.

Peter looked at his sleeping daughter, but she was too tired to be disturbed.

"I wonder if Herr Lükemeier suspects anything?"

"You worry too much, darling," he said reassuringly.

The storm blew over as quickly as it had come, and Peter soon opened the shutters again. One of the old oaks had been split by a lightning strike. A hay wagon was lying on its side, and the ground all around was full of twigs and branches.

"I'd be pleased to help you tidy up," he said later to Herr Lükemeier as they sat down to the evening meal, savoring the bread that the girl had baked.

Lükemeier looked him up and down appraisingly. "You don't look like a man who's used to hard physical work."

"I won't deny it. But I can do my share," Peter replied.

"Brigitte, will you be so kind as to show the little girl our calves," Lükemeier said to his farmhand.

"You have calves?" Emma squealed, rejuvenated after her short nap.

"Yes, and you can help Brigitte feed them if you like."

Instead of replying, she bounded from her seat and ran out after the farmhand.

As their steps faded away, Lükemeier leaned forward, his hands folded on the table before him. "Now tell me, Frau Dölling, what brings you here?"

"Well"—Charlotte searched for Peter's hand under the table—"we used to run a jewelry business, but then our lease was terminated."

"Yes, these things happen." The farmer looked Peter in the eye. "Very well, I'll be happy to take you up on your offer."

Chapter 24

November 1935–summer 1936

Peter had never done any serious farm work, but he made every effort to conceal his inexperience from Lükemeier. And the farmer was clearly satisfied, as a few days later he formally took him and Charlotte on in return for board and lodging, and gave them use of a second room. Although at first she struggled, Emma gradually grew accustomed to her new life, and followed Brigitte everywhere.

During the first few weeks, the fear of being unmasked was overwhelming. They impressed upon Emma that she mustn't breathe a word, even to Brigitte, making her repeat the promise nightly. They kept out of sight at all times, though apart from the mailman and an occasional visit from a neighboring farmer, hardly anyone found their way to the estate.

The more time went by, the quieter Charlotte became. Her homesickness and the impossibility of making contact with their family weighed heavily on her, and some nights, Peter caught her sobbing quietly into her pillow. He couldn't count the hours he had spent turning things over in his mind, trying to find a better solution. He had done everything possible; the last time they had visited Uncle Max in Lübeck, to say goodbye, he had casually pressed a note into his uncle's hand.

Wait for our news from Cape Town. With love.

Uncle Max had read the note immediately before burning it in an ashtray. Peter remembered how he'd whispered "Look after yourselves" in his ear as they were leaving. The memory still gave him goose bumps.

Winter had come early that year, and Peter's unease grew as he watched the roads turning impassable with frost and ice. If only Lükemeier had a telephone, he could at least book them passage on the *Watussi* in April. But that kind of progress had not yet reached the countryside.

When the farmer told him in mid-March 1936 that the roads were now clear and he had some bank business to see to in town, Peter asked if he could go with him. Under the pretense of wanting to phone his family, he went to a post office outside the gates of Lübeck and had himself connected to the shipping company in Bremen. The crossing was long since fully booked, he was told impassively, as the *Watussi* was the last ship to set sail from Bremen for Cape Town that year. He should try the port at Hamburg, where a ship was to take the same route in December.

On the way back, Lükemeier tried to chat with him. When Peter replied in monosyllables, the farmer looked at him thoughtfully. "Bad news?"

"Yes, unfortunately," Peter replied. "But I can't complain; we're living in bad times."

Lükemeier didn't persist, but for the rest of the journey Peter couldn't shake off the terrible feeling that the man was watching him.

Back at the estate, Charlotte was mending Emma's skirt. Peter took her aside and broke the news as gently as he could. Their daughter was sitting on the bed, winding wool.

"We can't risk sailing from Hamburg," Charlotte said quietly.

"No, we can't. We have to wait for a better opportunity."

The summer went by at a lazy pace. August came around, and the peace of the countryside was a balm to their taut nerves.

Late one afternoon, Peter was digging a deep hole beneath the knotty oak in front of their bedroom window and paused to wipe the sweat from his brow. The day was unusually hot, with scarcely a breeze to stir the leaves. Lükemeier, who had been treating them less formally of late, was away selling some cattle, giving Peter an opportunity at last to hide their savings. Their new friend must know nothing about it. However good-natured the man, a widower of two years, might be, they had no intention of taking him into their confidence. His work done, Peter shoveled the last spadeful of earth onto the metal box with a sense of satisfaction.

At lunchtime a delicious smell enticed him back into the house, where he found Charlotte at the stove. The ladle in her hand was shaking as she stirred the vegetable soup. "Where's Emma?"

"She's helping Brigitte with the milking."

Peter frowned. The look in her eyes worried him, and he made her sit. "Is something wrong?"

She was clearly fighting to find the words. "It's nothing bad. But I have something to tell you."

Peter looked at her expectantly.

"We're going to have a baby."

He pulled her to him, and for a blissful moment he was overflowing with joy. "How lovely," he managed to stammer.

She took his hand. "I didn't know how to tell you."

"Why not?" He kissed her tenderly. "You've made me the happiest man in the world."

"Please be realistic. It's hard enough to hide with one child. But come spring there'll be four of us."

"We'll manage," he replied, doing his best to sound convincing. But in his mind's eye he saw his wife with a baby in her arms, Emma holding her hand, and his insides clenched. The weight of responsibility lay even heavier on his shoulders. His last image of his father suddenly appeared to him, as he was giving him the music box—the beautiful keepsake that his daughter now treasured so much she even clutched it in her sleep, although the silver had long since tarnished. Had his father not proved to him that it was possible to overcome his own fears and risk his life for the safety of his family?

Peter took a deep breath. "We're in good hands here, darling. If the thugs were on our trail, they'd have found us a long time ago. We won't make the crossing until our baby's safely born. Relax. I'll get you all to South Africa, so help me God."

She stroked his cheek, but the gesture contained mute despair.

At that moment, Friedrich entered the kitchen along with Emma and Brigitte.

"Time to wash your hands, little one," Brigitte said firmly to Emma before they vanished into the bathroom.

"What a lovely smell. My mouth's watering, I tell you," Friedrich exclaimed loudly. But then he fell silent. "Goodness, what's with the worried faces?" He threw his hat down on the table. For the first time since Peter had known him, his face turned grim, almost angry. "Sit."

They obeyed.

"I've felt for a long while that you're keeping something from me." He narrowed his eyes. "Do you remember that stormy day when you appeared at my door?"

"How could we ever forget it?" Charlotte replied.

"I trusted you," Friedrich continued, "and invited you into my house, although there are plenty of thieves and con men out here. Last year someone tried to steal my cattle. So I had every reason to shut the door on you. But I didn't, because my instincts told me to trust you, that you're good people. Now I expect the same trust from you." His voice had a hard edge. "Let me make one thing clear: I won't accept any more evasion. Tell me—have you done something wrong?"

Charlotte gave Peter an imperceptible nod.

"No, we've done nothing wrong," he began carefully. "But you're right. We've been keeping something from you—only because we don't want to get you into trouble."

"You can let me worry about that," he replied resolutely.

"It's not that simple," Peter countered, thinking as he spoke what an incredible relief it would be to finally tell the truth.

"We're baptized Christians," Charlotte said after a brief pause. "But according to the new laws, nothing matters but our Jewish origins. We're non-Aryans on the run from the SA."

Friedrich let out a low whistle. "I suspected something of the kind."

Brigitte and Emma came into the kitchen, and the conversation came to an abrupt halt. "The food isn't ready yet," Brigitte said, reading the silence and looking meaningfully at the little girl. "Come and help me fold the laundry."

Once they'd left, Peter continued, "We've lost everything we worked for all our lives. Do you understand now, Friedrich? If we tell you the details, you'll also be committing a crime."

Friedrich's expression darkened. "Out with it all, if you want us to stay friends!"

Peter took a deep breath, then told him the whole story, omitting only the forged passports.

Friedrich was visibly shocked. "I'm truly sorry, my friends. Personally, I don't care what religion someone belongs to, as long as they have a good heart, and they're honest and hardworking. You're all of those. Someone should put a stop to the whole lousy Nazi business if you ask me. First, people welcome the Jews as good business people. But once they begin to make money, they exploit them, steal their worldly goods, and call them vermin." He reached for a bottle of schnapps and offered them each a glass, but Peter and Charlotte declined. With a shrug he poured himself a generous shot and knocked the clear spirit back. "The hate has reached us here, too. Neighbors are moaning about the cowardly, lazy Jewish rabble. There's even talk of Jewish youths assaulting young Aryans. I've never believed it."

"They've been stirring people up by fabricating stories like that for years," Peter said.

The farmer nodded. "I came to that conclusion myself. There are good and bad in every race, aren't there? Tell me, Peter—your little girl carries a silver toy around with her all the time. Was that made in your workshop?"

"Yes, my father made it for me."

"Emma seems very attached to it," Friedrich said.

Peter gazed into the distance. "Just like I used to be."

They fell silent.

"So, what now?" Friedrich resumed.

"We were intending to move on in the spring. But now something's changed." Peter hesitated. He thought he caught a glimpse of Brigitte's blonde hair by the washhouse door. But everything was still. He must have been mistaken. *I'm seeing things,* he thought, before turning to Charlotte.

Her cheeks were flushed. "We originally planned to emigrate to South Africa this year," she said hurriedly. "But now we're expecting another baby. I know it's not good timing . . . Please don't worry; we won't be a burden. I'm sure I'll be able to work right to the end."

Friedrich poured himself another schnapps. "That's the least of my worries, Charlotte. Though I don't envy you being responsible for two children in this situation." A small smile lit up his face. "On the other hand, challenges are there to be overcome. Can I do anything to help you?"

"Please promise this conversation won't go any further," Peter replied.

"That goes without saying," Friedrich said. "You can stay here and work for me for as long as you want. When the time comes, I'll take you to the ship myself."

Peter pressed his hands to his eyes so his friend couldn't see the tears. "If we can stay here until the baby's born, we'd be most grateful to you."

"Yes, that would be such a help," Charlotte whispered.

Friedrich struck the table with the flat of his hand. "It's a deal," he said seriously. "But you must stop running around like headless chickens every time there's a knock at the door. It only makes you look suspicious."

Emma came into the kitchen and sat down by her father.

"That may be," Charlotte said quietly. "But what if someone asks about us?"

Friedrich waved her concerns away. "Don't be silly. The more normally you act here, the less attention you'll attract. You work for me and that's all there is to it."

Chapter 25

One evening in early October, Friedrich and Peter passed the time playing cards. Charlotte had gone to bed early, and Emma was sleeping soundly.

"I'm worried about your wife," Friedrich said as he dealt. "She's so often absent and agitated."

"Yes, she's worried about her father, who refuses to leave his home. And there's also our circumstances. It weighs more heavily on Charlotte than she lets on."

"I think she's a very thoughtful woman."

The men gathered up their cards.

"I've got to go to town tomorrow to collect some cattle feed. If you want to give me her father's telephone number—"

"Dr. Fisch hasn't had a telephone since he was forced to give up his practice," Peter replied.

"But your uncle in Lübeck must have one?"

"The connection point was in our main shop, the one he sold, so I'm not sure."

Friedrich threw an ace down on the table. "If you give me his address, I can deliver a message to him."

Peter lowered his glass. "You'd do that?"

"Why not? What do you want me to tell him?"

"Just that we're well and not to worry. That we're thinking of him. Thank you, my friend."

At the crack of dawn the next day, Friedrich harnessed up the horses, and when he returned home a few hours later, Peter hurried to meet him.

"Did you manage to find my uncle?"

Friedrich took off his good summer jacket and hung his hat on a peg. "I had to get past a rather forceful woman first," he replied with a grin. "Reminds me of my wife, God rest her soul." He drew Peter into the washhouse. "Charlotte can't hear us in here. Did you tell her about our plan?"

"No, it would have made her too nervous."

"I thought as much. Well, your uncle was glad to hear from you, and he'll pass on your news to Charlotte's father."

"Thank you. That's good. Charlotte will be pleased. No one saw you, I hope?" Peter whispered.

"Of course not," Friedrich said. "I left through the back door by the laundry, and I took a good look around to make sure the coast was clear."

Peter heaved a sigh of relief.

"I'm to send you his love and tell you he's well. But if you ask me, Peter, the poor man looks more like death on legs," Friedrich added.

He called them all to the kitchen table.

Charlotte beamed when he told her of his visit to Max. "I don't know how we can ever repay you."

"You scratch my back, I'll scratch yours," he said dismissively. Emma was sitting by him. He stroked her hair and pointed to the music box in her hand. "That's a beautiful toy. May I please have a look?"

Emma looked to her mother. When Charlotte nodded, she gave him the keepsake, but didn't take her eyes from it for a second.

"Don't worry, little one, I'll be careful," Friedrich murmured as he examined it from every angle. "What's this?" He fingered a button on the base.

"You mustn't open that!" Emma cried shrilly. "That's my secret compartment."

Friedrich exchanged a smile with Peter. "Very well. I didn't realize. But this music box needs a good polish. I'll show you how to do it later."

Emma nodded eagerly.

Brigitte had the day off to see her nephew being baptized, so Charlotte was preparing bean casserole. Peter lit the fire in the stove while his wife chopped onions and fresh vegetables from the garden. Friedrich sat at the kitchen table with Emma, patiently showing her how to polish her toy back to its old shine with potash. He was whistling along to an operatic melody that crackled from the radio, winning a smile from Peter.

They heard the sound of an engine outside, followed by a knock at the door.

"Who can that be?" Friedrich murmured, and shuffled off down the hallway in his slippers.

"Heil Hitler. Are you Friedrich Lükemeier?" said a man's voice with a Pomeranian accent.

Peter tiptoed closer and listened.

"Yes, that's me," Friedrich answered. "With whom do I have the pleasure of speaking?"

"Inspector Hildebrandt, Lübeck District Sturmabteilung. These are two of my colleagues. We've been informed that you're hiding persons wanted by the police."

Peter felt as though his heart stopped. *Brigitte!* He had often noticed the girl watching them. *She betrayed us,* he thought. As if in slow motion, he turned to Charlotte and Emma, who stared at him wide-eyed.

"Wanted persons here?" Friedrich said loudly. "There must be some mistake."

Peter waved Charlotte toward the storeroom and dropped onto all fours. He crawled through the kitchen. Charlotte took Emma into her arms, the little girl clinging desperately to her music box.

"We'd like to see for ourselves." The inspector's voice sent a shudder down Peter's spine. He was no more than four yards away from the storeroom.

"If you would step aside, Lükemeier!"

"Now, listen," Friedrich said indignantly. "Show me . . . show me some ID first."

Peter slipped into the storeroom, where his wife and child had hidden behind two full-height shelves. He held them close. Charlotte was trembling like a leaf, all the blood drained from her face, and Emma clung to him, terrified.

"Not a sound," he whispered as he strained to listen.

The front door slammed shut and steps approached.

"Open the doors, Lükemeier! Or do I have to force you?"

The words struck Peter like painful blows. Thoughts whipped through his head. The open stove door, the chopped vegetables, the potash on the table, and his father's diary in the bag.

His eyes fell to the carpet. The crawl space! He suddenly remembered Friedrich telling them to store the harvested fruit there. He raised the colorful carpet that covered the hatch and, a split second later, he helped Emma and Charlotte down.

"I was just preparing a meal," Peter thought he heard.

"You're lying! Where are they, Lükemeier?"

Peter finally crawled down behind them. He pulled the carpet back over the opening and closed the hatch. They huddled together, their hushed breathing the only sound in the pitch-black space. *Please don't abandon us, God,* he thought.

A door opened with a creak. They heard boots striking the floor above them. Emma jumped, and Peter held her tight.

"I don't know who or what you're looking for, gentlemen," he heard Friedrich say. "The only people who live here are my employees."

"And where are they now?"

"They've gone to town," Friedrich stammered.

"It's obviously all perfectly in order here, isn't it, Lükemeier?" the voice sneered.

Charlotte and Emma leaned against Peter, holding their breath. Suddenly, something fell with a dull clank to the crawl space floor.

An endless moment passed before the silence was torn apart by a cheerful bird's twittering. The music box.

Peter held his breath.

"What was that?" one of the men above them barked.

"The damned swallows and their brood," Friedrich replied quickly. "Would you like to look in the washhouse and barns?"

The men moved away. *God bless you, Friedrich,* Peter thought.

When all was still, he slowly pushed the hatch open. Seconds grew to minutes and minutes stretched away to eternity. When at last they heard an engine roar to life and a car moving away, they climbed quickly out of the crawl space. The storeroom had a second door that led outside. Peter tried to open it, but it stuck. Sweat ran from every pore. The lock finally gave way. "Come on!" he whispered, taking the two of them by the hand. Then he heard moans coming from somewhere, and paused.

"You two wait here," he said. He glanced around, then ran toward the barn.

He found Friedrich on the ground by the hay wagon, his hands pressed to his stomach.

Peter ran to him. "What did they do to you?"

Friedrich looked up with glazed eyes. "A few kicks to the belly."

Peter wanted to tell his friend how sorry he was, and how grateful. But he couldn't speak a word.

Friedrich rose unsteadily to his feet. "You'd better be on your way soon. The bastard said they'd be back. He assured me that if I'd lied to them, he'd personally see to it that I never walk again."

"For heaven's sake!" Peter said hoarsely. "Brigitte must've given us away."

Friedrich gripped Peter's arms. "If that's true, she'll get what's coming to her." He gave Peter an imploring look. "You've got to get away from here. Today. God help you if they catch you." He suddenly turned thoughtful. "But not right away and not via the main road. We have to assume . . ."

"That they've posted spies."

"Exactly. But I have an idea. You see the woods over there?"

"Yes."

"Before it gets dark, make your way along the path between the fields toward it. On the left-hand edge of the wood, about two hours' walk, you'll find a hut. It belongs to a friend of mine. We stay there when we're hunting boar. He's away in the south with his wife at the moment. Spend the night there. Make sure you leave no trace." Friedrich grimaced in pain.

"Of course." Peter was thankful, but not at all happy about the idea of creeping through the woods with Charlotte and Emma like thieves.

Friedrich tightened his grip. "You have to leave the hut before dawn; otherwise they might find you."

Peter nodded.

"Keep to the far side of the road toward Rondeshagen and Berkenthin, following the Elbe-Lübeck canal. From there you can go on toward Ratzeburg or Lüneburg. It doesn't matter. But take care. The roads around there are well-used trade routes."

"Thank you for all you've done, my friend." Peter embraced him.

The older man pushed him away in embarrassment. "It was only what any decent person would do. Don't get sentimental now. You have to go and pack! Take plenty of food with you."

Friedrich was about to turn, but Peter held him back.

"What now?" Friedrich asked.

Now it was Peter's turn to be embarrassed. "I buried our savings in a metal box in the garden."

Friedrich rolled his eyes. "Oh, boy. I suppose you want to take it with you."

"Impossible." He showed him the place beneath the oak tree. "We'll sew some of it into our clothes. Take good care of the rest until we meet again."

"I can't do that."

"We trust you." He turned on his heel and went back to Charlotte and Emma. When he saw Emma, her cheeks wet with tears, he crouched down before her. "Why are you crying, little one?"

She held up the music box with a sob. "Look. One of the corners is broken. It's all my fault. Those nasty men almost found us because I dropped it." She looked up at him. "Did they hurt Uncle Friedrich?"

Charlotte and Peter's eyes met. "Not too badly," he said. "Don't cry now, we'll repair it."

A little later, they were sitting at the kitchen table. But although the bean casserole smelled delicious, they could hardly eat. Even Friedrich, with his legendary appetite, soon pushed his plate away.

Emma had hardly said a word since the incident. "I don't want to leave here, Papa," she whispered after she had finished eating.

"I know. But we're not safe anymore."

She didn't reply. Peter looked with concern at her red cheeks. Ever since she was a baby, she had tended toward fever when she was upset. But they had no choice.

In silence, they prepared to leave. After putting Emma to bed for a quick nap, Charlotte took scraps of fabric and made little bags to sew into their clothing. Meanwhile, Friedrich and Peter were examining the music box.

"The top left corner is dented," Friedrich remarked.

"And the trigger mechanism's sticking," Peter replied. "I'd need tools to repair the damage. Poor Emma's blaming herself."

"Anyone could have dropped it."

"Of course. But try telling that to my daughter, who swore that she'd look after it. She's very conscientious for her age."

Friedrich sighed. "Go to Lüneburg. The town is full of places to stay. There are some excellent roads out of Lüneburg to Bremen and the emigrant ships."

Peter exchanged a meaningful look with Friedrich. "Wish us luck."

"Of course. I wish you all the best for the future."

Chapter 26

By early afternoon, the house looked as though they had never been there. They kept their leave-taking from Friedrich brief, not wanting Emma to realize how significant their departure was, or suspect the difficulties ahead. Her fever had failed to materialize, but Peter and Charlotte were still worried about their daughter. The hardest thing for Peter was the agonizing question of how long she would have to live under constant threat.

The little girl tried bravely to keep pace with her parents, but as daylight faded, she gripped Charlotte's hand fearfully. When she was too tired to go on, Peter lifted her onto his back. His nerves grew worse, but after a while his flashlight picked out the silhouette of the hut. Emma collapsed on a wool blanket in the tiny room, and they took turns keeping watch until Peter told his wife to sleep, too. How could he possibly close his own eyes with all that lay ahead of them?

The birds were beginning their dawn chorus as the family set out again in silence. A little under two hours later they reached the village of Rondeshagen. The road was wider there and fairly busy by that time, which forced them to take detours across fields and meadows along the canal. Soon they passed the pretty little village of Berkenthin, and saw spread out before them a lovely, hilly landscape, radiant in rich autumn colors. When the hamlet of Kulpin came into view, nestled peacefully by a lake, they set up camp in a thicket of trees. Charlotte was exhausted and feeling ill, so they decided to stop and rest there for a day. The starry night was clear and warm, and Peter thought he glimpsed a number of figures moving like ghosts through the little wood. Were they also on the run?

Two days later, their food almost gone, they reached Ratzeburg. Worried for his family's health, Peter decided to risk renting a room in an inn under the common surname Meier. While Charlotte and Emma rested, he walked to the station. With a sharp breath he saw there was a train to Lüneburg, and he bought tickets for the next day.

"Do you think that's wise?" Charlotte asked later, once he was back in the room.

"Yes, I do," Peter said, placing a hand on her slightly swollen belly. "We have to look after our children—both of them. It's just as risky on foot, and we'll make better progress this way."

Charlotte smiled, but Peter knew she was struggling not to let her fear show.

Emma withdrew into a corner with her music box.

"What's the matter, darling?" he asked.

She was stiff-backed as she turned to face him. "What do you care? You never tell me anything anyway, because you think I'm too little."

Peter blinked in surprise.

"Why can't we go home?" she burst out. "I don't want to sleep outside. Where are we going?"

He ran his finger gently down her twitching face. "We're going to where your grandma lives. Once your little brother or sister is born, we're going to sail on a big ship. That's our secret. I'm sorry; we should have told you sooner."

She threw her arms around his neck. "It's OK. You see? I'm big enough."

"Yes, you certainly are," he replied, moved.

"I want a sister, Papa," she said, her eyes shining. "I pray to God every night for one."

The next day, the train carried them to Lüneburg without incident. Peter was getting better at putting on a happy face for his family, hiding his own turmoil. He remembered a line from his father's diary. *If there's one thing that keeps me going from day to day, it's the thought of holding them in my arms again.*

Emma didn't ask any more questions. The sun was sinking low over the rooftops when they came to an inn on the edge of the town. A young man around Peter's age opened the door. There was a room free, he said, sizing them up, but only for a few days.

They bought more provisions, took warm baths, and ate a hearty dinner in a neighboring restaurant. The curious stares of the other diners burned into their backs.

"I want to get away from here," Charlotte said once their daughter was asleep.

"Me too," he admitted. "I guarantee we'll be closely checked at Bremen station if not before."

Charlotte leaned against him. "I'm so tired. I've had enough of hiding."

"We have to keep going, my love," he said, looking deep into her eyes. "Only a few months to go. When we get to Bremen, I'm sure I can find work and lodgings for us. And once we reach Cape Town, we'll soon forget all our hardships and fears."

"I wish we could stay out in the country until then," she said wistfully. "The towns are swarming with SA troopers."

"You know that's out of the question," he said gently. "What if there were complications with the baby? Where would I find a doctor out in the country? No, we'll be safer in Bremen. I'll protect you."

The next morning they were woken early by activity outside.

"I'm going into town to see about getting us to Bremen," Peter said. "Get some more rest if you can."

"Come back soon, Papa," Emma said.

Peter found a quiet café and casually asked a waiter about the best way to Bremen. "We're visiting relatives," he bluffed.

"Well, if you don't mind walking, it'll take you about five days on foot. The heathland around here is very popular with tourists. Lots of them around this time of year."

Another five days, Peter thought.

He left the café deep in thought and wandered through the busy streets of Lüneburg, keeping an eye out for people who looked like hikers. He kept his ears open, but was beginning to despair of getting any more information, when he happened upon a little store. One side was packed with worthless souvenirs, but the other was well stocked with travel guides and maps. Peter soon found what he was looking for and headed back to the inn with a spring in his step.

He leafed through the book, making notes, and studied the map. Then he spread it out on the table in their room. "I found a good route."

Charlotte and Emma seemed remarkably calm; clearly the rest had done them good.

"It'll take us about three days to reach Tostedt," Peter explained. "There should be a few guesthouses for hikers along the way, but otherwise the area seems quite secluded."

Charlotte and Emma said nothing, so he opened the guidebook and continued. "Look, there's a train from Tostedt several times a day. We can travel to Zeven and from there on to Worpswede." He looked up. "We'll continue by boat from Worpswede."

"Is that the big ship?" Emma asked.

"Not yet, little one," Charlotte replied, brushing a wayward lock of hair from her brow.

Peter smiled. "But it'll still be special! We can ride on a peat barge. Here, read this," he said to Charlotte, passing her the guide.

She exclaimed in surprise. "I'd never have imagined a peat barge would be a tourist attraction."

That night they didn't get to sleep until late. Emma could hardly wait for the boat ride. Charlotte and Peter were kept awake by worry; they lay wrapped in each other's arms listening to Emma's breathing.

After breakfast, they set off on foot and made good progress in the gentle autumn wind.

A few days later, waiting at Tostedt station, Peter's palms turned sweaty. The swarming, noisy crowds reminded him of a beehive, and after the isolation of their long hike, he felt dangerously exposed. Once on the train, he glanced around, wondering if there were other refugees on the train.

They got off a stop before Worpswede, hoping to avoid the SA troopers sure to be patrolling a larger station. Just a few miles from their destination, they were caught by heavy rain showers and forced to take refuge in a dilapidated barn. Half the space was filled with bales of hay. Emma fiddled nervously with her music box, but it was unharmed by the water. They took off their wet clothes and hung them on pitchforks to dry, then wrapped themselves in blankets and huddled against the haystacks, listening to the pattering rain.

"We'll stay here tonight," Peter announced. "No one will be driving their herds out to the fields in this weather."

Neither Charlotte nor Emma objected, but Peter wished he could offer them a warmer place to sleep.

Hungry and stiff, the three of them continued on their way the next morning, the rising sun warming their numb hands. At last they passed a farm with a roadside stand where they could buy bread, milk, butter, and a little honey. Peter noticed the suspicion in the eyes of the farmer's wife.

It was easy to find the mooring at Worpswede—people saw their meager luggage and willingly told them the way. Some were dressed in their Sunday best, perhaps for a wedding in one of the nearby villages. Peter, Charlotte, and Emma were also wearing their good clothes; they might be homeless, but they were determined to look respectable.

The small village of Worpswede lay in a picturesque location by a river in the middle of the Teufelsmoor fenland. The neat timbered houses that lined the road housed exhibitions of works by local artists. Inns and cafés beckoned from among stands of tall trees. A few elegantly dressed people moved indifferently among the swelling throng of visitors.

Peter grew increasingly nervous as he watched the people, around fifty of them, waiting for the peat barge that would transport them to remote villages in the marshes or to Bremen. Among them was a couple well past seventy, looking lost among the cheerful crowd. Peter and Charlotte were moved by the way they held hands. Looking closer, they were struck by the man's ill-fitting pants and the patched sleeves of the woman's blouse. Peter and Charlotte made their way toward them, keeping tight hold of Emma.

"It's a beautiful day," Charlotte said.

The petite old lady peered up at them. "Warm for the time of year." She indicated the two suitcases at their feet. "We have a long journey ahead of us. We're sailing from Bremen on the SS *Bremen* to New York tomorrow. Our son lives there. What about you? Are you going abroad?"

"We're heading for Bremen, too," Peter said. "We'll be traveling on to Cape Town next year."

The man looked surprised. "Cape Town, did you say?"

"That's right."

"Listen, it's a while till the barge leaves, and they make wonderful coffee in that café over there. Would you join me for a cup?"

Charlotte flashed Peter a look of warning.

"Please don't worry," the man said, searching her eyes. "I'll bring your husband right back."

Peter's bewilderment grew as the older man led him to the café. "I don't understand, sir."

"I want to talk to you in private," the old man said quietly. "Am I right in assuming that you're 'undesirables,' like we are?"

"Um, no, we . . . ," Peter stammered, but the old man understood and nodded, putting a finger to his lips.

"I take it you haven't seen the latest news?"

"No. Why?"

The man ordered coffee and waited until the waitress was out of earshot. "There was a report in all the papers the day before yesterday. A few days ago, the SS *Stuttgart* made for port in Cape Town carrying over five hundred Jewish emigrants. They were temporarily refused permission to dock."

Peter stared at the man aghast. "Why?"

But the waitress was on her way with their coffee. The two men thanked her with feigned smiles.

"It was because of a demonstration by National Socialists," the man continued at last. "When the passengers were finally able to disembark, they were threatened and mobbed."

Peter's head spun. "Has this madness spread to the ends of the earth?"

"I'm very sorry to say it has," the man said anxiously, polishing his glasses. "As a result, they're severely tightening the entry regulations for Jews. I'm sorry to tell you that there'll be no emigrant ship leaving for Cape Town in the foreseeable future."

It suddenly seemed as though all sound was reaching him through wads of cotton, and Peter was grateful for the cup he was holding, which gave his hands something to do. His heart beat dully and heavily against his ribs as the man's words echoed through his head. Would this never end?

Chapter 27

Lilian

London, 1963

When the Second World War ended in Europe on May 8, 1945, in a sea of blood and tears, the silver music box lay almost forgotten in a safe-deposit box. No light fell on it, no one clutched it, listened to its cheerful birdsong, or hid letters in its little compartment. The silver treasure still guarded secrets.

But the person it should have belonged to suspected nothing.

An icy wind was blowing one February day, adding to the melancholy of Kensal Green Cemetery. A life-size marble angel watched over an elaborate, circular grave. After sweeping away leaves and twigs, a gardener in green overalls placed a dried flower arrangement against the headstone. Behind him, relatives stood with bowed heads.

The chapel clock struck three.

A little way off were two newly dug graves. A young woman stood motionless by the fresh heap of earth. From a distance she looked like a teenager, a colorful cap adorning long hair that blew in the wind. With the wool collar of her A-line coat turned up against the cold, she stared at the inscription on the simple markers.

Lilian shivered. Only three weeks had passed since Steve and Heather Morrison died, and she still couldn't fathom that her parents were gone, hit by a drunk driver. Instead of grief, she felt nothing but a bewildering emptiness. She brushed a chestnut-colored strand of hair from her face and crouched down. The bouquet of bright yellow roses she had laid on the grave stood out in the wintry cemetery.

Her thoughts returned to that fateful morning when her life had been turned upside down.

"Your father and I are just going out shopping. We thought it'd be nice to meet for tea," her mother had said on the phone. Lilian could never have imagined it would be the last time she'd hear her voice. And her father's, as he'd yelled in the background for her to be sure to be on time.

She remembered her resentment as she left her two-room apartment on Sutherland Avenue. As retired civil servants, neither of her parents understood how difficult it was for a freelance translator under tight deadlines to just drop everything and rush off to tea. But now, looking at their graves, none of that mattered anymore.

She heard footsteps approaching. As she raised her head and saw a tall young man in jeans and a black leather jacket, she offered a faint smile.

"I thought I'd find you here," Sam Flynt said.

Once again Lilian was struck by the uncanny way her best friend seemed to read her thoughts. They had met only a year ago, at a mutual friend's birthday party. It was hard to believe how perfectly they understood one another, how it felt like they'd been friends forever.

Sam was a primary school teacher but had the day off. He kissed her cheek. "Nervous?"

"A little."

"Come on, get it over with. Don't keep the solicitor waiting," he said, and gently led her from the cemetery.

The law office was on Hampstead Road, not far from the British Museum. Lilian closed her eyes, wishing the whole business of her parents' will was already behind her. They caught the bus from the Kilburn Lane / Harrow Road stop to Euston Square and walked the last few yards. He hugged her outside the time-honored building.

"I'll wait here for you."

Lilian nodded and went in.

A while later she emerged.

"Everything OK, Lil?"

"I don't know." She clutched a copper container the size of a shoe box. "I really need some fresh air."

He tried to carry the strange object for her, but Lilian shook her head. How long had her parents held on to it? Handing it over to someone else seemed somehow . . . disrespectful. It must have been important in some way for them to have left it to her.

Sam led her to a park by Euston Station. They sat down on a bench, surrounded by the sound of passing traffic, and watched a few birds searching for earthworms among the damp leaves.

"They've left me their property and a bank account," Lilian began. "It says in the will I should use the money to buy myself a flat."

"Great," her friend said in amazement. "Are you going to?"

"I'll think about it. In any case, I'll rent out Mum and Dad's flat. There are too many memories there." She looked up at him. "Will you come back with me?"

"You're worried about that box, aren't you?"

Lilian laughed in embarrassment. "Yes. I don't like the idea of being alone when I open it."

His velvety-brown eyes were comforting. "Of course I'll come." He winked and pointed to his leather bag. "There's a pomegranate-colored Barolo in here waiting to be uncorked."

"You know just how to make me happy."

He grinned and on the way home regaled her with anecdotes of teaching life. Lilian glanced at him sidelong. Sam was one of the most interesting men she had ever met. With his dark-blond hair and his brow frequently furrowed in thought, he looked more like Bob Dylan than a teacher. His sharply drawn features were a delightful contrast to his gentle manner. But whenever he talked about his dream of traveling the world, his eyes lit up. She was grateful that he lived only a few doors away.

In her first-floor flat, Lilian fetched fruit, cheese, and glasses from the kitchen, and they sat down together on the sofa. She pulled up her legs and stared at the box on the table.

"Are you practicing telekinesis and hoping the thing will open itself?"

She threw a cushion at him. He caught it with a grin.

"Open it, for goodness' sake. The curiosity's killing me."

Lilian hesitated. The small copper box with old-fashioned handles didn't seem at all like her parents. Her parents had liked all things modern—to them, antiques were nothing but an expression of meaningless nostalgia.

The lid creaked as she opened it, releasing a musty smell. Two envelopes, one bigger than the other, caught her eye, together with an object carefully wrapped in stiff fabric. Lilian recognized her mother's handwriting immediately.

She tore the small envelope open.

> *Dear Lilian,*
> *If you're reading this letter, it means I didn't find the strength while I was alive to tell you how you came to us. I would never have thought we would find it so difficult to explain that we took you in as a foster child when you were two.*

Lilian stared, transfixed, reading the words over and over again. Time seemed to stand still. Then something in her snapped and she went to tear the letter to pieces.

Sam cried out in horror. "Lil! Stop!"

He took the letter from her hand and laid it out of reach on the table. "Calm down. Whatever that letter says, it's from your mother."

"They lied to me," she gasped. "All my life, get it?" Her voice was tinged with bitterness. "Anyway, she isn't my mother."

"I don't understand."

"Read it yourself."

Lilian fought doggedly to open the wine bottle with shaking fingers, and poured them each a glass, watching Sam's expression as he read.

He lowered the letter to his lap. "Incredible. I understand you're upset, but please read through to the end. Then you can decide whether you want to keep it."

Lilian leaned back and gulped some wine. *What's the point?* she wondered. The easiest thing by far would be to throw the letter away and forget it had ever existed. How could they do this to her?

"No, Sam," she said angrily. "I don't give a damn what else it says! The only thing that matters is that they didn't deem it necessary to tell me the truth."

"Your parents aren't here to defend themselves," Sam said. "And this letter is part of your inheritance. You know how much your parents cared about you. Don't do something rash just because you're angry."

Lilian pulled a face.

"You can be a real pain," she said. She took a deep breath, and he pressed the paper back into her hands.

I know you'll be angry and disappointed. I can imagine you wondering how we could keep something like this from you. In case you're thinking we did it out of cowardice, you're wrong. The truth is far more complicated than that. We did our best for you in every other way—it may have been wrong, but we just wanted to spare you the grief of your origins. And I'll admit there was a small part of me that couldn't bring myself to spoil our happy little world.

Your father and I always dreamed of having a big family. But it wasn't going to happen. The doctors could find no explanation for our inability to conceive. Maybe it was simply God's will. Then, in 1939, we read in the papers that they were desperately looking for foster parents for a little girl who had been brought out of Germany on the Kindertransport. We contacted the authorities and visited you in the children's home. You were such a sweet little thing. A few weeks later, we were delighted to bring you home.

We were told that your family was in a terrible situation when they sent you and your older sister to England, but I'm afraid we know nothing about them. We don't even know their names. How desperate must parents be to give away their own flesh and blood?

Among your belongings we found the object we have placed in this box for you. The warden of the children's home told us that your sister gave it to you when you were separated. That is all we have been able to find out. Please don't blame us for not telling you. We thought it would be best for you, but it was a mistake. Everyone has the right to know their roots. I hope you can forgive us one day.

God bless you,

Mum

Lilian lowered the letter. Then she snatched up the other envelope in the box. It contained the adoption papers, dated March 10, 1942. Lilly Dölling, the date of birth the same as hers.

She shuddered, then handed the papers to Sam and ran out onto the balcony.

He followed after a moment and passed her a cigarette. She inhaled the smoke gratefully. "'Parents missing.' That's all it says. Nothing about who my parents were."

"Strange," he replied. "But you know that they went to great lengths to make sure you were safe, that you got out of there even though it meant giving you up. Isn't that the most important thing?"

"Maybe." She struggled to resist the need to lean on him. "But . . ."

After she'd finished her cigarette, he led her back inside without a further word.

Lilian took the object from the box. Looking closer, she could see that it was not wrapped in fabric, but soft leather. It was about the size of her palm. The leather was worn shiny in places from handling, and there were a few patches of mildew. She gently felt the edges. It had been sewn together to form a bag, apparently in a hurry or by someone unpracticed, judging from the uneven stitches. But it had nevertheless fulfilled its purpose for many years. She carefully took the object from its sleeve.

It was an old-fashioned box made of silver, tarnished but intricately decorated. She saw a line on one of the feet where someone had once soldered it back in place. Time had also left its mark on the upper part, where there was a dent in one corner. Someone must have dropped it.

Sam shuffled closer. "May I have a look?"

"Of course."

He put on his reading glasses—now he did look like a teacher—and examined the box.

"Hard to make out the pattern, it's so worn." He squinted and brought it even closer. "Wow," he breathed in amazement. "Look, there's a storybook scene here. Some birds singing to a little boy. My God, what a beautiful piece." He handed it to her. "Just needs a little polish and it'll be absolutely stunning."

"Do you think it's worth much?"

"No idea, Lil."

Her fingers touched a protruding point and a circular lid sprang open. A little filigree bird appeared and started twittering.

Sam laughed. "That's fun. I've never seen anything like it."

"Neither have I." Lilian turned it over to look at the base, where she found some engraved words. "Can I borrow your glasses, Sam?"

"Johann Blumenthal, Altona 1914. For Paul, with love," she read softly.

"1914? It must have belonged to a relative. You could find out where you came from!"

Lilian placed the heirloom back in the box. "Whatever. I'm not interested."

He frowned at her. "Are you sure?"

"Totally. I'm also sure your wine's had enough time to breathe. Or am I drinking alone?"

He picked up his glass. "What shall we drink to? An exciting future?"

Lilian waved him away. "To tonight. There's a new dance club opening nearby. Will you come with me?"

Sam shook his head in feigned despair. "A dance club? For goodness' sake. I've got two left feet. And besides, you look worn out."

"I feel fine. And I need to forget everything for a night." She stuck out her chin. "Are you coming with me or will I have to dance by myself?"

He grinned. "You're unstoppable, aren't you?"

Chapter 28

Ever since the old box with its secret had shaken Lilian's life like an earthquake, time seemed to stretch away endlessly before her. During the day, she sat in front of the textbooks she was supposed to be translating from German, unable to keep her thoughts from wandering. She hammered away at her Olympia typewriter in frustration, crumpling one half-typed page after another into a ball and cursing as she knocked over her coffee mug, ruining a pile of papers. In the evenings she escaped to the new club, where she lost herself in the latest dance crazes until the small hours.

More than a week went by. Late one morning, Lilian sat listlessly in her bedroom office, chewing her bottom lip as she stared at her work. Translating textbooks was never one of her favorite jobs, and especially not when the subject matter was this dull.

Words kept popping into her head, blinding her to the ones on the page: *Kindertransport. Older sister. Music box. Johann Blumenthal. 1914.* One sentence in particular was burned into her mind: *How desperate must parents be to give away their own flesh and blood?*

She had to concede that her mother was right about that. Gazing out of the window, she watched thick snowflakes falling silently from the sky, gradually enshrouding the sidewalks and parked cars in a blanket of white. There certainly must have been good reason for sending their own children abroad into the care of strangers.

Lost in thought, she switched on the desk lamp. Her initial anger toward her parents had faded to bitter disappointment. Why hadn't they trusted her?

Although the betrayal still hurt, more complex feelings had begun to surface. Things that had bothered her all her life suddenly seemed to take on new meaning. The times when her mother had comforted her, and yet, while still in her arms, she had felt a distance that she couldn't put into words. How often had she caught them looking at her with a longing and concern that didn't make any sense?

It was as though everything in her past snapped into focus. As long as she could remember, she'd felt like a stranger in her own home and family, half-conscious of something terrible and unspoken. If only her parents had told her the truth.

The dancing snowflakes swam before her eyes. *Damn it to hell!*

Lilian chewed the end of her pencil. If only they'd told her the truth, talked through it all, maybe they could have looked one another in the eye and for the first time seen genuine understanding and unguarded affection there. She had missed out on so much.

Every night, her mysterious older sister slipped into her dreams like an uninvited guest. When Lilian woke in the mornings, fragmented images echoed in her consciousness. She suddenly remembered that, when she was little, she had asked her parents if the God to whom they prayed every day could send her a brother or sister. But her mother had told her that she was too old for that.

Lilian threw the pencil down on the desk. It was hard enough to suppress thoughts of relatives in faraway Germany, but it was downright impossible to get this older sister business out of her head.

What if she lived nearby without either of them knowing? Maybe her sister still remembered her real parents, even a few details from their time together in the children's home.

Lilian hurried over to the copper box and returned to the desk with the adoption papers. They were stamped by Hampshire Court, a children's home in Bristol in the southwest. She looked again at the name on the papers—Lilly Dölling, not Blumenthal like on the music box. What did that mean?

On impulse she threw on a coat, fumbled around for her purse and keys, and ran out to the nearest telephone box.

She asked the lady at the exchange to put her through to Hampshire Court. The warden of the home promised to search the archives for children from the Kindertransport. They made an appointment for the following week, and Lilian hung up, feeling strangely elated. She decided to visit Sam that evening.

On entering his living room, she was met by a jumble of voices. He was engaged in a passionate discussion with a handful of young men about an anti–atomic bomb demonstration in April. When they saw Lilian, they greeted her noisily.

"Hi, Lil. So glad you're here. There's a lot of planning to do," said Sam's old buddy Mark, patting the seat next to him.

"I'd love to help out next time, but I don't have much time today," she said, trying to catch Sam's eye as he passed her a plate of cheese on toast.

"I bet you've hardly eaten today. Am I right?"

"Guilty as charged." To keep him happy, Lilian bit into a slice. "Can I have a word with you alone?"

Sam walked out into his little garden. "What's up?"

She told him what she'd discovered. "Do you fancy coming with me to the children's home next Friday? There's a train every hour from Paddington to Bristol."

Sam's eyebrows shot sky-high. "So you do want to make some inquiries about your family?"

She lowered her head to hide her embarrassment. "My sister, at least. She can't be much older than I am. It's just . . ."

His smile touched her heart. "You don't have to explain. I'm delighted."

"So you'll come with me?"

Sam shook his head doubtfully. "I'd absolutely love to. I've got work, but I'll ask the headmaster if I can take a day for 'family matters.' We are looking for your family after all, Lil!" He smiled. "Are you sure you don't want to stay for the meeting?"

"No, not tonight." They had a whole crowd of fellow activist friends, but when it came down to personal stuff, Sam was the only one Lilian trusted. "I'll see you," she said.

A warm gleam lit up his eyes. "Yes, looking forward to it."

But she hardly saw him over the next few days, mainly due to the fact that she had a tight deadline and was determined to clear her desk before the trip to Bristol. Late one evening, after finishing work and covering her typewriter, she reexamined the music box from every angle. *Time to take care of it*, she thought. So she polished the silver until the fine designs once again saw the light of day. Lilian marveled at the loving attention to detail. This Johann Blumenthal must have spent a huge sum on the gift. As she slid the piece back into its leather pouch, a small drawer fell into her lap. It was empty, but the scratches on it suggested it had been well used.

Friday finally came around. Lilian had mailed her translation off that morning, and Sam's school had given him the day off. Early in the afternoon they boarded the train for Bristol.

"You were right," she said to Sam in a whisper too low for the elderly lady sitting opposite to hear. "I polished the music box and now I see how beautiful it is."

He grinned. "I bet."

Mixed feelings washed over Lilian as the train gradually approached its destination. Sam must have sensed that she needed space to think, as he'd busied himself with some schoolwork he'd brought along. How different he looked when he concentrated like that, his reading glasses slipping down his nose. The nearer they got to Bristol and the children's home, the stronger the butterflies in her stomach became.

The nineteenth-century building was set back from a well-tended avenue on the edge of the city and looked respectable but plain. A six-foot-high wall shielded Hampshire Court from prying eyes.

Sam looked at her. "Are you ready?"

"Yes, of course," she said as she rang the bell.

Chapter 29

A young woman in her thirties introduced herself as Ellen Lynwood, the warden. The blonde woman led them down endless corridors with brightly painted walls. A few drawings by the occupants completed the cheerful atmosphere. Children of all ages ran past, and a large group of adolescents was playing soccer outside. Mrs. Lynwood ushered Lilian and Sam into her office, and they took seats in comfy armchairs.

The warden spoke first. "I'm delighted to meet you in person. You know, it's very rare that our former charges come to visit. And it's certainly the first time we've welcomed someone from the Kindertransport back here."

"I'm afraid I don't remember anything. I was too little," Lilian said.

"Of course you don't." Mrs. Lynwood gave her a friendly smile. "May I offer you a cup of tea?"

"Thank you, that would be nice." Sam and Lilian replied as one.

The warden passed the request on to her secretary before clearing her throat. "Now, to move on to your inquiry. I've searched our archive thoroughly, but unfortunately the information is sparse. A lot of papers were destroyed during the war or else lost in the general confusion."

Lilian leaned forward. "I'd be grateful for anything you can tell me." She gripped her purse tightly and felt the contours of the music box beneath her fingers.

Mrs. Lynwood nodded. "I understand. I'm afraid your admission papers are no longer here, but I did find your sister's."

She handed Lilian a file.

Emma. Emma Dölling. Born November 12, 1931, in Schwerin.

The old photo was faded, but nevertheless clear. Her heart jumped with excitement. Emma's face was narrow, her cheeks sunken, and dark rings showed beneath her eyes. Her snub nose, the defiant set of her mouth, and her raised head confirmed it. The seven-year-old was the spitting image of Lilian as a child.

"I'm afraid I haven't been in this position very long," the warden said. "So I've asked a colleague to join us—provided you agree, of course. Our former head, Mrs. Dunningham, has been retired for a few years now. She's kindly agreed to help us with your investigations." She glanced at her watch. "She should be here any moment."

As she spoke, Mrs. Lynwood poured tea and offered them buns. Sam tucked in eagerly, while Lilian declined politely. It was all she could do to sit still.

The door was flung open to reveal a formidable lady in her mid-sixties. She was wearing a fashionable green sack dress and tucked her silvery hair behind her ear as she entered.

"Miss Morrison, I take it? I'm Anna Dunningham. I was in charge of Hampshire Court before the war."

Lilian and Sam quickly got to their feet.

"Yes, I'm Lilian Morrison, and this is my friend Sam Flynt. I'm really grateful to you for taking the time to meet us."

"I'm only too pleased." Mrs. Dunningham took a seat, and Lilian met her thoughtful eyes. "How can I help you?"

"Do you remember anything about my sister?" Lilian handed her the file.

"I'm sorry," Mrs. Dunningham said after staring at the photo for a minute. "This little girl looks familiar, but . . ."

"Emma had a special toy," Lilian prompted, and handed her the music box. "Have you ever seen this before?"

Mrs. Dunningham peered at the silver toy. "Ah, of course!"

Sam and Lilian exchanged a quick glance.

"The little girl carried it around with her constantly," Mrs. Dunningham continued, smiling. "I remember admonishing her on several occasions to take good care of it. It was really far too valuable an item for a child. But Emma said it had been a gift from her father and she'd promised to look after it." Mrs. Dunningham gazed into the distance. "We wondered at the time how she managed to smuggle it into the country."

"What do you mean?" Lilian asked, baffled.

"Every child chosen for the Kindertransport was only allowed to bring one suitcase, a small bag, ten Reichsmarks, and a photograph," Mrs. Lynwood said. "Any valuables were confiscated. The Nazis inspected them and made no exceptions."

"But that must have been horrible for the children." Lilian's voice faltered. She wondered if Emma had found some kind of ingenious hiding place. But would a seven-year-old have been capable of that?

"If I remember correctly," Mrs. Dunningham said, "you and Emma were only with us briefly."

"That's right; just a few months," Mrs. Lynwood confirmed.

"What was my sister like?" Lilian asked breathlessly. As the older woman took her time to reply, she added, "I only found out about her a few days ago."

"Oh my. I'm sorry to hear it," Mrs. Dunningham replied, holding her cup out to Mrs. Lynwood for more tea. "Now, Miss Morrison, to be honest I'm struggling to think of an answer. You see, the Jewish refugees had been through terrible times; they were traumatized and disoriented by the loss of their homes and families."

"But my sister and I weren't Jews, were we?" Lilian asked as though electrified.

"According to the papers, your parents were Catholic but you were unbaptized," Mrs. Dunningham said. "That was unusual, but my employees and I didn't ask questions. It looks as though you and Emma were among the minority of the Kindertransport children who were Christian."

Lilian nodded. "My adoptive parents had me baptized as a Catholic later. Please forgive me asking all these questions."

"Not at all. I'm only sorry I can't remember more details," Mrs. Dunningham continued. "Of course, the language barrier also made things more difficult—our new charges couldn't make themselves understood for quite a while. Just think what it was like for them."

"We can't begin to imagine," Lilian whispered.

"Quite so. Some of them wet their beds, others developed emotional problems. They all suffered, and the situation was hard for us, too." She sighed. "My memories of Emma are beginning to come back to me. The child was terribly homesick. She was very reserved with us, and kept apart from the other children. I believe she would have liked to make friends, but was overwhelmed by their problems and difficult behavior."

"That's understandable," Lilian said softly. "Who knows what we had experienced before we arrived here." Her thoughts wandered to her adoptive parents. *How dare you not tell me I had a sister.*

"But when Emma played with you, she was transformed," Mrs. Dunningham said. "She was always telling you stories, and you always laughed when the lid of the music box sprang open and the little bird began to chirp." She smiled. "Is the mechanism still working?"

Lilian activated the music box and the little bird sang its heart out.

"Oh my, that takes me back. I remember now the troubles we had with Emma. She couldn't understand why she wasn't allowed to sleep with you in the infants' dormitory."

Lilian gratefully felt Sam squeeze her hand.

"We kept having to send Emma back to her own dorm, because she would go and lie down by you whenever you cried."

Lilian pictured Emma creeping through the corridors in her nightgown. She smiled; her sister sounded just as she had imagined.

"Despite our rules, she couldn't be dissuaded," Mrs. Dunningham said. "We finally came to the conclusion that you would both be happier if we had you fostered."

Lilian shuddered.

Sam poured a glass of water. "Have a drink, Lil. You're white as a sheet."

She drank for his sake.

Mrs. Lynwood placed a sympathetic hand on her arm. "I'm sorry, but you must understand: the disturbance Emma was creating would have been terribly disruptive for the other children, especially since they would themselves have been feeling abandoned—they were far too young to understand that their parents had saved them from persecution and even death by their sacrifice. I can imagine how upsetting this all must be for you, Miss Morrison."

Mrs. Dunningham nodded in sympathy. "Do you want to continue this conversation some other time?"

"No, I'm fine."

"Very well." Mrs. Dunningham crossed her legs. "We tried to find out about your family. But your sister refused to learn English. She probably kept hoping that it wouldn't be long before someone came to fetch her."

Lilian looked back and forth between the two ladies. "Do you know who took my sister in eventually? You must have kept a list of where children from the home went."

"We did, of course," Mrs. Lynwood said. "But unfortunately some of our documents were lost in an air raid in early 1941. I'm so sorry."

An air raid. The hairs on Lilian's arms stood on end. She was suddenly overtaken by a memory of running for cover with her parents.

She could still hear the sirens howling, followed by the sinister sound of the fighter planes above, and then the ear-splitting roar when bombs or shells fell. But the worst thing had been the deathly silence, and the stink of fire and burned flesh that hung in the air for days afterward.

Mrs. Dunningham rose and thanked her colleague for the tea. She handed Lilian a card with her address on the back. "I'll ask my former colleagues and see if they remember anything more."

"Thank you, that would be a great help," Lilian said. "And I'll continue the search myself, in any case."

"Could Emma have gone back to Germany after the war?" Sam asked.

"It's possible, Mr. Flynt," Mrs. Dunningham replied. "May I ask you a personal question, Miss Morrison?"

"Yes, of course."

"Were you happy with your adoptive parents?"

"They did the best they could," Lilian replied evasively.

"That's good to hear. Those were dreadful times. We were always pleased to be able to find a home for our children. It wasn't easy."

"I can believe that." Lilian shook her hand.

"I hope you're successful in your search," Mrs. Dunningham said. "Please get in touch if you think of any further questions."

Mrs. Lynwood accompanied Lilian and Sam out. The air was clear but shimmering with cold, and their breath came out in plumes.

"Huh," Sam said at the gate. "It's a good place, but I'm glad to be outside."

"It smelled like fear and loneliness in there," Lilian murmured. She looked around one last time and hooked her arm through her friend's. "Come on, let's go. I have to get away from here."

"I have an idea." Sam flagged down a blue taxi.

Lilian glanced at him questioningly as he gave an address to the driver. A few minutes later they stopped on Park Street.

"Can't you just tell me where you're taking me?"

"It's a surprise. We're going for a walk."

He led her past Charlotte Street to a classical church with Greek columns, crowned by a dome. "This is St. George's, built in the nineteenth century. There's a wonderful view of Brandon Hill from here," he said, mimicking a tour guide.

Lilian smiled. Why did life feel so much lighter and more carefree when Sam was with her? She looked in the direction of his outstretched hand. The extravagant park with its evergreens was a pleasure to look at. They strolled along a watercourse, ice crusting its surface. A tower soon came into view.

"May I present—the Cabot Tower."

They climbed a spiral staircase. The wind tugged at Lilian's hair as they stepped out onto the viewing platform to see the whole of Bristol laid out at their feet.

"How beautiful," she sighed. "But why are we here?"

Sam cupped her face in his hands. "I'm hoping the view might do you as much good as it does me. Whenever I need to feel calm, I seek out high places. They give us perspective on things."

"Sometimes I marvel at your wisdom, Professor Flynt." She released herself from him and breathed the clear air deep into her lungs. "Thank you."

Chapter 30

Lilian was on tenterhooks for the next few weeks as she cleaned out her parents' flat, saving only a few little keepsakes and photo albums, and donating everything else to charity. She hired contractors to renovate the place, and found new tenants. In early March, as Lilian closed the door behind her for the last time, her sadness was mingled with relief.

She threw herself back into her work. The silver music box now had pride of place on her desk. Lilian couldn't explain why, but it helped her to be able to look at it whenever she wanted. The memento was her only link to her sister.

She had spent the first few days after the visit to Hampshire Court waiting impatiently for a message from the former warden. When she finally made a follow-up call to Mrs. Dunningham, her excitement vanished. No one knew anything about the family who had taken Emma in.

But Lilian wouldn't and couldn't give up. She spent a weekend in Bristol, poring over the church baptism registers. It was a Sisyphean task. A week later, she returned, expanding her search to the surrounding towns.

One rainy morning, Lilian had already spent two hours poring over the books in a church vestry when an employee appeared. "Can I help you?"

Lilian told her what she was looking for.

The young woman, about her own age, shook her head doubtfully. "My goodness, that's a difficult task. You know, after all these years, people are still coming to us on a daily basis looking for relatives who went missing during the war. I'm sorry to be blunt, but have you tried looking in the registers of deaths?"

Lilian shook her head. "I wanted to leave that until I'd exhausted all the other possibilities."

"But since you're here," the young woman said sympathetically, "let's just have a look."

They combed through the index cards for Emma's date of birth, but there was still no trace of her.

"It's hopeless," the employee said finally. "You need more information. If only you knew her last address."

Lilian shook her head in frustration.

"I have an idea." The young woman leafed through a book and wrote something on a piece of paper. "This is the address of the electoral registration office."

"That's a good idea, thanks. I'm also going to try the patient registers of the local hospitals."

"Good luck."

But these registers yielded no new information either. Back at home, Lilian thought hard about any options she might have overlooked. But she could think of nothing.

It was now the end of March and that Sunday dawned foggy. Over breakfast, Lilian's eyes fell on the silver music box. There was no going back. The need to know more about her roots had taken over all her waking thoughts. At the beginning, she had felt slightly disloyal to her adoptive parents, even though their relationship had never been close or problem-free. But even they had sensed the significance her roots would have for her, otherwise they wouldn't have kept the adoption from her. But what twist of fate linked her to Paul and Johann Blumenthal?

She resolutely fed a new sheet of paper into her typewriter and began to type. Her efforts were thwarted when the doorbell rang.

Sam stood there in sneakers and running clothes, smiling. "Hi, Lil. I thought I'd call and check that you hadn't vanished from the face of the earth. I haven't heard a peep from you for at least a week."

"Sorry, Sam, I've been working. Well, trying to. Do you want to come in for a cup of tea?"

"It's the least you can do to make up for the neglect," he said as he edged past her. His aftershave tickled her nose.

He sat down on the sofa and watched her make the tea through the open kitchen door. When they were sitting together, he slipped two sugar cubes into his cup and gestured at the desk. "What are you translating there?"

She followed his gaze. "Oh, that. It's not a translation, it's a letter to the International Tracing Service in Germany."

Sam stared at her. "Sounds like I've come at exactly the right time. I thought we could go for a run in Hyde Park. You can tell me everything. If you don't get some fresh air and exercise soon, you'll turn into a slug."

Lilian made a face. "Does it have to be running?"

"I think so," he replied with his best teacher's face. "And I'm really hoping you'll spend the rest of Sunday with me, and everything that means."

She saw a gleam of amusement in his eyes. "And what does it mean?" she asked in a similarly lighthearted tone.

"I'm sure you can think of something."

Lilian gave in. Hyde Park was only a mile or so from her flat. They turned off Bayswater Road, followed the course of Long Water, and settled into an easy jog. The only people out in the park were a few scattered cyclists and dog walkers. Fleecy clouds drifted across the sky, and on the trees lining the footpaths they spotted the first buds heralding spring. An elderly couple cuddled close on one of the benches by the lake.

Sam asked Lilian about her visits to the churches and archives.

"Well, I'd been hoping to find Emma myself, but I'm not getting anywhere. So I've changed my strategy. I'll write to the Tracing Service with the details I have about Emma, and send a photograph of the music box and the dedication on its base."

"Good idea, Lil. They say the Tracing Service has reunited a lot of families."

She looked at him with a frown. "If you knew that, why didn't you suggest it before?"

He unfastened his jacket as he ran. "Because the normal procedure is for you to search for your family yourself first. The Tracing Service only comes into play once the relatives have exhausted all the possibilities." He smiled. "You will let me know if you find anything, won't you?"

"Yes, of course," she replied with a sigh. "How are you getting on with organizing the protest?"

"Imagine this—we've already had over thirty thousand people sign up, including the scientific journalist Professor Calder and even some church leaders. Mark and I are taking care of the permits and all the other paperwork. John, Claire, Mal, and Stuart are distributing leaflets."

"Claire? Who's that?" Lilian sank onto a bench.

He sat down and turned to face her. "Claire's recently joined us. She works with Stuart. A wonderfully pretty girl with impossibly long legs. I never realized before how sexy a girl can look in a simple dress." His features took on a rapturous expression. "We're going dancing next week."

Lilian stiffened. "Really? How nice for you," she replied, taking care to sound indifferent. She wasn't going to let him see how his words had affected her. And why should they? He could go out with whomever he wanted. They were just friends. But hearing about Claire still hurt. Until that moment, she had never given a moment's thought to how it would feel if Sam fell in love with someone. *I should have known,* she thought bitterly.

Sam was looking at her intently. "Is something wrong, Lil?"

"No, I'm fine." She got up and started running. As he caught up with her, he began to talk about trivialities, but his words sailed over her head. She felt like running all the way home, but she didn't want to give herself away. How could she have assumed that Sam belonged to her alone? How stupid of her. Staring straight ahead, she ran on. After eight miles, Sam declared he was satisfied and invited her to grab a bite. Not wanting to be a spoilsport, Lilian agreed. After they'd eaten, she claimed she had to go—there was more work to do.

"Are you coming to our next meeting on Friday?" he asked as they said goodbye outside her building.

"Sure." She shut the door firmly behind her and took the stairs two at a time.

Back in her flat she reflected cynically on what she'd just said. "Sure" she wouldn't miss seeing this Claire who Sam had his eye on, not for anything in the world. She put a Shadows record on the turntable, threw herself down on the sofa, and berated herself for the tears that were welling up.

Lilian avoided Sam for the next few days. He came to her door one evening, but she didn't even answer. She checked the mail several times a day, but there was no reply from Germany. Fortunately the crime novel she was translating from German was absorbing, a welcome distraction.

That Friday, she finally met the object of Sam's affections—and wondered what on earth he saw in her. Claire talked too loudly, laughed too shrilly. He probably liked her long blonde hair and her flirtatious repartee, something Lilian lacked completely. She left the meeting early, with a nagging feeling that she had lost something precious.

The protest against continued nuclear weapons testing was a huge success, with seventy thousand people marching through the streets of London. Japanese people from Hiroshima paraded silently past Windsor Castle. Young men played guitars, sang, and waved banners with skulls and peace symbols. A group of young mothers followed the march, pushing strollers. "No nuclear weapons for our babies!" they chanted through megaphones.

The weeks went by. Sam didn't talk about Claire, and Lilian swallowed any questions she might be tempted to ask. Meanwhile she had finished her novel translation and had nothing new in the pipeline, which made waiting for a letter from the Tracing Service all the harder to bear.

One rainy day in May, Lilian was leafing through *The Times* when her attention was caught by the missing persons section. A thought struck her. Why hadn't she considered it before?

She jumped to her feet and paced the living room, vaguely recalling a few journalists she had spoken to last year at a party. Hadn't they written for newspapers in Hamburg and Frankfurt? She quickly gathered together a few papers, grabbed her raincoat, and headed to a newspaper office where a friend worked.

She was smiling from ear to ear as she returned home. Moved by Lilian's story, the friend had put her in touch with a colleague from Germany. He in turn agreed to run missing persons ads with Lilian's prepared text in both newspapers, each with a photo of the music box.

Lilian's excitement grew, but then nothing happened.

The days grew ever longer, and summer arrived. One morning at the end of June, Lilian decided to spend the day at Battersea Park on the Thames. If she stayed home, she would only prowl around like a caged lion, keeping a lookout for the mailman.

The bright summer flowers and the rich green lawns were a balm to her spirits. She spent a few sunny hours by the water and ate a double scoop of ice cream. All the same, surrounded by loving couples and young families playing boisterously, she felt lonely as she never had before.

She returned home in the early afternoon and saw a thick envelope on her doorstep. Her heart rate shot up. Once inside she threw her bag down carelessly, kicked off her shoes, and tore open the letter. A smaller envelope was inside, and with it a note from the International Tracing Service, asking her to call them to discuss the next steps.

Copies of a few documents fell into her hands—sadly nothing about Emma, but the music box had been a good lead, as there were copies of birth certificates for Johann, Max, and Martha Blumenthal of Lübeck. They must have been siblings—their parents' details were identical. There was also a birth certificate for Paul, issued in Altona. "Parents: Johann and Lotte Blumenthal," she read. "Religion: Jewish."

Jewish. The word echoed in Lilian's head. A shiver ran down her spine. Then Mrs. Dunningham's words came into her mind. *According to the papers, your parents were Catholic but you were unbaptized.*

That meant the Blumenthals couldn't be her family. Yet young Emma had insisted the music box was a gift from her father. What if Johann Blumenthal had merely been the craftsman who had made the piece? Lilian's thoughts tumbled around her head.

Jewish.

In the early thirties, had a Christian even been allowed to buy from a Jewish jeweler? She suddenly recalled the dreadful images of overcrowded trains carrying their human cargo to annihilation. She recalled the inscription "Arbeit Macht Frei" from a report she had read on the concentration camps.

It made no sense. Or did it? Lilian took a deep breath. Her knowledge of the period was seriously lacking.

She examined the next document. It was Max Blumenthal's death certificate, issued on March 29, 1942, in Lübeck.

Lilian compared the documents. Max had clearly been the oldest of the three.

She brooded for a while longer, then hurried to the phone box, where she requested an international connection to the Tracing Service.

Chapter 31

"We haven't managed to find anything about your sister yet," the International Tracing Service historian said.

"Please keep looking; I'll pay whatever it costs," Lilian said, thinking to herself, *What's Mum and Dad's inheritance for, after all?*

"Yes, ma'am. We'll let you know if we find anything. But to answer your question: yes, some Jews did convert when the Nazis' sanctions became unbearable for them and they were effectively excluded from society. Unfortunately, such drastic measures didn't protect them for long."

Lilian stared out into the hazy summer sunshine. She felt as though she were on a never-ending emotional roller coaster. *What did Emma and the Blumenthals have to go through?* she wondered with a shudder. Among her innumerable questions there were two that plagued her day and night: What had become of Emma, and what did the Blumenthals have to do with her and her sister? Were they—could they have been—her real parents?

Lilian spent the next few days in the British Library. She wanted to find out as much as she could about the Nazi period and the Kindertransport. One muggy warm day, as she was entering the newspaper offices for a meeting about some translation work, she ran into her acquaintance.

"I heard you were coming today." She handed Lilian a letter with a foreign stamp. "This was received by my colleague in Hamburg. I hope it helps you."

Lilian turned hot and cold. She thanked her hoarsely and hurried on to the conference room. Her fingertips were tingling, and she wished she could read the letter at once. It took all her self-control to pay attention during the meeting, the letter rustling in her pocket every time she moved. She finally set off for home, having secured a new project. Her heart thumping, she rushed to the Tube and headed for Sam's building.

She found him in the garden; fortunately he was alone.

"Hi! Lovely to see you." He seemed genuinely pleased, and she sat down by him.

Sam's eyes widened as she placed the letter on the table.

"Why haven't you opened it yet?"

"Because I wanted to do it with you."

"Go on, then. Don't keep me waiting!" He shuffled closer.

> *To Box No. 1458.*
> *According to your advertisement in the* Hamburger Abendblatt *of June 28, you're looking for the owner of the silver music box in the photo. I recognized it immediately. If you're interested, please contact me.*
> *Yours sincerely, Friedrich Lükemeier.*

Beneath the name was an address in the Eppendorf district of Hamburg.

Lilian tensed. "Sorry, I've got to go. I have to book a flight."

But Sam placed a pacifying hand on her arm. She looked at him. His breath softly brushed her neck. If only she could lean against him, tell him what he meant to her. That he was the best thing that had ever happened to her. But what about Claire with all her superficial mannerisms? He let his hand slide down her arm and drew her closer.

"You're flying to Germany?" he said quietly.

She had always loved his deep voice, but now it sounded even more velvety and attractive. Their eyes met, and for a fraction of a second she couldn't think. *Don't do anything silly,* she thought and wriggled from his grasp. "Yes, as soon as possible," she managed to reply, getting up, ready to leave. "I can't wait any longer, and the man didn't include a telephone number. Besides, it's better to talk about something like this in person. Sam, what if he knew them?"

He stood to join her. "Why don't we call the airport right now?"

Lilian paused a moment as the words sank in. "You want to come with me?"

"I've heard that Hamburg and Lübeck are fascinating," he replied. He touched her cheek, sending lightning bolts through her body. "In any case, it's summer break and I've got all the time in the world. Let's have an adventure!"

Lilian didn't move; she wanted to enjoy the feel of his hand on her skin for a moment longer. "That would be lovely," she stammered.

The next morning they were sitting on the first flight to Hamburg, watching London disappear into the distance. Lilian had hardly slept a wink, and she was barely able to contain her nerves. After arriving, they got two rooms in a small hotel near the airport.

Once Lilian had freshened up and changed, she went to meet Sam in the lobby, where he was getting directions to Herr Lükemeier's.

Sam took her arm. "It should only take us half an hour. Are you ready?"

They were soon sitting in the train on its elevated track. How did Herr Lükemeier know her sister? Lilian wondered. Was it impolite to turn up at his door unannounced?

A short while later, they knocked at the door of a small, historic house.

A strong-looking man in his seventies answered.

Lilian had never been more grateful for her knowledge of German. "*Guten Tag.* Are you Herr Lükemeier?"

"I certainly am," he replied in a friendly voice, then paused. "Do we know each other?"

"No. I'm sorry to arrive unannounced. We've just come from London. My name is Lilian Morrison, and this is my friend Sam Flynt. You responded to my advertisement. About the music box."

Lükemeier looked at her thoughtfully. "I understand. Come in."

He showed them into an old-fashioned but elegant Biedermeier living room.

"Have a seat," he said good-naturedly, and indicated two armchairs. He studied them intently through rimless spectacles. "I take it you own the music box?"

"That's right." In a nervous rush, Lilian told him her story and held out the copy of Emma's registration papers from Hampshire Court. "That's my older sister. Do you know her?"

"You could say that." A melancholy smile came to his lips. "I also know your parents. What was your name again?"

"Lilian." Her pulse was racing.

"I'm a friend of the family, Lilian. My, you do look a lot like Emma." He let out a sigh. "Let me explain. Until a few years ago, I had a farm outside Lübeck. I only moved here to Eppendorf when I retired. The Döllings lived with me for a while in 1935 and '36. Peter and Charlotte worked for me on the farm."

Lilian listened in astonishment as Lükemeier told her how the Döllings had arrived at the farmhouse one stormy night and about the later confession that they were fleeing.

"Do you remember where they came from, how they made their living, anything?" Sam asked in broken German.

Lükemeier scratched his thick neck. "They said they ran a jewelry business in the Mecklenburg region."

"A jewelry business?" Lilian's voice faltered. "Did they say who made the music box?"

"Hm, let me think. Can I offer you a glass of lemonade?"

Wanting to be polite, Lilian and Sam nodded and waited until Lükemeier had brought them each a glass.

"Peter said he'd inherited it from his father," he continued. "Yes, I remember—when I laughed at how little Emma worshipped the thing, he said he'd been just the same."

Sam and Lilian glanced at one another. *Did Johann Blumenthal make the music box for his son?* she wondered. *But if that was the case, his son, Paul, or his descendants should have it.*

"The Döllings had converted to Catholicism," Lükemeier continued, "but all that counted to the Nazis was their Jewish blood. I'm sure there were things the two of them weren't telling me."

"Can you give me an example?"

"Well, yes. One thing seemed strange to me from the start," Lükemeier replied. "They certainly weren't from Mecklenburg. I know that accent. Hamburg or thereabouts for sure."

A rush of thoughts flitted through Lilian's head without her being able to grasp one.

Lükemeier laughed. "And Peter had no idea about gardening or farming. But he was a fast learner." Lükemeier told them about the morning when the SA had suddenly turned up and he had denied his friends' presence to protect them. "Of course the bastards didn't believe me and beat me up. The Döllings left that same day. I never saw them again, but I've thought about them so often over the years. Later, when we heard about what the Nazis were doing . . ." Lükemeier's voice grew thick and he dropped his head.

"Do you know where they were going?"

"To Bremen, I think," he said, shaking it off. "They were going to emigrate, but had to postpone their plans because Charlotte was pregnant."

"Emigrating? Where to?" Lilian asked with excitement.

"South Africa. Peter's mother was there." Lükemeier looked Lilian in the eye. "Do you know when you were born?"

"Of course. April 8, 1937."

His expression changed. "So it's true! You're the baby who was on the way. My goodness!" He shook his head again as though to push back the memories. "I took a photo of them, the Christmas they were with me." He rose nimbly, went over to an old wooden cupboard, and dug in an overstuffed drawer. "Damned mess. Just a minute." With his gray head bent over the drawer, he let out the occasional curse as he rummaged.

Lilian felt like she had been staring at Lükemeier's broad back for ages.

"Here it is!" Triumphantly, he held up a photograph with tattered edges and returned to his seat. "My God. Now I know why I thought I'd seen you before." He gestured to her to come and sit beside him on the sofa.

Lilian was trembling as she looked at the photo. A slim young man was standing in front of a tiled stove, his hand resting protectively on the shoulder of the woman in front of him. The gesture moved her. It was as though he was saying, "This is my wife, and no one will ever harm her." But it was his gentle smile that moved her the most.

Lükemeier pointed to him. "That's Peter."

In turmoil, Lilian stared at the clean-shaven face with its gentle, yet so expressive features. His eyes were unusually bright and bewitching.

Sam followed her gaze. "Lil! I must be going crazy! When you're embarrassed, you pull up the corner of your mouth just like him."

Lilian nodded, incapable of speaking.

Standing in front of Peter was a little girl of around four—Emma. Her short hair curled around her ears. She was holding the hand of a graceful woman in a high-necked blouse. Lilian blinked in shock. She felt as if she were looking at her own reflection.

"That's Charlotte." Lükemeier's voice sounded distant. "The resemblance is incredible; don't you think, Sam?"

There was a moment of utter silence.

"Definitely," Sam replied hoarsely. "You're the spitting image of your mother, Lil!"

The room seemed to spin. All Lilian could focus on was the picture of the three people in their old-fashioned clothes. After steadying herself for several long moments, she looked up. "Could I please borrow this for a few days?"

"Provided you promise to give it back to me. It's the only memento I have of my friends."

Lilian tried to answer, but there was a lump in her throat.

"Of course," Sam replied in her place. "You say you never saw them again, but maybe you heard something? A letter?"

"I'm afraid not," the old man said sadly. "After they left I did find a piece of paper with an address on it in my pocket. 'Please send mail here after summer 1937. To be forwarded,' it said. Peter must have slipped it in there."

"Do you still have it?" Lilian said. "And why didn't you write to them?"

"I don't have the paper, but I noted the address." Lükemeier shrugged. "And, well, it wasn't so simple—I didn't know the addressee. Those were such dangerous times, and I wasn't sure I could trust him. I was scared of tipping off the SA. Things were hard enough for the Döllings." He reached for a little address book and copied something onto a notepad. "Then the war came, and I was so worried about the three of them. I did send one letter, but I never received a reply." He tore off the piece of paper and handed it to Lilian.

Gregor Oetting, Farmsen-Berne.

"I often wondered what became of my friends," Lükemeier added. "And I have no idea whether this Oetting is still alive. He'd be an old man by now." He banged his hand on the table with a smile. "I just remembered something else."

Lükemeier hurried from the room.

Sam took her hand. "You OK?"

"I don't know," she whispered. "It's a lot to take in."

As the Döllings' old friend returned to the living room, he was blowing dust from a fabric pouch, which he laid on the table. "The day they left, Peter entrusted me with a box containing their savings. There were forty bundles of hundred-Reichsmark bills. Shortly before the war I changed the money to silver ingots, and a few years ago into German marks. It's yours now."

Lilian leaned forward. "You never stopped hoping you'd see them again."

"No, and I didn't want to watch their hard-earned money become worthless." Lükemeier helped her to untie the many knots safeguarding the bag. "You'll have to take it now, Lilian. No arguments. I was only holding it for them."

"Oh my God!" Lilian counted the money. Over twenty thousand German marks. "Thank you for your foresight." She took a deep breath, put the address and the pouch in her bag, and stood. "Thank you so much for everything."

"You're welcome." He smiled mournfully. "I wish you luck. If you find my friends, please give them my love."

"Of course," she replied.

They said goodbye warmly, and Lilian and Sam promised to keep Lükemeier up-to-date.

They found a nearby restaurant and sat at a table in the shade of some old trees. They ordered beef goulash and sparkling water.

"Let's go see Herr Oetting right away, Sam," she said after their plates had been cleared away. "I don't want to waste a moment's time."

"Of course. But maybe we should wait an hour or two. Older people often take a nap in the afternoon. And anyway, you need a minute to take in everything Lükemeier said. We could take a walk before we go? See the town a little?"

She looked at Sam. "You're right. I'm so glad you're here with me."

"So am I," he said with a smile.

Later that afternoon they arrived at the address Lükemeier had given them in Farmsen-Berne, and found themselves in front of a pretty, red bungalow. Without knowing how it had happened, Lilian realized her hand had been in Sam's the whole way over, as if it belonged there. She ought to let go, she thought, but she couldn't.

Lilian rang the doorbell and a man in his fifties with receding blond hair and a long nose answered. He studied them through his round spectacles.

"My name's Lilian Morrison." She introduced Sam. "I hope we're not disturbing you."

"Dieter Oetting. What can I do for you?"

Lilian cleared her throat awkwardly. "We're looking for Herr Gregor Oetting."

Dieter Oetting shook his head. "My father died in 1943 when the English bombed Hamburg. What's this about?"

"I'm very sorry to hear it," Lilian whispered with resignation. Another clue that led nowhere. "That dreadful war." She gazed at the tips of her shoes, trying to think how to explain. "Well, I'm searching for my family, who were trying to emigrate to South Africa before the Second World War. Herr Lükemeier gave me your address."

Oetting rumpled his brow. "Lükemeier? I've never heard the name. But come in." He opened the door and showed them to the garden.

A woman with dark hair shot through with the first strands of silver rose as Gregor Oetting's son introduced them and outlined the reason for their visit. "My wife, Sylvia."

"Please call me Lilian. This is Sam."

Sylvia Oetting smiled warmly. "So pleased to meet you! Make yourselves comfortable." She poured them a drink. "You're lucky to find us here. After my father-in-law died, the house was rented out for ages—it was too small for us when the children still lived at home. We only moved here a few years ago." She looked at Lilian for a long moment. "How sad that you don't know your family. But what does Gregor have to do with it?"

"We don't know exactly. We hoped you could help us," Sam said.

Lilian told the couple about the silver music box. "Before me, it belonged to my family: Peter, Charlotte, and Emma Dölling. They were fleeing from the Nazis." She looked at Dieter Oetting. "They must have really trusted your father, because they gave this address to a farmer who hid them for a while. The idea was that your father would forward their mail once they escaped the country." Lilian took the photo from her purse. "Herr Lükemeier gave us this. That's my father, Peter, my mother, Charlotte, and my older sister, Emma."

Oetting took the photo and held it up in front of his nose. He lowered it slowly and pointed to the young man in the middle. "I recognize him. But from where?" He thought deeply, and then his expression brightened. "Yes, of course! That's Uncle Paul, a friend of Papa's. I only saw him a few times; I was a child back then."

Paul echoed through Lilian's head. *Paul, not Peter.* "Paul what? Blumenthal?" Her heart was racing. "What was his surname?"

"I can't remember."

"Do you have the address your father would have forwarded their mail to?" she asked. "Maybe in South Africa?"

Oetting shrugged. "I'm afraid I don't. It's possible that Papa had it on him when he died. But if anyone knows anything about Uncle Paul, it's Papa's old friend August Konrad. They fought in the same brigade in the First World War.

"Is he still alive?" Butterflies fluttered in Lilian's stomach.

"Oh yes, he's very sprightly for his age," Sylvia Oetting said. "We see him every now and then. Shall we give him a call now? We have our own telephone here."

"That would be really kind," Lilian said gratefully.

Lilian followed Sylvia Oetting into the house, surreptitiously wiping her sweaty palms on her dress.

"Hello, Uncle August!" Sylvia Oetting told him the reason for Lilian's visit. "Wait, I'll put her on."

"August Konrad here. You're related to our Paul?" he yelled into the phone, making Lilian hold the receiver away from her ear.

"I think so," she replied, grinning involuntarily.

"But you're not from Hamburg."

"No, I'm not. I'm from London. I'm here searching for my family. Can you help me?"

The voice at the other end of the line was silent for a moment. "How about we meet at half past five by the Bismarck monument in the Alter Elbpark?"

Lilian looked at her watch. "Yes, that would be great. You can't imagine what this means to me, Herr Konrad."

Chapter 32

Sam and Lilian reached the Alter Elbpark half an hour early. They sat down on the grass in the warm sun.

Sam flicked an insect from Lilian's shoulder. "You're so quiet. Penny for your thoughts."

"I'm just thinking that, until Emma and I were registered at the children's home, there's no trace of the Dölling family. What if their name is really Blumenthal? Like on the music box. And what if Herr Konrad has their address?" Lilian hugged her knees to her chin. "I'm so excited."

"Look! Over there! I think that's him." Sam pointed to an old man in a beret approaching on a bicycle, one leg stretched out almost straight as he pedaled.

He must be around eighty, Lilian thought in amazement.

The man with wavy, snow-white hair dismounted and looked around.

She and Sam made their way toward him. When the old man caught sight of Lilian, he froze and muttered something she didn't catch.

"Herr Konrad?" she asked haltingly.

"That's me." He shook her hand firmly. "You must be Lilian Morrison."

"Yes, and this is my friend Sam."

August Konrad stared at her with sharp eyes. "Shall we find somewhere to sit? It gets harder for me to stand with every year that goes by." He indicated his unnaturally straight left leg and an orthopedic boot. "I took a bullet in the war."

They found a free bench beneath a row of maples. A tense silence hung over them.

August Konrad stretched out his leg and turned to her. "May I call you Lilian?"

"Of course." She was taken aback to see the shimmer of tears in his eyes. "Are you in pain?"

"No, no." The old man blew his nose ponderously and wiped his eyes. "You look so much like Clara that I thought I was seeing a ghost."

Sam got up. "I'm going to explore the park, give you some time with Herr Konrad. I'll be back in a little while."

Lilian nodded. "Thank you."

Lilian gave Konrad the photograph.

"Lord almighty! That's Paul and Clara." August Konrad's voice was husky as he pointed to the little girl. "Our little Margarethe. She was such a sweetheart. Gregor and I often used to take her for walks." He gave her the photo back.

"What . . . what was Margarethe, Clara, and Paul's surname?"

"Blumenthal, of course," he said, astonished. "Didn't you know?"

Johann Blumenthal, Altona 1914. For Paul, with love.

Johann had made the music box for his son, Paul. The same music box that lay safely in her purse. It confirmed everything she had sensed when she saw "Peter" in Lükemeier's photo. Paul Blumenthal was her father, Clara her mother, and Margarethe her older sister. The Döllings had never existed. Tears filled her eyes.

Konrad's face turned serious. "I served with Johann in the First World War. We thought we'd make short work of the French. I hated every minute, but we were sure we'd be back home before long. We had no idea how many years of carnage awaited us." He gazed into the distance. "Many men lost their minds on those battlefields. No one came out of that hell undamaged. I'm telling you, even the bravest man in the world was scared shitless when the orders came to advance."

"I believe it, Herr Konrad."

"It's August, child."

She smiled. "OK."

"No need for formality with me. Well, our Johann was a fine young man. He didn't say much, but when he did, everyone took notice. I looked up to him." August leaned forward. "We were friends. When my son came into the world and I couldn't be there, he helped me not to go mad." He spoke more urgently. "It's thanks to him that I'm sitting here with you now." In a quiet voice, he told her how Johann had died saving him. "After the war, Gregor and I kept in touch with Paul's family."

"What were they like? How come they were called Blumenthal, not Dölling? Are they . . . are they still alive?"

"Easy!" he laughed. "One thing at a time." He shifted his leg. "Paul was a loving husband and father, and a good businessman, just like his father. Then Clara was barred from teaching, Paul's shop was trashed by the brownshirts, and he was beaten almost senseless, so they decided to go live with his mother in Cape Town."

Lilian thought of that day in the British Library when she'd discovered so many shocking details about life under the Nazis. "I've read about how Jews and non-Aryans were harassed and taxed punitively and had to give up everything to be allowed to leave the country."

The old man nodded. "The Reich Flight Tax. But Paul—he was so proud of that business, of defending his father's legacy. He had no intention of letting the authorities turn them into paupers. His plan was to leave the country using fake passports." He paused. "What was the other name you mentioned?"

"Dölling."

"That must have been their new identity," August said, nodding. "Gregor and I did everything we possibly could to help them."

Remembering their worries brought the lines on his face out in sharper relief. "But I have no idea whether they ever reached South Africa."

She closed her eyes briefly in anguish. "I understand. Germany was at war; mail wasn't secure. But why didn't you write to them after the war ended?"

August's eyes shone with terrible memories. "Lilian, in 1943 and 1944 I lost my wife and son in short succession. A little later the English bombed my house and workshop. Thank God I was able to save my daughter, but things were very hard for a long time."

Shocked, she lowered her eyes. "Oh God. I'm sorry, that was so tactless of me." With a shudder she wondered how this man could bear so much pain without letting it break him.

"You couldn't know." He heaved a heavy sigh. "And to make matters worse, Gregor was also killed in the bombing. He was the only one who knew Paul's new address. If I'd known about the name Dölling, who knows, maybe I'd have been able to find them."

She looked at him in confusion. "I don't understand. Wasn't there a name together with the address?"

"Not Dölling. It wouldn't have been safe to connect the new name to their Jewish family. Gregor was supposed to forward anything to Martha and Hermann. Damn it, what was their name?" His brow creased in thought. "Severin, that's it! I think Martha was Paul's aunt."

They were silent for a moment, each sunk in their own thoughts.

Lilian stared at the photo. "My family hid on a farm for a while. I got this picture from the farmer who ran it. But the SA came looking, so they fled. Two years later, Emma and I were sent to England on the Kindertransport. 'Parents missing.' That's what it says on the papers."

He smiled sadly. "Smart move. We'll do anything to protect our children, you know." He gave a start. "Just a minute. What about Paul's uncle in Lübeck?"

"Max died in 1942." It was enough to drive her crazy. Every straw she grasped slipped through her fingers.

"And his housekeeper?" August asked. "She never left his side. We met a few times on holidays and the like. Her name was Alma."

"Where did she live?"

"With Max on Holstenstrasse, I think."

"Thank you, August. I'll go to Lübeck tomorrow morning. Please wish me luck finding her."

"Of course." He turned to her with a new look in his eyes. "My daughter's waiting for me, but why don't you and Sam come back to my place for a while? I don't know anything about you or your life. We should get to know each other better. Paul and Clara's baby."

His words warmed Lilian's heart. "I should go, but we'll come and see you on our way back, I promise."

"That would be lovely. I look forward to it." He noted something on a piece of paper. "Call me, please."

"Of course." She stood up and waved to Sam, who was sitting on a bench some distance away.

August hugged her warmly. "I see so much of your father in you, Lilian. Take care of yourself."

Chapter 33

Despite the early hour, it was already very warm in Lübeck, the sky a deep, clear blue. Lilian gazed in wonder at the Holsten Gate as they passed. The old brick gabled houses and merchants' villas, the waterways with sailboats gently rocking in the July sunshine—it all radiated a special charm. A little later they were in the sitting room of their guesthouse, drinking a cup of tea. Lilian was wearing a new flowery dress with a full skirt, her thick hair pinned up.

"We need to go to the registry office first and ask about Alma," she said to Sam as she poured milk in her tea. She hadn't slept a wink the previous night, but she was far too excited to feel tired.

His gaze seemed to caress her. "Just remember what we talked about—don't get your hopes up too high. What if she died a long time ago like Max and Gregor?"

"I know, Sam. But I'm not going to leave any stone unturned. Alma might know how to reach the Blumenthals in Cape Town."

He reached across the table for her hand. "But what if we don't find them, Lil? I see how caught up you're getting in all of this, and I'm a little worried. I don't want you to spend the rest of your life torturing yourself with unanswered questions."

She looked at their intertwined fingers. "I'll never give up the search for my family. I've spent my whole life missing them and not even knowing it, but now . . ." She pulled her hand away and stood abruptly. "Let's go."

They found out from their host that the local registry office was in a mansion in the old town, close to the cathedral.

Their route led them down Holstenstrasse, where the Blumenthals' shop and home had once stood. But the buildings there were mostly new, giving no hint of their former appearance or occupants. Sam studied the map and guided them to Mühlenstrasse. At last they reached the gleaming white mansion. Lilian smoothed her dress and licked her lips before entering. An official took their request and asked them to wait. Lilian paced up and down the corridor, the heels of her shoes clicking on the polished floor of the office building.

"Here you are," the official finally told them. "Alma Schott, born in 1892. We don't have a death certificate. If she still lives in Lübeck, you can get more information from the residents' registration office. But you'll have to hurry; they close at twelve."

They walked quickly to the address they were given and entered a redbrick building. After paying a fee, Lilian learned that Alma Schott was still alive. With hope stirring anew and Alma's address in her pocket, she wanted to go there immediately, but Sam held her back gently.

"It's time for a break. You're doing that thing where you forget to eat." He led her to a restaurant, where they ordered lemonade, steaks, and salad.

Fortified, they took the bus to the edge of the city. Alma Schott's address led them to a quiet side street. Lilian looked thoughtfully at the plain buildings. The windows were adorned with ruched curtains, and plastic flowers added a touch of color to the balconies. An elderly man was leaning over his railing, eyeing the newcomers curiously. It reminded her of the working-class flats in London.

Lilian rang the bell several times and peered through the glass panes of the door, but there was no sign of life. She was about to turn away when a stout woman in her seventies, wearing a headscarf and glasses, came down the stairs. She peered at them suspiciously through her thick lenses.

"Good afternoon, Frau Schott," Lilian began cautiously.

"If you're selling something, you can go right now," the old woman said firmly.

"Please wait a moment," Lilian insisted as Alma began to close the door. "I'm Lilian Morrison. I'm a relative of Max Blumenthal."

"Max Blumenthal," Frau Schott repeated flatly.

The mere sound of his name brought a softness to her spirited features.

As the woman remained silent, Lilian leaned in closer and added, "I'm Paul Blumenthal's youngest daughter."

Frau Schott turned pale.

"I'm searching for my family," Lilian explained in growing desperation. "Do you think you could help me?"

The color slowly returned to Alma's cheeks. She folded her arms across her chest. "Really? Anyone could say that. Can you identify yourself?"

"My passport wouldn't help. I was adopted in England. But I can prove it." Carefully, Lilian pulled the photo from her purse and handed it to her. "Maybe you'll recognize this, too." She unwrapped the music box and held it out in the afternoon light.

"My God," Alma murmured. "Of course I recognize it. Please come in."

She lived in a spotlessly clean, spartan flat on the ground floor. The three of them sat down in the living room. In pride of place on the table was a beautifully crafted, five-armed silver candelabrum. "My employer, God rest his soul, made that for me. To thank me for my faithful service." She blew her nose noisily. "How can I help you?"

Sam gave Lilian a nod of encouragement.

"Well, I know that my parents were on the run from the Nazis. They managed to get me and my sister to England on the Kindertransport,"

Lilian said. "But no one has heard anything about them since. Can you tell me whether they succeeded in emigrating to South Africa?"

The former housekeeper kneaded her handkerchief between her fingers. "I'm sorry, I don't know." She looked up. "Herr Blumenthal was in a difficult situation at that time. You know, in 1939 he was forced to sell our house for far less than it was worth." Her cheeks reddened with anger. "He had to move into a 'Jewish house.' Herr Blumenthal complained because he could only write to his sister in Cape Town through a messenger and couldn't get any information about Paul. Those damned Nazi swine would read his letters, and my employer wouldn't have betrayed Paul and Clara for the world."

Lilian couldn't find the words to express the dismay she felt at Alma's words.

"Men, women, and children were crammed together like cattle in those houses," the old woman continued. "He was assigned a tiny, drafty room without a bathroom. Imagine! It was dreadfully cold and bleak there, the old people wept uncontrollably, and many were starving. One widow was raped. And I daresay she wasn't the only one. At night, the residents had to gather for roll calls. One time, Herr Blumenthal was brutally beaten by the SA. His body was black-and-blue."

Lilian could see her struggling to hold herself together.

"It caused him such suffering not to see his beloved St. Mary's Church and the Holsten Gate from his window." She broke off. "I'm sorry, I'm being rude. Can I get you anything?"

Lilian and Sam thanked her but declined.

The elderly woman took a leather suitcase from a cupboard and set it down on her lap. "Herr Blumenthal wasn't even allowed a radio. From 1941 he had to wear the Star of David and adopt the name *Israel.* Then he received an order to list all his private possessions. Bed, toothbrush, razor, dishes, mattress, and the silver trinkets he kept to remind him of his life's work. Everything. Herr Blumenthal said to me, 'Now they're stripping us of the last of our dignity.' They auctioned off all the Polish

Jews' belongings because they wanted to deport them back to their own country. I saw one of those auctions." Frau Schott snorted. "Those so-called 'Aryans' sniffed around their things like jackals around a corpse. They couldn't leave even the most paltry objects alone. As if they hadn't already stolen everything from their Jewish neighbors. Never have I been more ashamed of my own people."

"It's unimaginable," Lilian murmured.

Frau Schott picked up a framed photo from the side table. "Just look what a splendid man Herr Blumenthal was."

Dressed in a sleek suit with his hair neatly combed back and a cigar in the corner of his mouth, Max was laughing into the camera with a challenging expression in his dark eyes. His face was unforgettable. Lilian noted a clear resemblance to Paul.

Sam nodded appreciatively. "An interesting-looking man."

"Were you allowed to enter the Jewish house?" Lilian asked. "Since you're a Christian?"

Alma's mouth hardened to a bitter line. "Of course I wasn't supposed to. I felt the brunt of their batons often enough, not to mention the cursing and shoving. A man in uniform . . . assaulted me. He got a knee in his privates for his trouble. The next day I didn't go to visit my employer. Heaven knows what would have happened if he'd seen me in that state."

A pained silence hung over them.

"Fortunately, Dr. Fisch never let him down, even though he had to travel all the way from Hamburg."

"Was he a friend of the family?" Lilian asked.

"He was Clara's father—your grandfather!" Frau Schott crossed herself. "Oh, the good doctor. May his soul rest in peace."

Lilian pricked up her ears. "So he's no longer alive?"

"That's right," she answered sadly. "He was killed early in 1942 in the Riga Jungfernhof concentration camp. Fortunately that was something Herr Blumenthal didn't have to experience."

Lilian reached out and took Sam's hand. "How did Max die?"

"Once the war started, the air-raid sirens were always going off—practically every day." Frau Schott's face betrayed deep-seated trauma. "We'd run to the bunkers. I'll never forget; it was Palm Sunday, 1942, shortly after eleven at night, and the sirens started up. A few minutes later we heard the bombs dropping. Fire was shooting up to the sky. It spread so fast. When I saw the flames near the synagogue, I was afraid for Herr Blumenthal, since the Jewish house was right on St. Annen-Strasse. I simply ran." She caught Lilian's eye. "Fortunately the Jewish house hadn't been hit. The residents were running into the street in their pajamas, screaming, but Herr Blumenthal wasn't among them." Alma Schott sat motionless for several long moments; only the occasional blinking of her eyes revealing that she had not turned to stone. "He had hung himself from a roof beam. I don't remember how I . . . got him down. Oh, the poor man. I prayed for him. I couldn't move, just kept looking at him. Suddenly the floor shook from another hit. There was a postcard on the nightstand. On the back it said, 'You've been destroyed, my beloved homeland.' I tucked the card and his address book in this bag."

Lilian gripped Sam's hand like a shipwrecked sailor clinging to a buoy.

Frau Schott wiped her eyes. "I ran back to my flat as fast as I could. On the way I heard more bombs falling." Her fingers were shaking as she handed Lilian the leather bag.

"Did you tell the family?" Sam asked.

"I sent a message to their contact's address, asking them to pass it on. But I never received a reply."

"I'm not surprised. Things must have been chaotic at the time," Lilian replied sadly. "And their contact also died in the bombings."

The leather briefcase was old-fashioned and well-worn. Lilian could imagine Max striding through the streets of Lübeck in his hat and long coat, briefcase in his hand, raising his hat in a polite greeting, aware of the impression he made on people. She found it difficult to tear her gaze from it. "His address book is in there?"

"Of course."

"Thank you." Lilian placed a piece of paper with her own address on the table. "Not only for taking the time to see us, but for standing by my great-uncle right to the end."

"I loved him," Frau Schott said simply. "Whether or not it was sensible. Ultimately it made no difference that he only saw me as a friend. Love doesn't listen to reason, does it?"

No, Lilian thought, glancing at Sam, *but if a man doesn't love you, or even loves someone else . . .*

The three of them clasped hands. "We'll stay in touch, Frau Schott."

"Please do. I've always longed to hear that Paul, Clara, and Margarethe made it. Just seeing you, child, it's a balm to my heart."

No journey had ever seemed so long as the one back to Sam and Lilian's guesthouse. Once there, they sat down on the bed and Lilian opened the briefcase. Maybe it was her imagination, but she thought she could detect a faint smell of smoke from the black leather address book. She felt strange looking at the large, neat handwriting that so perfectly matched her image of Max.

Among the telephone numbers and company addresses, listings for a pharmacy and Dr. Nathan Fisch, she saw Gregor's address. She suddenly saw Uncle Max's sharp eyes from the photo, and her mind began to race. Pressing her lips together, she held the little book closer. In the top right-hand corners of some of the pages he had drawn sketches, most of them faces in a variety of grimaces. Lilian smiled; she also doodled when she was frustrated or bored with her work. But in the bottom left-hand corners he had noted down one or more numbers or letters.

"Everything OK, Lil?" Sam asked.

"Yes, just let me think for a while." She continued leafing through the pages. About halfway through, the doodles stopped. "Can you pass me something to write with?" she murmured.

"What are you doing?"

Lilian didn't reply, but jotted down the sequence of numbers and letters. They made no sense, so she rearranged them over and over like puzzle pieces, working backward from what she knew, like Max's sister's name. She and Sam stared at the result.

Martha und Hermann Severin, 12 Kent Road, Cape Town.

"My God, how clever!" Sam exclaimed.

"Yes!" Lilian hugged him wildly. "At last!" She pressed her cheek against his and felt his arms enfolding her. "I knew Max was too clever to risk betraying Paul."

"You've missed your calling as a detective, Lil. Is there a telephone number?"

"Well, there's one number in the book that isn't labeled. It's all by itself on the last page and it's definitely not German." Her voice was quivering with excitement. Laughing, she stood to go to the phone, pulling him along behind her.

The operator confirmed the number was in Cape Town and put Lilian through. She shook like a leaf as she waited, listening to the crackling on the line. Sam didn't take his eyes off her.

A woman's voice came from a great distance. "Hello?"

Lilian's knees wobbled. "Hello," she said in English. "My name is Lilian Morrison and I'm calling from Lübeck. Am I talking to Mrs. Martha Severin?"

"No. Mrs. Severin and her husband died a few years ago. My name is Kuipers. I'm their sister-in-law. Can I help you?"

The woman spoke with a distinct German accent. Lilian's mind raced. *Sister-in-law? But wasn't Martha's sister-in-law Lotte Blumenthal?*

"I don't know," she said finally. "I'm looking for Herr Paul Blumenthal, but he may go by the name of Peter—Peter Dölling." She gulped. "Do you know where my father is?"

"Father?" the women whispered. "You're confusing me."

Lilian locked her gaze on Sam's inquiring eyes. "My older sister, Margarethe, was born on November 12, 1931, in Altona. I was born on April 8, 1937. I was adopted in England and they baptized me as Lilian." She struggled for breath. "Please, I have to know. Is my father alive?"

She heard rapid breathing. For an endless moment no one said a word.

"Hello? Are you still there?" Lilian asked, her voice rising.

Then she heard a noise that sounded like suppressed sobbing. "Oh, Lord, thank you. You've answered my prayers." The woman's voice was soft. "Your real name is Gesa. Gesa Blumenthal. I've hoped beyond hope to hear your voice one day. Yes, your father's alive."

Gesa Blumenthal. Tears blurred her vision.

"He's at work now, but he'll be overjoyed! I'm your grandmother, Lotte."

"My God," Lilian stammered. "I found you. Please tell everyone I'm coming as soon as I can."

"I will. I can't believe it. Come home, little one, and we'll explain everything. You've made an old woman very happy. We'll see you soon."

Chapter 34

Lilian stared at the receiver until Sam gently took it from her. His arm around her shoulders, he led her to the Lower Trave River and sat her down on a low wall overlooking the water. They watched the crowded tourist boats pass by. After all the months of confusion, she would get to meet her father and her grandmother. But the woman had mentioned Paul. Did that mean Margarethe and her mother weren't with him? Were they alive? One question in particular plagued Lilian: Had her family ever looked for her?

"How do you feel?" Sam asked.

"I can't begin to tell you how happy I am. And I've got the music box to thank for it all. Without it, I might never have found them." She could feel the weight of the memento now in the bag on her knee. "There's so much I still don't know. But my father's alive and I'm going to meet him! I'll find out the rest then."

"Let's head back to Hamburg," Sam suggested. "We can tell Herr Lükemeier what we've found so far, and get a flight from there to Cape Town. What do you think?"

"Do you have time to go all the way to South Africa? And what about Claire?"

Sam stared at her. "You still think we're going out?"

His smile confused her. "So you're not?"

Sam drew her closer, his eyes locked on hers. "There was never anything between us. I was just testing you."

"You were what?"

"I wanted to see if you'd be jealous. It worked."

She sat there thunderstruck.

"Why don't you admit it, Lil?"

"It hurt me to think of you with her. I always thought there was something special between us."

Sam kissed her gently on the tip of her nose, then lifted her chin. "Yes. There is. I've loved you ever since we met. It was obvious to everyone else—even Claire!" He grinned. "I thought the time had come for you to realize that we belong together. And if you still don't believe me, I'll say it again. I love you, Lilian—or Gesa, if you prefer. Just tell me which name you choose and I'll call you that forever. There'll never be anyone else for me but you."

Deeply shaken, she gazed at his familiar features, listened to the gentle tone of his voice. "That was a lousy way of going about things," she whispered.

"But it worked."

She threw her arms around his neck. "You win. I couldn't be mad at you if I tried. But never play games like that with me again."

"Cross my heart!"

She traced the lines of his face. Her heart leapt as she saw the love in his eyes. "And I can't choose: I'm both Gesa Blumenthal and Lilian Morrison. Who else can claim such a thing? And if you want to know, Sam Flynt: I love you, too."

Their lips met in a gentle kiss, the lovers completely unaware of the amused glances of passersby.

"I don't think Claire's pretty at all," she murmured.

"Too much makeup," he replied, trying to sound serious.

"You called her sexy."

Sam shrugged. "I couldn't think of anything better to say."

Lilian grinned with relief.

They sat for a long while in a close embrace, watching the boats go by and the children throwing bread crumbs to the ducks. Later, they called Friedrich Lükemeier and arranged to see him that evening.

"You can stay with me. I have a guest room, and one of you could sleep on the sofa if you like."

Sam suppressed a smile. "No need; we'll be happy with just the guest room. Thank you very much." After hanging up, he caught Lilian's raised eyebrow and blushed. "I'm sorry, Lil, I shouldn't assume, it's just—"

She silenced him with a kiss.

On the train to Hamburg, Lilian gazed out of the window, deep in thought. How could one brief phone conversation and a kiss be enough to make this the best day of her life?

Friedrich Lükemeier was visibly delighted to see them back and had supper ready and waiting. He showed them the guest room, then led them out to the garden.

"When are you going to Cape Town?" he asked after Lilian had told him the whole story.

"As soon as we can get a flight," she replied. "I don't want to wait any longer. But I'm scared, too. They're my family, but they're strangers. What if we can't think of anything to say to each other?"

"You worry too much," Sam said.

Lükemeier looked from one to the other, slowly turning his beer glass in his hand. "I don't want to intrude, but would you mind if I came, too?"

Lilian and Sam exchanged a look of surprise and stared wide-eyed at the old farmer.

Lükemeier folded his hands on his large belly. "I've always wished I could see my friends again one day. I feel strong enough for a long flight, but how much longer will I be able to say that? And I've got some savings. What else is money for?" He smiled. "What do you think? Can you put up with my company a little while longer?"

Lilian felt warmth spread through her. "It's a wonderful idea."

"I think so, too," Sam added. "Your father will be thrilled!"

Lükemeier clapped his hands. "It's settled, then. This is a day to remember—let's drink to it!"

They clinked glasses.

Lükemeier suddenly leaned forward. "What will you do with the money in the pouch? I doubt they'll let us take that much into South Africa."

"My father should get it back. I'll think of something."

A little while later they sat around a small table in the garden sharing sausage rolls, cheese straws, and freshly baked bread. The next day they had lots to do, not least arranging a flight. They had also promised to visit August again.

But that could all wait for tomorrow. The three of them sat up talking about what they expected to find in Cape Town, making plans. Lilian relished the fluttering in her stomach whenever she looked at Sam. After a happy evening, the oil lamps in the garden began to go out.

As Sam closed the door to the guest room, Lilian felt giddy. How many times had she longed to feel his hands running through her hair, his skin touching hers? She could hardly believe her dream was coming true. She smiled dizzily as she listened to his heartbeat, melted into his embrace, gazed into his eyes.

"I think I might be happier if we were sleeping in separate rooms after all," he murmured into her neck.

"Why would you think that?"

"To feel you so close is putting my self-control to the test. But we're guests here."

Lilian giggled. "We have the rest of our lives ahead of us."

Chapter 35

Lilian had insisted on paying for Sam's flight, and he had reluctantly accepted. August had been delighted to hear the good news and noted down Lotte's phone number with tears of relief in his eyes.

Two days later, Lilian, Sam, and Friedrich boarded a South African Airways plane as the sun sank in the western sky. Lilian's hands were clammy with anticipation.

She picked up one of the glossy magazines offered by a flight attendant and read a report on Kennedy's visit to West Berlin a few weeks earlier. But her thoughts kept wandering to her family. As the plane took off and rapidly gained altitude, she wondered if they were as excited as she was.

She sensed Sam looking at her, and laid her head on his shoulder. Would it be possible to overcome the feeling of strangeness, and to be a family after all they'd lost over the years? The indifferent humming of the jet engines and the light snoring of the passengers eventually made even her sleepy, and she nodded off.

When she opened her eyes, the sky was red with the first light of dawn. The captain informed them that they were beginning their descent into South Africa.

As they walked down the gangway, Lilian's heart beat harder. The air was warm and smelled of rain. A light breeze cooled her hot cheeks. Sam held her hand on the way to the exit.

They scanned the waiting crowds. Black people in colorful clothing called out in greeting to their friends and family. But all Lilian could see was the tanned man in a straw hat and white shirt, standing motionless by a group of women who were singing joyfully as they waved at someone. He had his arm around an elderly woman in dark glasses.

Their eyes met and he smiled a little crookedly, just like in the photo. Lilian stood rooted to the spot. Everything seemed to be reaching her through a veil. Then, she began to walk toward him as if in a trance, and saw her own image reflected in his features. The old woman pressed her hand to her heart. Lilian found herself running, seeing only a pair of widespread arms—and sank, sobbing, against his breast. All her fears, her worries, were suddenly gone, vanished into thin air. His embrace enfolded her like a protective cocoon. Here, in this moment, Lilian found what it was she had been missing her whole life long.

"Gesa," he sobbed. "I can't believe you're here. Thank God."

There was something familiar about his voice, and the way he said her name stirred a memory of gently murmured words she had heard time and again in her dreams. She'd been remembering the sound of her father's voice.

She blinked at him through her tears. "Yes, it's me."

She felt her grandmother's hand on her cheek. "Welcome home."

"Grandma." She sank into a soft, rose-scented embrace.

Finally, she introduced Sam to her family.

Then her father looked up and his jaw fell open. He stared at the broad-shouldered man standing behind Sam. "Friedrich?"

"Yes, Peter. I've waited so long to see you."

A little later, Peter Dölling was skillfully maneuvering the jeep along narrow, crowded streets, while Friedrich talked quietly with Sam and Lotte. From the passenger seat, Lilian took the opportunity to study her father closely. He had a handsome profile and lightly curved lips. His gray-flecked temples seemed incongruous with his otherwise youthful appearance.

But it was his melancholy smile that moved her the most deeply.

"You look just like your mother," he said with a sigh as he turned uphill onto a side street lined on both sides by white houses with low garden walls. Flowering shrubs and cactuses added pretty flashes of color. A little girl ran out of one of the houses, chasing a cat.

"Here we are." Peter steered the car into the garage and led them into the garden of a neat little house. The view over the Atlantic with Table Mountain in the background was breathtaking.

"It's stunning," Sam said.

"Yes, the view's priceless, although the house itself is modest enough. We don't need much." Lilian's father invited them in.

Lotte and her son lived in four rooms with an eat-in kitchen that had space for the whole family. After Peter had shown them around, his mother took over. "Go and take a seat in the garden," she said to Lilian and her father. "Friedrich, we also have a cozy little guesthouse out back. I hope you'll stay here with us."

"I'd be obliged," he replied.

"Lovely. Come with me. Let's get your luggage inside."

Sam and Friedrich followed Lotte out.

Once Lilian and her father were sitting alone in the garden, a timid silence settled between them.

Peter was the first to speak. "How did you find us?"

Hesitantly at first, but soon warming to the subject, Lilian told him about her months-long search. About August, Friedrich, Dr. Fisch and his tragic death, Alma Schott, and how Gregor had been killed in an air raid.

"My God, Gregor," Peter murmured. "I've missed him, and I kept hoping I'd see him again one day. It explains why my letters were returned. I tried to reach him by telephone, too, but I was simply told he didn't live there anymore."

Lilian nodded. "They rented out his house."

They sat in silence again, searching for words. This time it was Lilian who broke the silence.

"Where's my mother? Is she here?"

He shook his head. "Your mother's dead, my love."

She caught sight of Sam and Friedrich, who glanced at them and quickly withdrew into the house.

"The Nazis shot her." Her father stopped as his face crumpled.

The pain Lilian felt took her breath away. She sat with her father and cried, cried all the tears she'd been saving up since losing her adoptive parents, since finding out about her family, since beginning to understand the terrible atrocities people had committed.

Once their tears had run dry, he explained how he had managed to get to Bremen with Charlotte and Emma. The fact that he still used the assumed names vital for their safety reminded Lilian of how desperate their situation had been. Once in Bremen, they'd found a room in the backyard of an ironmonger's, just in time before the onset of winter. A few months later, on April 8, 1937, she, little Gesa, was born, making them proud, grateful parents once again. During this time he supported the family by working as a buyer for the ironmonger, who appreciated his intellect enough not to ask questions. The next ship bound for Cape Town wasn't due to leave until January 1939, forcing them to wait and watch as the situation in their homeland grew darker still.

In November 1938, they went to buy their tickets—a huge risk. "The officials were on the lookout for Jews trying to escape. I was terrified about the fake passports. The SS officer scrutinized me for a long time. I was sure we'd be exposed." Lilian's father stared straight ahead, as though the ghosts of the past had come to life before him. "Then the man came nearer and spoke under his breath. 'Do you recognize me? It's me, Martin.' Martin Holz had been my friend when I was a boy, but we hadn't seen each other for so many years. 'You're Paul, the boy with the music box, aren't you?' I was so shocked I couldn't even deny it. I just stood there like a statue. Then he proclaimed in a loud voice that the papers were all in order and there was nothing to stand in the way of our departure."

"He did that because of your old friendship?"

"Partly," Peter said dismissively. "Also, my parents had often helped his family, slipping them food. He probably felt it was his way of repaying that debt."

"What happened then? Tell me about my mother."

"We were doing all right at the ironmonger's." Peter licked his lips. "When I came home with the tickets, we were so happy and relieved. We dreamed of our new life in Cape Town, sure the years of deprivation and persecution would finally be behind us." Lilian winced at the bitterness in his voice. "But late that evening, we heard shouting and the sound of shattering glass. A gang of brownshirts had smashed in the window of a Jewish shop across the street. They were throwing furniture and goods out onto the street and destroying everything they could lay their hands on." His lips were thin. "People were screaming. Then the SS stormed into the shop and dragged the owner at gunpoint out into the street in his underwear, in the bitter cold. They kicked him until he stopped moving." He wiped a hand across his face. "That night's now known as Kristallnacht."

Lilian shivered despite the sunshine. "I've read about it."

"We watched the ironmonger run up to the SS men and point to his house. We immediately realized he suspected us and wanted to give us up rather than risk trouble himself."

"For heaven's sake! What did you do?"

"We panicked, grabbed you two from your beds, and wrapped you in sheets. There was a small park behind the building with a tiny underground shelter. We hid you there, told Emma to look after you. Then we ran, looking for somewhere to hide." He paused, tormented by the memory. "But the men stormed after us. 'Stop!' they yelled. 'Stop! Surrender!' Charlotte cried, 'We have to lead them farther away, or they'll find the girls.' So we ran and ran. Then they fired. Charlotte collapsed. She was dead on the spot. You . . . you can't imagine what it was like—having to leave her there . . ."

"But you couldn't risk dying, too." Lilian drew her jacket tighter around her shoulders. "You had Emma and me to think of."

"That's right," her father replied, tears running down his cheeks. "There was a cemetery opposite the park. I jumped into an open grave and covered myself in dirt." Peter's voice was husky with sadness. "They ran off in the other direction and, after a few minutes, I crept back to find you. I was so relieved that you were OK. But you weren't safe with me; the SS were on my trail, and I knew they wouldn't hesitate to shoot children."

He stared into space. "The first night, I booked us into an inn under a false name. Not like that was anything new. I was worried about you because you weren't used to bottled milk. But we had to make do."

He paused briefly, and Lilian took his words in.

"As the inn was on the outskirts of town, we were relatively safe there. On November 23, I heard on the radio that the British government had agreed to take in ten thousand persecuted children. That's our salvation, I thought. So, the very next morning, I took you to an aid organization. There was a long line of people waiting. When they handed out the forms, I assumed that the three of us could go together. But then I was told the British were only taking children—not their parents. I had to decide whether to pay for your safety with separation."

"You had no choice," Lilian whispered.

"Most importantly, I had no time to lose. The SS could find us at any moment. Can you imagine how terrified I was when I had to prove my identity? All I could think was, what if they discovered that our passports were fake? The lady behind the desk saw how young you were and took pity. She told me to be at the Altona rail station on December 1. She had two spots left."

"Altona! But people would recognize you!" Lilian said.

"Exactly," Peter said. "Emma was so devastated by her mother's death, and on top of that I had to tell her we were going to be parted. It broke my heart. I promised your sister that I'd get you to Cape Town as soon as I could. But she had to swear that she'd never tell anyone about our plan."

"What a huge burden for a seven-year-old," Lilian said.

"Yes, but I didn't know of any other way. That weekend we went to meet Gregor in Stade. He urgently advised me to vanish, and offered to smuggle you to Hamburg himself. There, his elderly aunt would look after you until December. Gregor also offered to act as your official sponsor for the transport and to take you to the station when you left for England." He looked into her eyes. "I'll never forget the moment I had to say goodbye. Emma sobbed, and you . . . you looked at me with your big eyes as though you understood what was happening. The hardest thing I've ever done was letting you go."

Lilian pressed her lips together. She didn't want to burst into tears again. When she had collected herself, she asked, "But didn't August know about the plans you made with Gregor? He didn't mention any of this."

Peter nodded. "Gregor promised to only tell August face-to-face. The situation was too dangerous. It sounds like they never got the chance."

They sat together in another long silence. Then Lilian handed him the silver music box.

He looked at it, turning it over in his hands, and pressed it to his heart. "Emma loved this so much—as much as I did."

Lilian looked at him steadily. "Where's my sister now?"

"She's dead, like your mother."

Lilian remembered the warden at Hampshire Court describing how Emma sang to her baby sister and made the little bird chirp to calm her. She felt like she couldn't breathe.

"When the German Luftwaffe bombed London in December 1940, Emma and her foster family took cover in an air-raid shelter. She suddenly remembered they'd left the dog in the house and ran out before they could stop her." He fell silent. When he looked up, his face seemed set in stone. "That very moment, a bomb fell."

"Oh no." Lilian pressed her hands to her face. The loss hit her with a violence she could never have imagined. How much she had wished to find her sister, to laugh with her, to discover all their similarities and differences. She had only been nine years old.

"As I was registered as missing, Emma sent postcards to Gregor, who forwarded them to Martha. From the things she wrote, I knew she was horribly homesick," her father continued. "Maybe that was why she was so attached to the dog. She had scribbled something on the edge of her last postcard, in tiny writing so it wouldn't be noticed: *Come get me. Bring me home.*"

Lilian was overcome with shame as she thought of her adoptive parents. She had always loved them, and still did, despite her disappointment. It was not her place to be resentful; she had lived a sheltered life. Why couldn't her sister have had that? "But why did Emma have to make sure the writing wouldn't be noticed?"

Her father reached for her hand. "The messages couldn't be more than twenty words long and they were censored. 'We eat a lot of blancmange. I'm well and I'm learning English. The dog is so sweet. I love you, Emma.'" He kissed Lilian's palm. "She always hated blancmange. That's how I knew she was unhappy."

Lilian pulled away from him. The hairs on her neck stood on end. "I feel so sorry for her." She looked at him. "Why do you still go by Peter? Are you trying to forget who you were?"

"Far from it." His bright eyes regarded her seriously. "Once the war was finally over, I wanted to go back to my real name. But then you would never have found me, since your papers were issued under the name Dölling."

"So you did it for me?" Her heart clenched.

"Yes, of course. I hoped so much that I'd see you again. But tell me, what do you want me to call you, Lilian or Gesa?"

"Whichever you prefer."

"Then I'll stick with Lilian—it's who you've always been, and I'm enormously grateful to the people who took you in and named you that," he said. "You know, at first I hated the name Dölling, but I've come to terms with it now. To people here, I'm the jeweler, Peter Dölling."

"The best jeweler in the whole of Cape Town," Lotte said with undisguised pride as she came toward them with a tray of drinks and snacks, set it down, and moved away again.

"Thank you, Mama," Peter called after her. He poured a glass of juice for Lilian and himself. Then he met his daughter's eyes again.

"Did you find out anything else about my Uncle Max?" he asked. "I heard nothing from him after 1941. His telephone number doesn't work anymore. I contacted the Tracing Service after the war, but they just sent me his death certificate. It seems there aren't any other records."

Lilian took his uncle's postcard from her bag and handed it to him. "He took his own life in 1942."

Peter read the brief text. His face changed color. "I understand. Seeing his beloved city under attack was too much for him. I feared it was something like that."

"I'm sorry," Lilian said. "I wish I could have met him."

"He'd have liked you. You know, Max and my father-in-law refused to the bitter end to leave their homeland." Peter's voice was sharp with agitation. "They simply couldn't let go. They couldn't begin to imagine what people are capable of."

Lilian looked him firmly in the eyes as another thought came to the surface. "Why didn't you look for me?"

She saw the pain her words caused him.

"I did," he replied finally. "It's best if I tell you the whole story. For a long time, South Africa refused to take in any more Jewish refugees. But I'm glad to say the regulations were eventually relaxed. They agreed to take in those who could be expected to integrate rapidly. Like me. When I arrived in Cape Town, I dreamed of building a new life here. But as long as the National Socialists were in power, I wasn't allowed to make contact with you or your foster parents. During all those years, I lived in hope of bringing you to me safely. Shortly after the end of the war I found out from the Tracing Service that your sister had been killed and that the Morrisons had adopted you in 1942."

"But surely they would have needed your consent," she said, aghast.

"That's what I thought, too," he replied huskily. "But there was a new British law that enabled foster families to adopt a child who had lived in the country for several years and whose parents hadn't been found. They said it was for the good of the children."

Lilian gasped. "So the sacrifice you made to save us prevented us from being a family."

"Yes." His face twitched. "I was prepared to raise the dead to have you here with me, and I flew to London to search for you. But my lawyer couldn't do anything—your foster parents had the legal right to decide whether to tell you about your blood family or allow contact. And for the sake of your 'spiritual welfare,' they decided not to." His voice broke and he dropped his head. "They wouldn't let me near you. When you came of age, they were supposed to tell you so you could decide for yourself whether you wanted to get to know me, us." Peter raised his head and looked his daughter straight in the eye. "My lawyer said the Morrisons wanted to do everything they could to give you a carefree childhood. They were offering an intact family, a living father and mother. Something I could never give you, they said. It was so hard to accept, and I've never come to terms with it." He smiled through tears. "But looking at you now, I'm just glad you were happy."

"Yet I never truly was," Lilian said quietly. "I was missing you; I know that now."

"We'll just have to make up for everything we've missed," he said. "All these years I've been waiting for a letter from you, a phone call, anything."

"But that wasn't possible," Lilian burst out. "I only found out about you a few months ago, when I read my parents' will."

"The Morrisons died? I'm so sorry." Peter stood and pulled her into his arms. "Were they good to you?"

"Yes, they were," she whispered.

"I'm so happy you're here," he said softly.

Lilian allowed his warmth and the sun's rays on her back to enfold her. All at once she felt a weariness in every limb.

"You're tired." Her father stroked her hair. "Go and get some rest. Today has been a lot at once."

"That's a good idea." She smiled at him, and the sadness in his eyes vanished for a moment. "Wait, I've got something else for you."

She took two envelopes from her purse.

Peter opened the first one. "A check?" he said, baffled.

"Friedrich took good care of your savings."

He thanked her, clearly moved. "If it hadn't been for Friedrich, August, and Gregor, none of us would have survived. I'm so sad to hear that Gregor didn't make it."

"And I so wish I could have known my mother." She looked at him thoughtfully. "Have you remarried?"

"No, Lilian. I had a few relationships over the years after I got fed up with being alone, but none of them could hold a candle to your mother. There's no one like her. I'm probably one of those people who only loves once in their lives."

"I understand," Lilian said, smiling. She couldn't imagine ever being with anyone but Sam. She kissed her father on the cheek. "Alma Schott said that love doesn't listen to reason. She was right."

Chapter 36

The days in Cape Town flew by, and when Lilian lay next to Sam at night, listening to his heart beat, she still couldn't believe her luck. Her father had given them a room at the far end of the house, and they enjoyed their privacy. She spent the days with her family and the nights with Sam. When the young couple were alone in the evenings, they shared all their new discoveries and surprises. The landscape, the colors, the open people who affectionately called Cape Town "Mother City," and the wide expanse of the ocean—all of it moved something deep inside her.

When she and Sam stood, closely entwined, in the garden, the mountains at their backs and the ocean before them, Lilian thought she was in paradise. But she soon learned that the sun cast shadows in paradise, too. The Jewish immigrants had always been viewed with some suspicion in Cape Town, and the country had its own Nazis. Lilian therefore found it all the more remarkable to discover a flourishing Jewish community there. The streets of the little Sea Point neighborhood were full of Jewish grocery stores, schools, and synagogues. But the coast was reserved for white South Africans, who had restricted the black population to the edges of the city. Lilian and Sam saw signs declaring "White Persons Only" in front of the idyllic, picture-postcard beaches, as well as on park benches and public transport. Of course Lilian and Sam had heard of apartheid, but they were shaken to see racial segregation up close.

One evening, the whole family got together to celebrate the family reunion; even Martha and Hermann's sons, Michael and Robert, came along with their wives.

"I think it's dreadful," Lilian said. "It reminds me of what Dad and Grandma have told us about the Nazi period. It's history repeating itself, but with a different enemy."

"You're right," Lotte said, reaching out and brushing Lilian's cheek with her fingers. "When I arrived here, people tried to stir up hostility against us. Now they've forgotten about us—we Jews have become part of Mother City. But the way the Afrikaners treat the blacks is almost as inhuman and cruel as what Hitler did to us."

"I wonder if it will ever change," Friedrich mused, shifting closer to the older woman. "Humans always seem to need an enemy. But our Lotte reminds us that it doesn't have to be like that."

Lilian smiled at Friedrich. She admired her grandmother, who had married the restaurateur Antoon Kuipers many years ago. Lotte had assured her that Johann would always be the love of her life, but cheerful Antoon knew how to see something positive in every day, and had given her life new meaning. He had died a few years ago. "I'm grateful for the happy years I had with him," she'd told Lilian.

After his death, her grandmother had converted the restaurant that adjoined their house to a meeting place for young single mothers. "I don't want to sit around just waiting till I breathe my last. I need a purpose. When I met Ewa shortly after I arrived here—she'd come to Cape Town completely on her own—I knew I had something to give to women with experiences like my own." Her grandmother smiled. "I love to see children playing in my home, and to give their mothers a little reprieve."

It made no difference to Lotte Kuipers whether the women were white or black—but she did have to take care not to be seen with the black women. During her stay, Lilian made time every day to help Lotte look after the little ones or prepare hot food for their mothers.

Her father and Friedrich were clearly enjoying their reunion and making the most of their time together. And when August telephoned one morning, her father was delighted.

Time went by, and before the young couple knew it, their departure was fast approaching as Sam's summer break came to an end. Lilian got quieter every day.

Walking along the beach at Sea Point, Sam kissed her tenderly. "It's going to be hard for you to go home, isn't it?"

She put her arm around his waist, the wind playing in her long hair, and looked up at him. "I don't want to, Sam. My family is here. Do you understand? There's nothing to keep me in London but my work and a stupid rented flat." Her eyes filled with tears. "I don't want to leave my family again."

"What about us?" Sam asked, his face expressionless.

"I love you and I don't want to lose you," she said and rested her head on his chest. She had to make a decision, but whichever she chose, it would break her heart. "I'll come with you, Sam," she finally whispered, so quietly that her words were barely intelligible.

He wiped the tears from her cheek. "I have a better suggestion. I've always wanted to live abroad." With infinite tenderness, he brushed a lock of hair from her face. "I'm sure they need teachers and translators here, too. When we fly back to London, it can be for the last time. We'll pack, I'll give notice at school. We can make a new start here. Provided you agree, of course."

Lilian looked at him, stunned. "Are you serious?"

"I'm deadly serious." Sam held her at arm's length. "What do you say?"

Lilian gave him a meaningful look. "There's one condition."

"And that is?"

Sam's expression sent waves of happiness through her veins.

"You have to marry me. Here in our new homeland, the good old-fashioned way, with flowers, music, and a ring." She drew him close.

"Very well, because it's you, my love," he said with a grin, and sealed his words with a long kiss.

Author's note

There is a general misconception that only Christian German soldiers fought on the front lines of the two world wars to defend their homeland. In the First World War, around one hundred thousand Jewish volunteers fought for Germany, of whom some twelve thousand were killed in action. They were men who loved their homeland and felt morally obliged to fight, since they had lived for many years in safety and harmony with their Christian neighbors and felt like full members of German society. They could have no idea of the catastrophic times that lay ahead.

You may ask why my Jewish characters could move around without having to wear the Star of David. All the available information for Hamburg, Altona, Lübeck, and northern Germany indicates that the Jews did not have to wear the Star of David until the 1940s. By that time, Paul and his family had already left the country. Only Max Blumenthal and Dr. Nathan Fisch were unable to escape being marked in this way.

The call to boycott Jewish businesses actually began on what is known as the Shabbat boycott, April 1, 1933, in Hamburg and Altona. However, the changes could be described as creeping, since it can be shown that notaries, lawyers, and business proprietors continued to operate until September 1935. This was certainly the case in Lübeck, and the treatment of Jews in Hamburg and Altona was similar.

There was a "grace period" between 1933 and 1935. It was during this phase that the two jewelry businesses in my novel saw an upturn in their fortunes. The persecution of the Jews took hold slowly, and there were groups, such as the family of Rabbi Carlebach, who were able to continue living and working without great difficulties during this period. But even during that time there were some "Aryanization" measures and liquidation of Jewish businesses and companies, including in Hamburg, and further dismissals of Jewish employees. For this reason I have set the dramatic events surrounding the Blumenthals in 1935. Like certain members of this family, some Jews who were affected emigrated from Hamburg and Altona for fear of their livelihoods.

A further note on the adoption of a child from the Kindertransport out of Germany: it was only after 1946 that it was possible for foster parents to adopt a child, provided the child had lived in their care for at least five years, had become socialized there, and their natural parents had not been found. I have allowed myself to reduce this period for plot purposes.

In my novel I have described a number of real-life events. I would like to give the example of Fritz Lissauer, a member of the Lübeck Jewish Community Council. He was accused of requiring his Aryan employees to work too much overtime. They dragged him through the streets, with a sign hung around his neck stating: "I'm a vampire and suck the blood of my German workforce!"

Max Blumenthal's statement "I'm told that a Jew isn't a German citizen, that I'm supposed to be politically irrelevant and inferior . . ." is a quote from Simson Carlebach from a letter of April 30, 1933, to the Lübeck high school authority, when he removed his son from school because he was no longer safe there and had been ostracized. When I happened across the letter in the course of my research, Simson Carlebach's words expressed Max Blumenthal's feelings so perfectly that I have used his statement, with respect to this man from the famous rabbi's family.

The original text can be read (in German) at: http://www.jugend-ins-museum.de/files/judenverfolgung-holocaust/arbeitsblaetter/1933_aprilboykott.pdf.

Concerning the Jewish houses that were set up from 1938 onward throughout the Reich, I have found no reference to accommodation of this kind in Lübeck, since by then most of the city's Jews had long since left or been deported. In 1942, when Max Blumenthal took his life on the night of Palm Sunday, there were only elderly and sick people still living in the house on St. Annen-Strasse—in the winter of 1941–42, most of the residents had been sent, along with other citizens of Hamburg and Lübeck, to the Riga Jungfernhof concentration camp for extermination. For the sake of simplicity I have therefore called the accommodation a Jewish house.

It remains for me to tell you, my dear readers, a specific story that relates to August. He is a person based on historical fact, although he won't be found in any history book. I had to give him a different surname, since his own is typically Bavarian, which would not have been appropriate for my soldier from the northern Hanseatic city.

If Johann Blumenthal were not the product of my imagination, August Kastenhuber would surely have fought alongside him in the same division at the Battle of the Somme.

A master carpenter like the fictional August, he really was shot in the knee. His comrades carried him for a full day through muddy enemy territory to the field hospital. In my novel I gave this task to Johann, because it was in his character to do so. August begged his comrades to leave him to die, because he could no longer bear the pain. But they wouldn't be persuaded. In the hospital, they wanted to amputate his leg from the thigh, but August refused emphatically. He would rather die than return home a cripple and be unable to provide for his family. The doctors therefore merely removed the bullet and gave him morphine. It was not long before he was heavily dependent on it. It was only when a new doctor replaced the morphine with saline solution without August's knowledge that the seriously injured man's fortunes changed. The withdrawal was like a never-ending hell for him, but he managed it. August then spent a few more months in the hospital, and his left leg remained stiff and unnaturally straight. During his convalescence he helped the hospital staff, and was at last able to return to his wife, Guste, and his little son, Emil. In 1919, their daughter, Friedel, was born.

Despite his stiff leg, August built a house for his family and a workshop for himself. He later forbade his children from joining the Hitler Youth, justifying it by saying they couldn't afford the leather jackets. His wife died in 1943, and his son fell in the Second World War shortly afterward. And when his house and workshop were razed to the ground in an air raid in 1944, August, who had raised Friedel alone, rebuilt everything himself. And he constructed a bicycle that he could use despite his disability. August lived for many more years surrounded by his large family, and he was a loving father and grandfather. He was a clever, shrewd man who never despaired of his fate, but made the best of everything. He is still remembered by his descendants with loving affection.

I am grateful to the lovely Uschy Schlichtinger of Regensburg for telling me her grandfather's story. August Kastenhuber made such an impression on me that I felt compelled to immortalize him in my novel. He is but one example of the many men and women who surpassed themselves in times of crisis and rebuilt their lives with admirable courage. We owe them so much. They deserve to live on in our memories.

My most important sources:

Das Leben der Hamburger und Altonaer Juden unter dem Hakenkreuz [The Lives of the Jews of Hamburg and Altona Beneath the Shadow of the Swastika]. Selected letters of Dr. Joseph Carlebach, by Hilde Michael. Berlin: Lit Verlag, 2009.

Die Kindertransporte nach Großbritannien 1938/39 [The Kindertransports to Great Britain, 1938/39]. Experience of exiles based on interviews and life stories, by Christiane Berth. München-Hamburg: Dölling und Galitz Verlag, 2005.

Kleine deutsch-jüdische Geschichte [A Brief History of the German Jews]. From the beginnings to the present, by Dr. Peter Guttkuhn. Lübeck: Schmidt-Römhild, 2004.

Die Lübecker Geschwister Grünfeldt [The Grünfeldt Sisters of Lübeck]. About the lives, suffering, and deaths of female "non-Aryan" Christians, by Dr. Peter Guttkuhn. Lübeck: Schmidt-Römhild, 2001.

Bomber gegen Lübeck [Bombers Attack Lübeck]. A record of the destruction of Lübeck's old town in the air raid of March 1942, by Lutz Wilde. Lübeck: Schmidt-Römhild Verlag, 1999.

Für Kaiser und Vaterland [For Kaiser and Fatherland]. About Jewish Lübeck and the First World War. A small booklet on the history of the city, Book 23, by Albert Schreiber. Lübeck: Archive of the Hanseatic City of Lübeck, 2014.

"Die Nürnberger Gesetze" ["The Nuremberg Laws"], *Jüdische Rundschau* (Berlin), September 17, 1935.

Felix zieht in den Krieg [Felix Goes to War]. A story about the First World War and its consequences, by Michael Landgraf. Neustadt ad Weinstraße: Agiro Verlag, 2014.

The Steady Running of the Hour. A novel by Justin Go. New York: Simon & Schuster, 2014.

Human Failure. A film by Michael Verhoeven. Berlin: Arthaus, 2008.

Der große Raub [The Great Theft]. How the Jews were plundered in Hesse. A film by Henning Burk and Dietrich Wagner. Hessischer Rundfunk, 2007.

*Acknowledgments*

I want to thank a number of people for enabling my idea to become the book you are now holding in your hands. Without them, the story that I have been mulling over in my head for years would not have been written. And I consider that a huge gift.

My heartfelt thanks go to:

My agent, Lianne Kolf, and her assistants in Munich, for their wonderful work.

My lovely editor, Lena Woitkowiak, of Amazon Publishing, Munich, for her enthusiasm for my book.

My copyeditor for her sensitive editing.

All the hardworking people at Amazon Publishing for their support and the wonderful cover.

Silvia Kuttny-Walser and Ingeborg Castell, my two tremendous mentors, for their many years of advice and support.

My dear colleague, Dr. Barbara Ellermeier, for her historical advice and the many little "treasures" that have enriched my novel.

Simone Kühlewind for the proofreading. Her eagle eyes spot everything.

I would also like to thank my colleagues, companions, and friends. And, last but not least, my family. You mean everything to me.

But my greatest thanks go to you, my dear readers. You are the engine that drives me to continue bringing you exciting stories.

Shalom, all the best, and see you soon!

About the Author

Mina Baites has written stories for as long as she has been able to think, and she loves transporting her readers to new, mysterious worlds. She has published a number of successful contemporary romances under the pseudonym Anna Levin. She also cowrites historical novels set in her beloved Germany as one half of the pseudonymous author Gerit Bertram. Mina lives with her family in northern Germany and loves traveling.

About the Translator

Photo © 2016 Sandra Dalton

Alison Layland is a novelist and translator from German, French, and Welsh into English. A member of the Institute of Translation and Interpreting and the Society of Authors, she has won a number of prizes for her fiction writing and translation. Her debut novel, the literary thriller *Someone Else's Conflict*, was published in 2014 by Honno Press. She has also translated a number of novels, including Corina Bomann's *The Moonlit Garden* and *Storm Rose*. She lives and works in the beautiful and inspiring countryside of Wales, United Kingdom.